Prisoner of Powder River

Five men, heavily armed, watched as Quick Shot pushed Elinore Pruitt—still bound and gagged—to the ground.

"Some important folks are very upset with you," Quick Shot said. "The last straw was when you filed on that piece of property next to Stewart's spread. That's some of the finest grazing land in Powder River, and no damn *woman* is going to homestead it!"

Elinore looked around her, and decided that escape would be impossible. She remembered Clyde Stewart's warning, his offer of protection. What a fool she'd been to spurn his help out of spite! She felt the tears welling up in her eyes.

"No sense crying, little lady," Quick Shot said. "You're not going to die—not yet, anyway."

Elinore looked up at him, a question in her eyes. Quick Shot laughed obscenely.

"I plan to have my pleasure while there's still life in that pretty body . . ."

The
WOMEN WHO WON THE WEST
Series

Eighth in the Series

WOMEN WHO WON THE WEST

Princess of Powder River

Lee Davis Willoughby

A DELL/BRYANS BOOK

Published by
Dell Publishing Co., Inc.
1 Dag Hammarskjold Plaza
New York, New York 10017

Dell ® TM 681510, Dell Publishing Co., Inc.

ISBN: 0-440-06326-4

Printed in the United States of America

First printing—September 1982

Prologue

Powder River, Wyoming, November 1891

THERE IS something eerie about the casual behavior of people who don't know they are about to die.

Emma Timmons, better known as Cattle Kate, rode down to the river to buy some moccasins from an elderly Sioux trader. They had been friends since her arrival in Powder River. Tucker, a cowboy in her employ, rode along.

The Indians had come down from the mountains, as they did every season, bringing their wares. Emma carefully chose an embroidered pair of white moccasins and a variety of beads to adorn her full bosom. Then the old Indian took a turquoise ring from his pouch. In all her trading with the Sioux, Emma had never seen anything like it. The stone was heart-shaped and the silver setting was engraved. When the Indian mentioned the price the cowboy gasped.

"Why, Miss Emma, don't you think that's a little rich for a homesteader?" Tucker asked.

"Tucker, I'll be damned if I'll be a dirt-poor homesteader my whole life," Emma said. "Remember, I own

5

three dozen head of cattle. 'Sides, this ring's good for business. My men friends like to see their women friends adorned."

Emma Timmons had taken up her homestead on a valuable piece of land along Crazy Woman Creek in the middle of a huge tract of land questionably claimed by one of the largest and most arrogant of the cattle barons. Since then she had catered to the needs of the woman-starved cowboys.

Emma could afford the ring as she had had a particularly prosperous year between running what the West politely called a "hog farm" and the selling of yearlings she often took as recompense for her favors. She was also a natural agitator and was becoming a legend in her fight to organize the small ranchers and homesteaders against the cattle barons.

The old Indian agreed to the terms of the bargain—two yearlings to be fetched tomorrow—as Emma admired the ring on her finger. It was the most glamorous thing she had ever possessed.

Emma jumped up astride her horse, her full calico skirt flowing over the saddle and her sunbonnet tied around her neck and resting on her back. Tucker mounted his horse, looked toward town and said, "Miss Emma, that's the second time today I've seen those six men ride past. You suspect they're up to something?"

"Tucker, it's Shaunsey and his boys," Emma said. "I seen 'em, too. They been harassing me for three years and I ain't been afraid yet. Not going to start today. Now, you get on into town and get me that fencing I need."

"Don't you want me to ride you back to the ranch?" Tucker said.

"Ain't no time for that," Emma said. "I'll be fine."

Tucker rode off. Neither of them noticed the seventh man, who had been watching all along from atop the ridge. He sat on a fine horse with a European saddle and held a handkerchief to his face to shield it from the dust. The linen handkerchief bore his family's insignia.

Emma was well on her way back to the ranch when she first noticed the six men following her. She gently spurred the horse to quicken her pace. The men did the same.

For the first time Emma sensed real danger. In a full gallop, the men close behind her, she thought, "If only I can get past that next ridge, in sight of the ranch, I have a chance."

Within a hundred feet of the ridge, Emma turned to see Shaunsey at her heels. In a minute, he was alongside her. He grabbed at her reins. She kicked at him furiously. Finally he took hold of her reins. The horses halted less than ten feet from the ridge. The other men fixed their Winchesters on Emma.

"What do you want with me now, Shaunsey?" Emma asked the large, red-headed Irishman.

"We got a warrant for your arrest and mean to take you in," Shaunsey said.

"I'd like to see that warrant," Emma said confidently.

"Kate, you'll never get smart, will you?" Shaunsey asked. "You take up a homestead and raise cattle where no man is welcome, certainly no woman. To answer your question—these rifles is all the warrant we need. You getting smart yet?"

They took off, but not in the direction of town. There was only one thing out where they were headed. Independence Rock, Emma thought with a chill. My God, they're fixing to hang me, or at least scare me pretty bad. Well, I ain't gonna squirm like they expect of a woman.

But just to be cautious she slipped her new treasure off her finger and into her pocket.

* * *

The seventh man followed surreptitiously and watched from behind sagebrush as the party approached Independence Rock. Shaunsey grabbed Emma's hands and tied them behind her back. But as he tried to place the noose around her neck, she dodged her head so fiercely it took another man to hold her still. Shaunsey took the other end of the rope and tied it to a limb of a stunted pine.

"Be game and jump like the man you think you are, you little strumpet," Shaunsey said. "Or be reasonable. This is your last chance to leave Powder River. We'll buy you out fair and square or we'll just kill you."

"I ain't leaving my land," Emma said and spit down from her horse into Shaunsey's face.

His anger flared. He slapped the horse's bottom. Emma dropped. But the mere two-foot drop did not even give her the dignity of a broken neck and a quick death.

Emma hanged there, atop the ridge, slowly strangling for the best part of an hour. Her face swelled and discolored. Her tongue hung grotesquely from her mouth and her eyes bulged. After a few minutes, even Shaunsey had to turn away.

The struggle finally over, Emma's body hung limply. The little moccasins slipped from her feet. The six men drove off, their task finished.

Once the men were out of sight, the hidden man showed himself from behind the sagebrush. He reached for his handkerchief as he approached the body, for the odor of blood and defecation was already strong in the warm autumn sun.

To be cautious, he searched her. He found the ring in her pocket and took it out.

He looked up at the distorted face.

"Kate, I warned you," he said. "We have no use for homesteaders out here, particularly agitating women. I gave you a choice and you chose to die." He put the ring in his pocket and walked away.   ᴇ§

1

Denver, Colorado, November 1891

ELINORE PRUITT looked down at the wooden cross that marked her husband's grave. It was unlike the other markers that were battered and grey, for it had been placed there just this afternoon.

Elinore had stayed behind as the few mourners who attended Phillip's funeral paid their condolences and returned to their lives. She stood there and wept, wondering what her life would now be. Finally, as it began to get dark, she walked from the grave.

Elinore thought of only yesterday when she had begged Phillip not to go gambling at the hotel, how she had told him that gambling would never reap the prosperity he wanted so desperately. She had said she would be content to be a homesteader's wife, to work hard and gain the security of land that she most desired.

But Phillip had gone to the hotel anyway. He wanted her to be a lady instead of the wife of a hard-scrabble farmer. Now, this loving, passionate man was dead. All over a petty argument at a card table. She had not even asked what the row was about. It was of no consequence. All that mattered was that he was gone and she was alone.

An expensive carriage was parked outside the cemetery gate. A pretty blonde woman looked out as Elinore approached.

"Mrs. Pruitt," the woman called. "I'm Bette Iverson. I live at the Windsor Hotel and I knew your husband. Women in my profession know all the gamblers in town. Phillip often spoke of you and your little girl, Jerrine. Please, let me offer you a ride back to town."

There was such sincerity in the woman's voice that Elinore accepted the offer and stepped into the carriage.

"Jerrine is back East in boarding school," Elinore said. "I sent her when Phillip started his foolish gambling." Elinore nearly broke into tears again. "But I won't have the money to keep her there after this year."

"Yes, I knew that Phillip was losing heavily," Bette said. "May I be of help and loan you some money? You can send it to me when you're on your feet."

"Thank you for your kindness," Elinore said. "But I couldn't accept money. I'm going to try and find work until I can decide what's best for Jerrine and me. Jerrine's only seven years old and I want us to be together again soon."

"Well, if you're willing to work I'm certain I could help you find work at the Windsor. They're always in need of quality help."

"That would be wonderful," Elinore said. "I am a fine laundress, but I'd be willing to do anything."

"Why don't you come back to the hotel with me for some tea?" Bette said. "We can discuss it further. Besides, you shouldn't be alone this evening."

Elinore was reluctant but she realized that Bette Iverson was right. She did not want to be alone now.

"Tea sounds like a lovely idea," Elinore said.

The carriage continued toward town. In the silence, Elinore drifted off into her thoughts. She dreaded every day ahead.   ⋐§

2

Denver, New Year's Eve, 1891

JAMES ADRIAN waltzed with the loveliest woman in the ballroom. They spun faster and faster, their legs intertwined, until he swept her off to the end of the gallery. There, out of breath, they sat in a loveseat.

"Bette, I wanted you all to myself for a moment to compliment you on your beautiful gown and the sprigs of forget-me-nots in your hair," Adrian said.

Bette Iverson was striking in her deep blue gown. It complemented her fair complexion and blue eyes, while revealing her many charms. She possessed everything necessary to succeed in her profession and this dress made no secret of it.

"Why, James, thank you," Bette said. "I've been eager for your return to Denver and wanted so much to please you."

"I would have been back in Denver weeks ago but there've been some land disputes in Powder River," Adrian said. "A woman homesteader who had been giving the cattle barons a rough going was hanged by a group of unknown men. But now, I can stay in town for the winter. Besides," Adrian added lightly, "I wouldn't have missed escorting the most desirable woman in all of Denver to the New Year's ball. And I've brought you a special present."

"You're cruel, James Adrian," she said, smiling. "You've been teasing me about this gift ever since you arrived. I canceled all my appointments so that we might be together. My customers have been bad-tempered ever since. And yet you persist in teasing me. Haven't I been good to you since you returned to Denver?"

"Yes, you certainly have," Adrian said. "And haven't I promised you your gift at the stroke of midnight? Be patient, my pet. Now let's return to that table of bores so we may indulge in a fine meal. Aside from your company, I have most looked forward to a gracious dinner this evening. The Windsor, of course, is the best hotel in the West, rivaling Delmonico's in New York."

"I'll be glad to return to the table, James. But please, for my sake, be civil. It is New Year's Eve, darling," Bette said.

"Bette, you must understand," Adrian said. "I find those people boring but tolerable. It's that newly rich cowboy, Casper, I detest. You Americans take equality a bit too far when you allow a cowpuncher to dine with gentlemen."

"James Adrian, I like that man no more than you do," Bette said. "You British feel you are the only ones capable of being offended. But let's not argue, sweetheart. Come along."

As they strolled across the Windsor's parquet dance floor, the orchestra slowed its tempo, signaling the start of the meal. Floors and candelabras glowed all along the richly polished European paneling. The enormous crystal chandelier made the entire room sparkle. Potted palms and fresh flowers were abundant. Every table was attended by four waiters and a captain, who continually poured France's best champagne. The appointments were the finest crystal, china and silver. Richly colored rugs muffled the din of conversation.

Bette and Adrian approached the table. He stood behind her chair, pushed it in, and graciously took his seat next to Casper. The waiters scurried about distributing the consomme Chatelaine while others poured the amontillado. Even Adrian was impressed. At times he pretended to be back in England—the food and service were that good—until he was reminded of being in the States by the increasingly inebriated cowboy to his left.

Dinner continued with an equally sublime saumon Livonienns. A variety of entrees followed, complimented by a Chateau Margaux '48. After the sorbet, intended to lighten the palate, Adrian and Bette returned to the dance floor.

"James, I couldn't have anticipated a more delightful evening," Bette said. "Oh, James, hold still. Your stud has come undone again. Let me fix it."

"What, again?" Adrian said. "If it hadn't been for your help I wouldn't have gotten them in to begin with. This silk shirt is such a nuisance, but it's the only dress shirt that incompetent valet packed for me. American help! And now the rest of my luggage is late arriving. Oh, Bette, what would I do without you?"

"Why, thank you, James," she said, as he escorted her back to the table.

After the vegetable course, dessert, and coffee, everyone awaited the stroke of midnight, their glasses full. The maitre d' began the countdown—ten, nine, eight, seven, six, five, four, three, two, one—Happy New Year! Everyone shouted. Streamers flew. Horns blew. Bette and Adrian embraced as the orchestra struck up the Scottish "Auld Lang Syne."

Adrian reached into his vest pocket and produced a small package.

"Happy New Year, Bette," he said, as he handed it to her.

She opened it quickly.

"Oh, James. You found it. Just the ring I wanted," Bette cried.

Adrian placed the ring on her finger. She leaned over and kissed him. Just then Casper rose to propose a toast. But as he raised his glass he lost his balance. His madeira spilt down the front of Adrian's shirt. The rage came immediately to Adrian's face.

"You fool! I have taken your abuse all evening," Adrian said. "You Americans have to learn money does not make a gentleman. Get out of my sight, Casper, before I do something we both may regret."

Casper was so drunk he was immune to the insults. Two waiters led him away. The maitre d' rushed to attend to Adrian.

"Please, Henry, call for Elinore in the laundry," Bette said to the maitre d'. "She attends to all my finest things, James. I would trust no one else."

The maitre d' immediately sent a waiter to the laundry and escorted Adrian and Bette to a small lounge off the ballroom.

Elinore Pruitt brushed the red hair back from her face as she stepped back from the steaming pots of linens. She looked around the dismal laundry and to the ten-year-old children working past midnight. I don't mind working myself but I refuse to let this happen to Jerrine, she thought. Someday, with the Lord's help, we'll have land.

Suddenly her thoughts were interrupted by a man's voice from behind. She braced herself for the chastisement she was certain to receive for her day-dreaming.

"Miss Pruitt," the man said. "Come quickly. There's been an incident in the dining room. Miss Bette has asked for you."

"Just one moment," Elinore said, relieved. "I'll change my apron and gather some remedies." In an instant, they were climbing the stairs to the main floor.

"Thank you for coming so quickly, Elinore," Bette said, as Elinore entered the anteroom. "I've told everyone of your talents. Elinore Pruitt, this is James Adrian."

Adrian did not look up.

"I appreciate your confidence in me, Miss Bette, but has anyone gone for a fresh shirt just in case?" Elinore asked.

"If I had a fresh shirt would I be bothering you?" Adrian snapped, still looking down at his shirt.

"No, sir. Of course not. Please excuse me," Elinore said, as she knelt to examine the shirt.

"Quickly, Elinore, use some bleach," the maitre d' said, eager for a resolution.

"Excuse me, sir," Elinore said, looking up at him. "This is a fine silk shirt and bleach would yellow it permanently. I've brought some hydrogen peroxide and baking soda. Everything will be fine shortly."

"See, James, I told you she was exceptional," Bette said. "And pretty, too."

Adrian looked down at Elinore for the first time as she applied the peroxide and soda. She was fair-skinned. Her violet eyes radiated, though she was obviously exhausted. A sheen of perspiration on her face attested to her hard work. To Adrian's surprise, he found her incredibly attractive.

"The stain is gone, sir," Elinore said. "You'll just have to wait for it to dry."

"I thank you, miss," Adrian said. Not wanting her to leave, he added, "May I offer you some champagne to show my appreciation?"

"No, sir. I'm afraid I couldn't," Elinore said, glancing nervously at the maitre d'.

"Nonsense. Henry, bring a bottle of your finest and glasses for the ladies and me," Adrian said.

In a moment Henry was back with a table, linens, flowers, and a candle. The champagne was poured. Elinore delighted in its coolness. She looked into the ballroom and was reminded of Phillip. They had loved to dance.

"May I ask what brought you to Denver?" Adrian asked, after a moment of silence.

"I came with my husband," she said. "My daughter is back in St. Louis at school."

"What of your husband?" Adrian asked. He felt Bette nudge his arm.

"My husband died recently," Elinore said. "I am alone."

"Elinore, look at the ring Mr. Adrian gave me," Bette said, wanting to end the awkward silence. "It's just like the one I told you I wanted."

"You two seem to have quite a friendship," Adrian said.

"Yes, Mr. Adrian," Elinore said. "Bette has been very kind to me. In fact, she helped me get this job at the Windsor."

"Miss Pruitt, forgive me if I seem forward," Adrian said. "But what does a woman of your quality plan to do here alone in Denver?"

"Oh, I don't plan to stay here, Mr. Adrian," Elinore said. She sipped her champagne. "My dream is to homestead. I want the security for us that only land can bring."

Adrian was amused with her determination. "Do you have any knowledge of this business, Miss Pruitt?" he asked.

"No, sir," Elinore said. "I know my plan sounds foolish but I intend to find work on the frontier and learn what it takes. I read the advertisements for housekeepers every day. The Reverend Father Corrigan advises me."

"Homesteading is a dangerous business for any man,

but for a woman it's out of the question," he said. "The homesteaders' situation is desperate."

"Yes, Elinore," Bette said. "James has just told me of a woman homesteader who was hanged."

"Yes, it's true, Miss Pruitt," Adrian said. "But as for the other part of your plan, I have, by coincidence, a friend back in Powder River who's looking for a housekeeper. You two would be perfectly suited for one another. If you like I will begin correspondence with him right away."

"I would appreciate that, sir," Elinore said. "Could you tell me something about him?"

"Clyde Stewart is a gentleman, accustomed to servants," Adrian said. "But most quality help has no desire to see the frontier. He is a bachelor and . . ." Adrian noticed a sudden concern on Elinore's face.

"Don't worry, Miss Pruitt," he said. "You'll have no worries about your honor. Clyde is no newly rich cowboy. He's of the Stewart clan. He is a bit peculiar but undoubtedly a gentleman. You don't mind working for a Scotsman, do you?"

"No, sir, my only concern is that Mr. Stewart is a gentleman," Elinore said. She was elated. This was the opportunity she had prayed for. She did not care what Mr. Adrian thought of her scheme. She would homestead. "I'll never be able to thank you enough, sir." Suddenly she remembered Bette. "Oh, Bette, your ring is lovely."

Elinore glanced at it again. The ring certainly was unique.

"Please excuse me now," she said, sipping the last of her champagne. "I don't wish to interfere with your festivities any longer."

Elinore returned to the laundry, euphoric from the effects of the champagne and the excitement of her new opportunity. But she hesitated a moment on the stairs, frightened, and wondered if the frontier were as dangerous as Mr. Adrian had said.   ❦

3

Buffalo, Wyoming, April 1892

THREE MONTHS later the stage from Cheyenne carried Elinore Pruitt into Buffalo, the last stop of her long journey. Looking from the window, Elinore observed her new home. There was not a tree or shrub to be seen. The wide street was lined with cowboys in broad-brimmed sombreros and fringed-leather chaps. Big Mexican spurs jutted out from their boots. Even the horses were disappointing. They looked like sickly little ponies with their dejectedly hanging heads.

The stage stopped in front of the only brick building in town, the courthouse. Elinore anxiously searched the small group that awaited the stage for her new employer. One man, who was peering into the coach, stood out in the crowd. He was rotund, well-dressed, and middle-aged.

This must be Mr. Stewart, Elinore thought.

The driver took her hand as she stepped from the stage. Her patent leather boots sank into the mud. She and the middle-aged gentleman started toward each other. Just as she was to make her introduction, he continued past her. Elinore turned to see him shake the hand of a young gentleman she had been traveling with. The young man turned to Elinore, tipped his hat, and the pair walked off.

The crowd now dispersed quickly, leaving Elinore alone on the slatted-wood sidewalk.

"Ma'am, where would you like me to put your bags?" the driver asked.

"I'm to be met here. Please leave them on the sidewalk," Elinore said, wanting to appear self-assured.

Elinore looked down at herself. Her short, striped chintz skirt was terribly wrinkled. The Norfolk jacket she prized was disheveled, and her new patent leather boots were covered with mud. Her lovely red hair was full of dust and falling from her hat. It took all her strength to keep from crying.

Glancing up from under her parasol, she noticed a rough-looking cowboy approaching. He was long and lean, just as Elinore would have expected. As he stepped toward her he took off his hat, revealing a mass of dark, wavy hair. A pistol hung from his hip.

"Excuse me, ma'am. Are you Elinore Pruitt?" he asked.

Mr. Stewart has sent one of his cowhands to meet me, Elinore thought. A gentleman would never keep a lady waiting in this wilderness.

"Let me introduce myself," he said. "I'm Clyde Stewart."

Elinore could not hide her surprise. She was expecting a middle-aged Scot gentleman, not a young cowboy!

"You are no doubt surprised at my appearance, Miss Pruitt, but you'll soon find out formality has little place on the frontier," Stewart said, making no apology for his tardiness. His Scottish accent was now apparent.

Stewart placed the bags in a wagon that had been sitting there. Without a word, he took her hand and helped her into the front seat. He climbed in himself and they drove off.

Mr. Adrian did say he was peculiar, Elinore thought, trying to reassure herself. She found herself thinking longingly of the laundry at the Windsor Hotel.

No, she thought. I won't let myself be frightened or even think of the past. This is my new life. I must make it work.

Just as they reached the end of town a young man pulled his wagon next to Stewart's. A pretty, dark-haired woman sat beside him. Three children, the eldest perhaps six years old, played in the back.

"Hello, Stewart, what are you doing in town?" the man asked. He was not quite as large as Stewart. His hair was sandy-colored.

"I've come to meet Miss Pruitt, Tisdale," Stewart said. "I told you I had hired a housekeeper on James Adrian's recommendation."

Elinore noticed the disapproval on the man's face.

What must he think of me, Elinore wondered. A young woman come all this way to keep house for a young bachelor.

Stewart introduced Elinore to the Tisdales and their children. Mrs. Tisdale stretched out her hands to greet Elinore. Mrs. Tisdale was a frail woman, and her hands were rougher and redder even than her own, Elinore thought.

"Miss Pruitt, we're sincerely glad to have a new neighbor," Mrs. Tisdale said. "Although we're a few hours' ride from Mr. Stewart's, we're your closest neighbor. I can't tell you how nice it will be to have a lady to visit. Please call on me anytime."

She smiled at Elinore.

"Thank you very much," Elinore said, honestly pleased.

"How about that trouble we discussed, Tisdale?" Stewart asked.

Mrs. Tisdale went pale suddenly. Even the eldest boy stopped his play to hear his father's answer.

"Well, as far as I can tell nothing's changed," Tisdale said. "But I'll be damned if I'll be intimidated or run off my land. I suspect it's the same bunch that harrassed Cattle Kate. But they ain't dealing with no woman this time."

Elinore knew of Cattle Kate. It had been in all the Denver papers. Kate was a prostitute, desperate as any man, and handy with a six-shooter. She wore silks and diamonds, rode like a demon, and once shot a drunk dead for insulting her. In order to rid the community of such a menace a band of unknown men had lynched her. But Elinore could not understand what all this had to do with Tisdale and his land.

"We'll have to discuss this, Tisdale," Stewart said. "When you find the time, come by and we'll have a talk."

As they made their good-byes, Mrs. Tisdale reiterated her invitation to Elinore. Then Elinore and Stewart drove off into the prairie.

The midday sun beat down on the dreary landscape. It was too early for any wildflowers and the scrubby trees were just beginning to bud. The prairie was flat and uninteresting, covered with grass and studded with wide, shallow brooks. There was no cultivation.

About an hour out of town, they passed a Sioux village. It consisted of a few wooden shanties. As they rode by, the squaws with their papooses stared stolidly at Elinore.

Despite her parasol, her eyes began to burn from the glare of the sun and the alkali dust. Stewart, without a word, handed her his handkerchief, indicating that she should shield her eyes with it. The handkerchief was made of the finest linen and was embroidered with an insignia. Elinore guessed it must be the coat-of-arms of the Stewart clan.

This silly handkerchief is the only sign that this man has any breeding at all, Elinore thought.

"I want to thank you for your generous traveling expenses," Elinore said, wishing to end the long silence. "And insistence that I spend the night in Cheyenne at the Dyers. After such a tiring journey, a good hotel is such a pleasure."

"Very good," he said, and nothing more.

They drove on. Elinore's back and head were aching. She wondered again if she had made a mistake.

Late in the afternoon the wagon approached the ranch house. Even from afar it was an impressive building, more so than any of the ranches they had passed. The foundation was of stone and its porch wrapped around the entire house. From the second story roof two chimneys jutted out.

Stewart pulled up to the house and helped Elinore from the wagon.

"McPherren," he called to a man out in the yard. "Come help with Miss Pruitt's luggage."

They climbed the stairs and entered the house. It had been a pleasant surprise at first but as Elinore stood there she noticed the lack of furnishings, rugs, or even curtains. Everything was covered with a thick layer of dust.

"I've been told it needs a woman's touch," Stewart said, gruffly.

After showing Elinore the kitchen and offering her a glass of cloudy water Stewart said, "Well, Miss Pruitt, you must be tired from your travels. McPherren took your things upstairs. I thought you might like to wash up and take a nap."

"Mr. Stewart, I thought I would be sleeping downstairs, behind the kitchen," Elinore said, thinking the worst. Mr. Adrian promised me he was a gentleman, Elinore thought.

"No, Miss Pruitt, I suggest you sleep upstairs,"

Stewart said, oblivious to Elinore's innuendo. "I prefer to sleep downstairs in case of trouble."

Elinore was relieved, though a bit frightened by his mention of trouble.

Stewart showed her to her room. It faced the front of the house. The late afternoon sun shone through the windows. Disturbed by their entrance, the dust rose and speckled the rays of sunshine.

"Make yourself at home," Stewart said, nodded and left the room.

Elinore looked around and wondered if she could sleep in such filth. She put on her nightgown and tossed the covers on the bed to dispel some of the dust. She crawled in. Before she knew it, she was asleep.

With a start Elinore sat up in bed. It was dark. Still half asleep and frightened, she did not know where she was. A whining noise had woken her.

Again the whining came. And again. A long whining noise, like a child in distress. Without a thought she rushed down the stairs and into the sitting room. She was terrified.

As she entered the parlor, she saw Stewart sitting in a straight-backed chair. His large body was wrapped around the bagpipe he held in his lap.

Elinore suddenly remembered where she was.

"I'm sorry, Mr. Stewart," she stammered, realizing she was standing in front of this strange man in her dressing gown. "I . . . I heard a noise in my sleep."

Elinore's face was crimson.

"I play every evening. I am accustomed to being left alone," Stewart said.

Frightened, Elinore began to back out of the room.

"One bit of advice, Miss Pruitt," Stewart said, his blue eyes fixed on her. "This is a dangerous place, especially for women. You'll be best off if you keep to yourself. I wouldn't want to see anything happen to you."

"Yes, sir," Elinore replied. She turned and hurried up the stairs. *This man is not only peculiar*, as Mr. Adrian had warned, *he is eerie*, she thought.   ◅ৡ

4

McPHERREN AND two of the other hands were grumbling as they turned the soil in what would be Elinore's garden. Elinore had discussed the garden with Mr. Stewart that morning. He had shown little enthusiasm for her idea but now the disgruntled cowboys were turning the soil just where she had suggested. Mr. Stewart had shown himself to be peculiar time and time again these past two weeks.

Elinore looked out the kitchen window and thought what a frightfully difficult two weeks they had been. She had scrubbed the house from corner to corner and it still did not seem clean. From dawn till late in the evening, she had cooked, cleaned, washed, and mended. After serving dinner she would retire to her room to read or write a letter to her daughter in St. Louis. Stewart, meanwhile, would sit alone in the parlor, night after night, playing his bagpipes. She dared not go downstairs.

A knock at the back door pulled Elinore from her thoughts. She opened the door to find John Tisdale standing there, a basket in hand.

"Hello, Miss Pruitt," Tisdale said. "I've just come from town and wanted to speak with Stewart. Mrs. Tisdale baked these this morning and thought you and Stewart would enjoy them with your tea." He handed her the basket.

"Well, thank you, Mr. Tisdale," Elinore said, so thankful for a friendly voice. "That was very thoughtful of Mrs. Tisdale. I'm surprised she finds time to bake with three children and a house to keep."

"Yes, her chores seem to never end," Tisdale said. "But if I may say so myself, Mrs. Tisdale is a remarkable woman. That's why I made a special trip to town to pick up a mirror I had ordered for her birthday tomorrow. I'd be lost without her."

"And she without you, I'm certain," Elinore said. "Would you like some tea? I'll put the kettle on. Mr. Stewart should be in shortly."

As she filled the kettle and placed it on the stove, Stewart walked in.

"Well, Tisdale. Good to see you," Stewart said. He did not acknowledge Elinore.

"Hello, Stewart," Tisdale said. "I stopped by to see if we might have that talk you mentioned."

"Certainly," Stewart said. "This situation could get out of hand. Something must be done."

When the water was ready Elinore poured it into the cracked china teapot and set the tiny cakes on a plate. She placed the two unmatching cups on the table with sugar and spoons and began to pour the tea.

"Aren't you having any?" Stewart asked.

"Well, Mr. Stewart, I thought I'd leave you gentlemen to your conversation," Elinore replied.

"Nonsense," Stewart said forcefully. "Bring a cup. You've expressed an interest in homesteading. This conversation will dispel any romantic notions you might have."

Elinore dutifully took her tea at the table.

"Stewart, you seem to have found yourself a dandy," Tisdale said, looking around. "I've never seen this house so tidy and home-like. Miss Pruitt, you've done a fine job."

Stewart just shrugged.

"Thank you, Mr. Tisdale," Elinore said, quite pleased that someone had noticed.

Elinore remained silent during the conversation about cattle prices and the approaching spring round-up.

"So what's the news from town?" Stewart asked.

"Well, everyone is still talking about Cattle Kate," Tisdale said. "The tension is growing."

Elinore's interest was now aroused. This was a topic she knew something about.

"Why is everyone so concerned with seeking justice for a murderous prostitute?" Elinore asked. "Why, I read she had imposed a reign of terror on the community, shooting several men."

"Miss Pruitt, do you believe everything you read in the papers?" Stewart asked in a tone Elinore was beginning to despise. He treated her so disparagingly. His only comments to her were critical or even threatening.

"I knew Cattle Kate," he continued. "She'd been out here for years. She was a prostitute, but she never killed a soul."

"Then why did they lynch her?" Elinore asked.

"That's what all the talk in town is about," Tisdale said. "No one seems to know for sure but Jack Flagg is saying there'd been a dispute about some land or unbranded calves."

"You mean she was a rustler?" Elinore asked.

"Miss Pruitt, it's not that simple," Tisdale said. "The Cattlemen's Association has laid down some pretty unfair laws. We small ranchers and homesteaders are beginning to see the situation as a war of classes, not honorable men and thieves. The maverick law says that no mavericks—that's what we call unbranded calves, ma'am—born on the open range can be claimed and branded. They have to be put in a common pool at round-up time for auction by the Association. But in order to bid in the auction you have to post a three thousand dollar bond. None of us have three thousand dollars. So in other words we have to give our calves to the Association. Is that fair?"

Elinore sat back and sipped her tea.

I can't believe what Mr. Tisdale says is true, Elinore thought. They may see it as a war of classes, but to me rustling is plain thievery.

"What of your troubles, Tisdale?" Stewart asked.

"Well, there has been bad blood between me and Shaunsey, the Association detective, for a long while," Tisdale said. "They want me off my land but I'm not budging. Jack Flagg is a good man and Nick Ray and Nate Champion are strong leaders, but I'm the only educated voice the small ranchers have. Stewart, as a member of the Association, I don't mean to insult you but things have definitely gotten out of hand. Major Wolcott and his friends would just as soon kill off all us small ranchers if they could get away with it."

"There's a meeting this week of the Association. I'll try and reason with Adrian, Wolcott, and the rest," Stewart said.

"Stewart, I know Adrian is a friend of yours, but he's as ruthless as the others," Tisdale said. "I'm afraid there is no reasoning any longer. They intend to make every small rancher pay for their own mismanagement. I plan to lead the organization of small ranchers, now that Cattle Kate's dead. Jack Flagg, Nick Ray and Nate Champion are behind me all the way. We've got to protect ourselves. After losing eighty percent of their cattle this winter, the cattle barons expect to make it back by persecuting any man trying to make an honest living."

"Before you do anything drastic, let me have my chance at the Association meeting," Stewart said.

"I know you're a reasonable man, Stewart," Tisdale said. "I respect you for it. But I'm afraid the longer we wait to organize the more unexplained deaths we'll see. My wife lives in fear every time I leave . . ."

Tisdale was suddenly silent.

Elinore looked up to see James Adrian standing at the door. She hoped he hadn't heard the hateful things Tisdale had said.

"Associating with commoners again, Stewart?" Adrian said, glaring at Tisdale.

Tisdale jumped to his feet. Adrian lifted his fists.

But before either could strike, Stewart rushed between them. His chair fell to the ground. Stewart pushed the two men apart. Elinore sat frozen with fear.

"I won't tolerate this in my home. I'll take you both on if you insist on continuing this madness. Be civilized," Stewart demanded.

"That's fine with me," Tisdale said. "I'll have plenty to say to you, Adrian, soon enough."

Tisdale walked past Adrian, tipped his hat to Elinore, and left.

Elinore now understood Tisdale's disapproval when Stewart mentioned he'd hire her on Adrian's recommendation.

"That was uncalled for, Adrian," Stewart said angrily. "Never do that again in my presence."

"Yes, I apologize, Stewart," Adrian said. "But Tisdale is a trouble-maker. Besides, I didn't come to argue with you, ole boy. I came to see how Miss Pruitt is getting along. After all, I feel a bit responsible for her being in Powder River."

Adrian looked at Elinore. Suddenly she became very self-conscious. Her hair was unkempt and her dress dirty from her morning chores. Her hands looked worse than ever.

She glanced up at Adrian. He was incredibly handsome in his riding breeches and boots. His dark hair was oiled and combed. His nails were perfectly manicured.

"She's quite a little lady, eh Stewart?" Adrian said.

Stewart sat hunched over the table refusing to even acknowledge the question.

"Excuse me, gentlemen. I must return to my chores," Elinore said nervously.

"May I speak with you before I leave?" Adrian asked.

Stewart scowled at this.

"Certainly, sir. I'll be on the front porch," Elinore replied and turned to leave. She felt Adrian's eyes on her back.

Elinore had just swept a small portion of the porch when Adrian stepped through the front door. The sun was getting low and the porch glistened in the afternoon sunlight.

"You've done a fine job with this place, Miss Pruitt," Adrian said. "Isn't Stewart every bit as strange as I warned?" he added.

"Yes, sir. Every bit," she said. "I must admit I'm frightened of him at times. He has a horrible temper."

"Tell me if it ever becomes too much for you, Miss Pruitt. I really do feel responsible for you being here. But for now, I must be going. I've important business to attend to in town but I would like to come again, soon. Would that be all right with you?"

"Yes, I would like that," Elinore said.

"I imagine a little gentlemanly company is appreciated after weeks with Stewart and his cowboys," Adrian said.

Elinore nodded.

He reached for her hand and kissed her fingers. Elinore was embarrassed by his boldness but more so by the condition of her hands.

"I'll see you soon," Adrian said, as he mounted his horse.

Elinore was thoroughly infatuated as she watched this handsome gentleman ride off. A gentleman giving me serious attention, she thought with a thrill.

Elinore turned to enter the house.

As she stepped through the door she gasped. Stewart was standing there. After the initial fright, Elinore became angry at this breach of her privacy. He obviously had been standing there all along. She stared at Stewart but his menacing look wilted her.

"Miss Pruitt," Stewart said, "I advise you not to see that gentleman in my house again."

His fists were clenched. "If you choose to make a fool of yourself, do it elsewhere," he added and left the house.

My God, Elinore thought, he looked as though he wanted to strike me. I don't understand that man. She lifted her hands to her face and cried.

Every time the road dipped into one of the countless water-worn gulches that seamed the prairie, John Tisdale cursed and held on to his wife's mirror. He had creaked and crawled along in his wagon, making no more than three miles an hour. He was now two hours from Stewart's ranch with at least another hour before he reached home. He might not make it before dark.

Fifty feet from the next gulch, a man stood hidden, his horse tied to a tree.

As Tisdale reached the gulch, he braked his wagon and cursed again, looking down at his wife's mirror. The hidden man waited as the wagon began to make its climb. Then, he stepped out from behind a tree and raised his Winchester. John Tisdale's back now presented a perfect target.

The first shot rang out. It hit the six-shooter Tisdale was wearing in a shoulder sling and glanced off.

Tisdale reached for his shotgun. But as he cocked it, the second shot ripped into his back.

John Tisdale fell back dead, shattering his wife's mirror.

5

ELINORE BEGAN preparing the noonday meal, still uneasy about the quarrel she had had yesterday with Stewart. Suddenly the dogs started barking. She heard a horse galloping toward the house. She rushed to the front door, hoping it was Adrian. But as she looked out she saw a stranger dismounting his horse hurriedly. He went directly to the barn. Though she was curious, Elinore returned to her work.

A minute later Stewart and the stranger walked through the kitchen door.

"Miss Pruitt, this is Nick Ray," Stewart said. "Nick used to work for me but he now owns the K.C. ranch with Nate Champion."

Nick Ray was a large man, larger than Stewart, with thick black hair. His eyes were big and light blue, giving him a boyish quality. But his leathery, browned complexion and rough hands told of a hard-working man.

Nick had yet to catch his breath but as soon as he spoke with his soft drawl, Elinore knew he was a Texan.

"Miss Pruitt," Nick said. "There's been an accident

and we, I mean Nate and I, decided that maybe you could be the best help, seein' as you're a woman."

Elinore was puzzled. Nick continued.

"John Tisdale has been shot and we were hoping you would go out to Mrs. Tisdale."

"Is Mr. Tisdale hurt bad?" Elinore asked. She felt a terrible uneasiness in her stomach.

"John's dead," Nick replied. "Nate took his body out to the house and I came to get help."

Elinore sank into the chair. Her cheeks were feverish.

"Who would kill such a fine man?" Elinore asked.

"The same people that killed Cattle Kate," Nick said. "Any of the big cattlemen that consider the small ranchers a threat."

There was plenty of land for everyone, Elinore thought. Why did anyone have to kill a decent, hardworking man? What of his wife and children? Elinore began to cry.

After a moment she looked up at Stewart. They hadn't spoken since their argument yesterday. He put his hand on her shoulder and nodded gently.

"Miss Pruitt, I'll be glad to take you out there if you are willing," Stewart said. "You can't ride alone and this way Nick can go to town. People will be wanting to know."

Without a word Elinore got up and began packing the mess-box. In minutes they were off in the well-stocked wagon.

The ride was almost ten miles but it went quickly, as dreaded things often will.

Elinore saw the house on the horizon. It was made of logs and had a pitched roof. It was more elaborate than most houses on the plain, but not nearly as grand as Stewart's.

As they approached, the sickening sensation in Elinore's stomach worsened. What a fine present for Mrs. Tisdale's birthday, she thought. She remembered just yesterday the loving husband carrying home the special surprise for his wife—the mirror she had wanted so badly—and now he was dead.

Stewart helped her down from the wagon. They entered the house without knocking. The three children sat quietly in the front room. The eldest boy, whose sandy-colored hair was just like his father's, wept softly.

Elinore could hear wailing in the back of the house. She went to the sound to find Mr. Tisdale on the bed still in his blood-matted clothing. Mrs. Tisdale sat beside him, rocking and crying. Elinore looked up to see a man standing silently in the corner.

This must be Nate Champion, Elinore thought. He was stocky and his hair hung over his steely blue eyes. He nodded to Elinore.

Elinore sat down on the bed next to Mrs. Tisdale. She held her and they cried. After a long while Elinore took her arms from around Mrs. Tisdale and forced the woman to look into her face.

"Mrs. Tisdale," Elinore said. "I think it's time to clean Mr. Tisdale up and put on his Sunday clothes."

Mrs. Tisdale stared at Elinore with her red, swollen eyes for some time. Finally, she said, "We can dress him but we're not going to bury him."

Nate looked at Elinore in horror.

"Fine," Elinore said. "We'll talk about that later. But for now, if you'll find some clothes for Mr. Tisdale. . . ."

Mrs. Tisdale went to a large cedar chest and carefully chose Mr. Tisdale's finest clothes.

"He wore this shirt the day we were married," Mrs. Tisdale said, not looking up from the homespun linen shirt-waist.

Elinore led Mrs. Tisdale to the sitting room and directed Stewart to make some tea. As she entered the sitting room she saw the mirror laid against the side wall. It had a carved wooden frame. Elinore walked over to it. The mirror was covered with blood. In the shattered glass Elinore could see fragments of her reflection. She couldn't stand to look and quickly went to the kitchen to boil some water for the dreaded task ahead.

When the water was ready she went off alone to dress the body. She could barely look down as Mr. Tisdale lay there stiff, his clothes and hair matted with blood and dirt. It didn't seem possible that she had had tea with him yesterday. She began to cry; everything seemed so bleak. No, I mustn't, she told herself and quickly began the task.

Gently she removed his clothes and tied them in a bundle to be burned. She began washing his body. It took all her strength to turn him over and wash the huge hole in his back. She washed and combed his hair, then carefully dressed him. She saved the shirt-waist for last. The bosom was ruffled and tucked, all done by hand. It obviously was made by Mrs. Tisdale as a wedding present. She buttoned the lace cuffs and inspected him one last time. She wanted everything as nearly perfect as possible for Mrs. Tisdale.

In less than an hour she emerged from the room. She went directly to the kitchen to wash up and begin preparing dinner. Stewart followed her silently.

"Please take them and burn them," she said to Stewart, handing him the bundle of clothing. "And then if you would wipe the blood from that mirror."

She did not want to go near that mirror again.

"You're doing a fine job," he said. "We're all appreciative."

He turned and left the room. It seemed the first time he had ever said anything kind to her.

As the sun set people began appearing, all shocked and hungry. It seemed everyone had come for thirty miles carrying butter, chickens, bread, eggs, coffee, elk and deer meat, precious apples and assorted clothing. The men discussed the tragedy and how they would hire a man to help Mrs. Tisdale. The women wept.

By sundown the small front room was filled. The din was deafening. Elinore thought it was the oddest wake she had ever attended.

Suddenly a large woman burst into the room, carrying a roasted goose under her arm. She was tall and plump, with a mass of auburn hair atop her head. She was better dressed than most who had come. Elinore stood back and watched as this woman took command.

"Why, have you all lost your senses?" she began. The room went quiet. "It's past dark and the children aren't in bed."

She looked around the room and called to an elderly grey-haired woman. "Mrs. Louderer, please," she said, handing the goose to a young man who stood at the door.

Mrs. Louderer obediently went off with the children.

"Jack Flagg," she called to a light-haired man who sat with his wife. "Get my bag. Mrs. Tisdale is going to need something to help her sleep."

Amazed and a bit fearful of this commanding woman Elinore returned to the kitchen. But just as she began to clean up she heard that distinct voice behind her.

"I see someone was thinking before I got here," she said to Elinore. "I don't think we've met. I'm Mrs. O'Shaughnessy. My ranch is on the way to town."

"Pleasure, Mrs. O'Shaughnessy," Elinore said, though she wasn't sure she meant it. "My name is Elinore Pruitt."

"Why, I heard of you," Mrs. O'Shaughnessy said, with a chuckle. "You come to housekeep for that strange Scotsman, Stewart."

Elinore smiled at her reference to Stewart.

"You're the only one with any brains out here, excepting me, of course," Mrs. O'Shaughnessy continued.

"You did a fine job dressing Mr. Tisdale. I know it wasn't easy. I was expecting to have to do it."

She turned and left the room. Elinore was flattered but still uncertain about this bold woman.

Mrs. Tisdale had now been put to bed, along with the children, and suddenly it appeared a town meeting was in progress.

"What are we going to do?" Jack Flagg called out. "Sit back and let them pick us off one by one? Wolcott and his boys are too arrogant."

Elinore looked out from the kitchen at Jack Flagg. He was of medium height and fine-looking. Later she found out he owned the Red Fork ranch and lived there with his wife and step-son. He also worked for James Adrian.

"First Cattle Kate and now Tisdale," Nick Ray said. "Anyone that steps up and tries to organize the small ranchers and homesteaders they just get rid of."

"Gentlemen," Stewart called out, "before we do anything drastic let me have my chance with Wolcott and the others tomorrow. There's a meeting of the Association. Let's be reasonable."

"Yeah, that's what you been saying since they lynched Cattle Kate," called out a rough-looking cowboy.

The arguing continued without resolution. The small ranchers did not trust Stewart as he was a member of the dreaded Cattlemen's Association. They knew Stewart was right but Elinore was learning that it wasn't a cowboy's nature to be patient.

Tired from the day and further exhausted by the arguing, Elinore left the kitchen and made up a bed on the floor in the children's room. She thought of the children so innocent and now fatherless, like her own Jerrine. She laid her head down and cried herself to sleep.

*   *   *

As day began to break Elinore came out of her slumber. A familiar sickening sensation came over her. It was just like the sensation she had experienced the day after her husband's killing. She had awakened hoping desperately that all that had occurred the day before had been a nightmare. But as she came out of her sleep she knew John Tisdale had been murdered. She was nauseated.

Elinore sat up quickly, trying not to think, and dressed. She tiptoed past Mrs. O'Shaughnessy, who had made a bed up next to hers, and went to the kitchen to prepare breakfast for the Tisdales and Mr. Stewart.

After the coffee was ready Elinore went quietly into Mrs. Tisdale's room. Mrs. Tisdale lay on the bed, staring up at the rough-wood ceiling. She obviously had not slept.

Without a word, Elinore sat Mrs. Tisdale up in the bed and put the coffee cup in her hands. Mrs. Tisdale sipped at it. After a few minutes Elinore said, "Mrs. Tisdale, I know this is difficult, but Mr. Tisdale must be buried today."

Mrs. Tisdale looked up at Elinore and nodded. Tears came to her eyes. Elinore held her and again they cried.

When Elinore returned to the kitchen to get Mrs. Tisdale more coffee the house had begun to stir. She could hear Stewart out in the barn sawing and hammering what she knew would be Mr. Tisdale's coffin. Mrs. O'Shaughnessy had told her the night before that Stewart was an excellent carpenter and had asked to make it. Mrs. O'Shaughnessy would pad and line it. Then Stewart would trim it and cover it. It wasn't that they couldn't have afforded to buy a coffin but it was a sad pleasure to do everything themselves as a last goodwill gesture for their friend.

In the early afternoon a somber crowd stood around the hole that had been dug behind the barn.

Bishop Beeler, a Mormon but the only minister for

miles around, stood at the head of the grave. He wore a black frock coat and a wide-brimmed hat of the same color. Mrs. Tisdale and the children were at his side. When the bishop began to speak the quiet murmur of the crowd died.

"Let all bitterness and wrath and anger and clamor and evil-speaking be put away with all malice," he began. "Be ye kindly affectioned to one another, tender-hearted, forgiving as God hath forgiven you. Bless them that persecute you, bless, and curse not. For it is written, Vengeance is mine, I will repay, saith the Lord. Let us pray for John and his family."

Everyone bowed his head, Mrs. O'Shaughnessy came up and held Mrs. Tisdale on one side. Nate Champion took her other side. Six men lowered the coffin into the hole. Mrs. Tisdale knelt and tossed a handful of dirt into the grave. She rose and held her handkerchief to her face. To Elinore it was a bad dream repeated.

Mrs. Tisdale was led back to the house and put to bed. Shortly thereafter, the meeting of last night was resumed.

"What are we to do?" Elinore heard from the kitchen where the women had congregated.

Elinore peeked into the room to see who was talking. It was Nick Ray.

The other women had feigned disinterest but it was fear that kept them from listening, fear that it would be their husband or son next. Perhaps if they didn't listen the problem would go away. Elinore knew better.

"This is the worst I've ever seen it," Elinore heard from behind her.

It was Mrs. O'Shaughnessy. "These cowboys are after blood," she continued. "Those arrogant cattle barons have gone too far this time."

"How do you know who is responsible?" Elinore asked.

"Dear, this feud's been going on as long as there

have been cattle on the range," Mrs. O'Shaughnessy
said. "And now, as more and more homesteaders are
claiming land the barons considered theirs to exploit,
the tension builds daily. The big cattlemen came out
about ten years ago, right after the Indians were done
away with, bought up a herd, and watched their investment double in a year's time. Then they would go
back East to spend their money. The competition from
the independent cowboys was negligible but the ax fell
this winter. While the 'lords' were sipping champagne
at Delmonico's in New York their investment froze to
death. When the snow finally stopped, the cattle just
floated in a continuous stream down the creek."

Elinore couldn't believe what she was hearing. Mrs.
O'Shaughnessy just hated the rich cattlemen like all the
others, she thought. She would have to ask Mr. Adrian
about the situation next time she saw him. She hoped
that it would be soon.

"Miss Pruitt, do you know how to use a gun?" Mrs.
O'Shaughnessy asked, interrupting Elinore's thoughts.

"Why, no," Elinore replied.

"Well, you'd better learn," Mrs. O'Shaughnessy said.
"Get Stewart to teach you. He's one of the best shots
in the county. If he won't, you come out to my place
and we'll have a lesson or two."

Elinore nodded, though she remained unconvinced.
Why did she have to learn to shoot, she wondered.
All she wanted was a piece of land for Jerrine and
herself. She wanted no part of the cattle business or
this violence.   ᴥᣩ

6

THE CHEYENNE Club in Buffalo was a unique institution in the cow country. It was here that cattle barons from London, Boston, New York, and Philadelphia met to mingle among gentlemen of their own class. The club boasted the best steward and chef of any club in the United States, a wine cellar second to none—though many of the English complained that Americans did not know how to serve wine—and servants imported from Ottawa where, under the British flag, men were taught to be proper servants.

The club's roster contained titles out of Burke's Peerage and names familiar to the highest financial circles of Wall Street. The heady mixture of youth, money, and optimism bubbled in the high plains like the champagne the members consumed in such huge quantities. They came to speculate in what many considered an outdoor sport that paid handsome dividends, the cattle industry.

People on both sides of the Atlantic were talking about the fortunes to be made by raising cattle in the West. Free grass, by courtesy of Uncle Sam! No cost beyond the paltry wages of a handful of "cow servants". No capital investment worth mentioning—just a few rude log buildings set up on public domain. No risks—simply buy a herd, set up a "ranch"—and nature would do the rest.

The English felt particularly able as they were excellent horsemen. All they needed was a little practice throwing a rope. But it was the canny Scots who plunged the hardest. With the promise of at least twenty-five percent dividends, and with losses arising only from natural causes, there would be no speculation in cattle-raising.

The night following Tisdale's funeral Stewart entered the Cheyenne Club as the sun was setting. Tonight promised to be a gala evening. It was the first meeting of the Stock Growers Association that season. The members came in white tie and tails, which they facetiously dubbed their "Herefords," in reference to the popular breed of cow with dark coat and white chest. Steward went along with this formality, though he thought it utterly foolish.

The solid-walnut paneled rooms led off a great two-story hall that ran the entire length of the club. There were enormous fireplaces at each end of the hall. The walls were hung with buffalo robes, and antlered heads of elk and deer. The walnut staircase ran up to the "musicians' gallery" with its potted palms and vines climbing from the floor below. Downstairs, there was a dining room that could seat fifty comfortably, an extensive library, an office, and a central living room— seventy by seventy feet—where the meeting would take place after dinner. In the back was a huge kitchen and pantry. There was a game room lighted by Tiffany lamps, filled with pool tables and potted palms.

Stewart could smell the cigar smoke and could hear the din of conversation emanating from the living room where the gentlemen would certainly be sipping champagne and whiskey.

He entered the living room from the foyer to see the familiar faces of the Association members. The attendance was the lightest he could remember for the spring gala. Major Frank Wolcott stood by the podium in his "Hereford" though he was famous for his brown bowler hat, white collar, and riding breeches, and never, never dressed in the style of a lowly cowboy. Stewart had heard the cowboys refer to him as "the Dude," their variation of the English "Duke".

Frank Canton was also there, not in his usual long black overcoat and double-over black broad-brimmed hat, but in his "Hereford." Canton's long handlebar moustache was as black as his narrow black eyes.

Stewart looked to the far corner of the room to see Adrian signal him.

"Stewart, come over here, ole boy, and have a bit of bubbly with some gentlemen," Adrian called. "It's been a long time since we've all been together."

Stewart moved through the group, nodding and shaking hands with those gentlemen whose attention he caught. Finally, he reached Adrian. He shook hands with him and with Moreton Frewen. Frewen had come out years earlier for his health and had stayed on to gain his fortune. Stewart disliked him more than the others, for he was pretentious beyond imagination.

Frewen was constantly traveling back and forth from New York to court the lovely Clara Jerome, daughter of the New York financier Leonard Jerome and the sister of Jennie Jerome, who had married Lord Randolph Churchill. But Moreton's reputation for being fast had kept the conservative family cautious. Stewart suspected it was her position rather than the woman that kept Frewen so persistent.

"Well, ole boy," Adrian continued, "We must chat after dinner about the horrendous winter just past. Stewart, I still can't understand why you persist in staying out here off-season."

"Adrian, I've tried to explain this before," Stewart

said. "The cattle business is not like the opera. It requires attention all year long, particularly in the off-season, as you insist on calling it. When this group sobers up and talks to their foremen they're going to discover that many of them have lost fortunes."

"I've kept up with the business this winter," Adrian said. "I read the Cheyenne *Weekly Leader*. I was as well informed as you were in your snowbound house."

"Yes," Frewen said. "You needn't be so self-righteous. We're serious businessmen, too. It's just that we're not masochistic enough to spend the winters in this God-forsaken place when there is so much to do back East, or in Adrian's case, in Denver."

Frewen winked at Adrian. Adrian returned a smile.

"The *Leader* made many mentions of the trouble in Montana," Adrian said, "but it said repeatedly that the range cattle business in Wyoming had suffered no unusual loss."

"You know as well as I do," Stewart said, "the Cheyenne *Weekly Leader* is for all intents and purposes run by the Association. They print only what the members want to read or they would go out of business. Didn't you read any of the headlines in the Chicago papers?"

"Stewart," Frewen said confidently, "the *Leader* said that most accounts in the Eastern papers were greatly exaggerated. It seems to me that since they were writing from the source they would know better than their Eastern counterparts. And I've trusted the Leader."

"Yes, and I was out here with your fellows from the *Leader*," Stewart said. "We had fifty-four consecutive days of snow beginning in February. Many of the cattle died of thirst because the streams were frozen solid. My men had to go out and cut holes in the streams and tanks so that my cattle could drink."

"Well, then, what were your losses?" Frewen asked.

"My losses were negligible," Stewart said with some pride. "You see, I kept plenty of men on the payroll and they herded the cattle away from the death-traps. The men had to blacken their eyes with the deposits from kerosene lamps to ward off snow blindness. Some men died exerting themselves in the subzero weather. And all for forty dollars a month."

"You're always so sympathetic to your cowservants," Adrian said. "Why, give them half a chance and they would gladly rob you."

"I've had no thieving at my ranch," Stewart said defiantly.

"Enough of this sentimentality," Frewen said. "The situation couldn't be as bad as you describe it. You're just letting your cautious Scots nature get the better of you."

"Oh, thank God," Adrian said, "There is Stephan. You can always depend on good help to announce dinner when conversations are becoming tedious."

"When the round-up comes this July, gentlemen, I promise not to say I told you so," Stewart said.

"Well, Stewart," Adrian said. "Consider that if I hadn't gone to Denver you might not have the lovely Miss Pruitt to keep you company."

"Miss Pruitt does not keep me company. She keeps house for me."

"Good. I was hoping that would be your response," Adrian said. "Then you shouldn't have any objections to my riding out tomorrow afternoon to pay the fair maiden a visit."

"No, of course not," Stewart snapped. "Shall we?" he added, gesturing toward the dining room.

Dinner seemed endless. Stewart was always amazed by the ability of these men to sit for hours over a single meal. Although he liked to eat, an entire evening was too long for simply taking care of a biological necessity. There was soup, fish, vegetables, meat, wine, champagne, more vegetables, pastries and coffee. This display of opulence was upsetting as Stewart knew of people who had nothing but potatoes all winter and were grateful for them. Finally, the men adjourned to the sitting room and as soon as the cognac was poured and cigars lit the meeting began. Most of the members were half drunk by now.

Stewart couldn't help but compare the richly paneled room filled with these arrogant men with the bare-walled cabin of this morning filled with desperate men.

Thomas Sturgis, secretary of the Association, pounded the gavel and called the meeting to order. Sturgis was a short man, rather squat, approaching middle-age. He had brown hair and brown eyes. He was a member of a well-to-do New York importing family and had been a member of the Association since its fruition in 1873.

"Gentlemen," Sturgis began, "we have grave matters to discuss tonight. Graver than any this Association has had to deal with to date."

Stewart felt encouraged by this beginning. Perhaps Sturgis had kept in touch with the disastrous happening of this winter and knew of the tremendous losses that had occurred.

"There is a special menace," Sturgis continued, "to all honest cattle owners. Theft is being practiced with apparent impunity by men in the employ of well-known ranchmen. That's why we've had losses this winter."

Stewart was stunned. Sturgis was discussing rustling as the great threat! Why, if every cowboy and home-steader was a thief they couldn't have rustled all the cattle that these men lost this winter! But it seemed these men preferred to remain ignorant up to the last moment, the round-up this spring.

"Men with no cattle of their own and no means to buy any are filing brands of their own," Sturgis said. "In order to protect our investments, gentlemen, I resolve that we blacklist any cattle-owning cowboys. By this I mean that any cowboy who insisted on owning cattle would be denied employment by any member of the Association. But in order for this resolve to work it must be unanimous, so I will put it to a vote and the majority decision will be binding to all Association members."

Stewart stood.

"Gentlemen of the Association," he said, "I beg you to consider this proposal before a rash vote. If all cattle-owning cowboys are to be placed on this blacklist and denied employment permanently they will have no choice but to increase their herds, and put a claim in on a homestead, producing a greater competition to us in the long run. We should allow cowpunchers to own cattle. Ninety-nine percent of them are honest men. And if they are allowed, even encouraged to buy mavericks, the unbranded calves, it would give them a chance to get ahead and give them an interest in the range. This will do more than any other measure to stop rustling, as these boys are on the range all the time."

"These men are thieves and anarchists," Sturgis replied. "Why, if we let them go unpunished we will lose all power to govern the affairs of the cattle industry."

"Mr. Sturgis, with all due respect for your proposal," Stewart said, wanting to remain polite, "these cowboys are the most independent class of men on earth and they won't take this lying down for long. Why, this proposal requires no proof or even charge of wrong-doing, but simply ownership as presumptive evidence of guilt."

"Mr. Stewart, these men are guilty," Sturgis said. "How can a cowpuncher on a salary of forty dollars a month for six to ten months out of the year afford to invest in cattle?"

"Mr. Sturgis," Stewart replied, "there are foremen who make three times the average pay of a cowpuncher. These men became foremen because of their exceptional ability and know-how. Eventually, they wish to become independent, as any man would. You can't punish a man for a strong will. These are exactly the men we don't wish to cross."

"Stewart," Sturgis said, disregarding civilities and showing his temper, "you can't mean to say you are afraid of these men?"

"It's not a question of fear but good judgment," Stewart said. "You can't erect a wall between the big owners and the ambitious men in our employ and not expect repercussions. These men have rights, too."

"What then of our rights?" called Frewen from the back of the room, his alcoholic stupor evaporating momentarily.

"Hear, hear," was the general call from the meeting room.

"Quiet, gentlemen," Sturgis said, pounding the gavel on the podium. Despite his call to order, Sturgis' satisfaction with the consensus was apparent.

Stewart knew he had been defeated. He took a long swallow from his cognac.

"All in favor, say yea," Sturgis called.

"Yea!" rang out from the room.

"All those against," Sturgis called, his eyes on Stewart, "say nay."

There was silence.

"Then I submit to the Association a unanimous decision to blacklist all cattle-owning cowboys from the employment of any member of this Association," Sturgis announced, thoroughly pleased with himself.

Stewart thought of the men in his employ who had risked their lives maintaining his livestock this winter who did have cattle of their own. Now he would either have to disobey the Association resolution or his own conscience. For the moment he did not dare discuss Tisdale's death with the Association. After that vote they certainly would not be sympathetic to the homesteaders' plight. Stewart took another swallow of his cognac, and gestured to Stephan, the butler, to bring him another.

Stephan immediately set another cognac down in front of Stewart.

"Thank you, Stephan," Stewart said.

"You're welcome sir," Stephan replied with all the formality of the best English butlers.

He takes himself so seriously, Stewart thought. He must be sixty years old. His posture was perfect, his nose always upturned, and he never said anything except in response. Stewart had never seen him in anything except his "Hereford."

"Hey ole chap," someone behind Stewart said. "No hard feelings, eh?"

Stewart turned to see Adrian, who was quite drunk by now, standing there.

"No, of course not, James," Stewart murmured.

James Adrian continued past Stewart.

"Wait, James," Stewart said, "there is something I want to discuss with you."

"Does it have to do with women?" Adrian asked.

"No, James," Stewart said, "This is serious."

"Well, what is so damn serious now, you old Scot?" Adrian said, his eyes rolling slightly. "Don't you ever enjoy yourself, Clyde?"

"James, I want to talk to you about the death of John Tisdale," Stewart said.

Stewart's remark sobered Adrian.

"Why do you want to discuss this with me?" Adrian asked.

"I want to know who was behind it," Stewart said.

"Are you implying that I would know?" Adrian retorted.

"It's a pretty tight inner circle here," Stewart said. "I thought you might have heard something. The homesteaders are up in arms. Tisdale's death was outright murder. All evidence points back to this club. I meant to bring it up but Sturgis caught me off guard with that blacklist proposal."

"Listen, Clyde, like I said before, Tisdale was a troublemaker. He asked for it."

"He didn't ask to die, Adrian. And what of Cattle Kate?"

"The same goes for her," Adrian said. He turned his back on Stewart and began to walk away. "Don't go defending the little guys, Clyde. They always lose."

Stewart had known Adrian a long time and he was certain Adrian knew more than he was telling. After all, Adrian was out there the day Tisdale was shot. But he's not cold-blooded, Stewart thought. His biggest fault is that he is arrogant and heartless to those he considers beneath him. He also takes his pleasure a bit too seriously, particularly women.

Suddenly Stewart's thoughts jolted back to Miss Pruitt and Adrian's announced visit tomorrow. He swallowed his cognac in one gulp and signaled Stephan for another.

7

ELINORE STOOD in the center of the soil that McPherren had turned just two days before. It seemed an eternity since John Tisdale had stopped by for tea. Elinore couldn't understand why anyone would kill such a kind, hard-working man. Could he have been a rustler? The trouble with finding out was that everyone she asked had a different story and each believed it passionately.

She looked down at the soil. This was as close to her dream of homesteading as she had gotten so far. She knelt down and ran the dirt through her fingers. In this soil she would find her freedom and a respectable life for Jerrine and herself. Why, she had even heard that the Department of Agriculture in Washington would send enough of any seed, as much as you wanted, to make a thorough trial. And it didn't even cost postage! Elinore planned to write this very evening, as this was her day off. That was also why she had the full day to work in her garden.

Elinore had asked Mr. Stewart if the garden could be directly behind the kitchen window, as the light was good there. But just as importantly, she wanted to have the pleasure of watching it grow as she did her other chores.

Mr. Stewart had given her a bunch of potatoes that morning. She made neat furrows with a small shovel she had taken from the barn and dropped the cut potatoes into the holes. Now, all that was left was to water them. And if they grew she would have a fine crop of potatoes this fall.

She laid the shovel down and went to the kitchen to fetch a pail. She carried it back and forth many times until the garden was well watered. When she was finally done she turned the pail upside down and sat on it to admire her hard work.

As she sat on the pail she thought of being poor in Denver. Once she had her own land she would do chores for no one but herself and there would be no house rent to pay. Even if improving her own place went slowly, it would be that much done that would stay done, unlike washing other people's laundry.

"Miss Pruitt," someone said. She looked up to see Adrian standing over her.

"I've come to call," Adrian said, "to see if you would take a ride with me."

He was looking down at her. She was in her oldest dress, now spotted with the soil she had been so fond of minutes ago.

"Didn't Stewart tell you I was coming?" Adrian asked.

"No," she murmured, looking down at herself.

What a hateful thing to do, she thought. Mr. Stewart does these things just to spite me. I haven't done anything to deserve such a reproach. Then she remembered his warning about visiting with Adrian in his home.

"Mr. Adrian," she said, "if you don't mind waiting I could change my dress and be ready in no time."

"For a fair maiden such as you, I would wait forever," he said, bowing slightly.

Just then Elinore noticed Stewart coming from the barn. She was angry with him for not telling her of Adrian's intentions, but she was even more afraid of what he would say to them.

"Hello, Adrian," Stewart called. "Slipped my mind that you were coming out today."

"After the condition you were in last night it's no wonder," Adrian said jokingly.

Somewhat relieved, Elinore picked up the pail and started toward the house.

"Miss Pruitt," Stewart called, "who gave you these tools?"

He pointed to the shovel.

"No one, sir," she said, "I helped myself."

"In the future I would appreciate your asking my permission to use my tools, as I value them highly," he said. "They are not easily replaced."

Elinore was humiliated. She knew she should have returned the shovel to the barn but in her desperation to get away from the two men she had forgotten it. Without a word she went to the shovel, picked it up and started toward the barn. Her fury rose though, for she knew that Stewart cared less for the shovel than he cared to humiliate her in front of Adrian.

When Elinore returned to the backyard she had replaced the old red gingham housedress with a blue calico dress she had made herself. The gored skirt's fullness emphasized her delicate waist. Atop her head sat a sunbonnet, with a narrow edging of lace around it. The sash at her waist had a pattern of forget-me-nots. Her slippers were patent leather. The white stockings made her legs look smooth and refined. Her hands were gloved in white crochet. She knew she looked lovely. When the two men saw her they stopped their conversation.

"Miss Pruitt," Adrian said, "you look like an angel in that dress."

Elinore was so pleased, for this was the first time she had had the opportunity to attend to her toilette for Adrian. Three times they had been together and three times she had looked her worst—their first meeting when she had come from the laundry, the second meeting when she had just finished her chores, and today when she was sitting atop a pail.

Stewart said nothing but continued to stare.

Elinore wore her thick red hair in a coronet braid, which added height and dignity, as well as being simple and becoming. This coiffure, tucked neatly under the sunbonnet, emphasized her violet eyes. It felt so lovely to be a woman again, even if it were just for the afternoon, she thought.

"Shall we?" Adrian asked, offering her his arm. He turned and called to Stewart, "See you later, ole boy."

They strolled arm-in-arm to the front of the ranch house. Elinore couldn't have been more delighted. For the first time since she had arrived in Powder River she felt certain she had made the correct decision in coming.

Adrian's carriage was waiting. It was a black surrey, drawn by a powerful black stallion. The horse neighed softly as they approached.

"Mr. Adrian, your carriage is lovely," Elinore said. "And such a fine horse."

"Thank you," Adrian said. "I was hoping you would like the surrey. I had it brought by rail from St. Louis. It arrived just yesterday. This is its maiden voyage."

Elinore was excited as Adrian helped her into the seat. He jumped in effortlessly beside her and they were off.

The horse trotted at first but soon Adrian clicked the reins and the horse broke into a canter. The wind whirled by as they drove northward. Elinore had to hold on to her sunbonnet.

To the south were the great somber, pine-clad Big Horn Mountains, while ahead and on every side were grass-covered hills with sloping sides and flat tops. There was a tang of sage in the air. All around were shrubs covered with flowers that looked and smelled like goldenrod. The sun was bright, the sky cloudless. Elinore couldn't have been more pleased.

"Miss Pruitt," Adrian said, "why don't you sit a bit closer?"

Timidly, Elinore moved closer. Adrian reached out his arm and put it around her waist.

"You look so lovely today, Miss Pruitt," Adrian said. "You truly dazzled me when you came out of the house. Even that dolt Stewart couldn't keep his eyes off of you."

"Thank you," Elinore said.

He pulled her closer. Their thighs were touching now. Elinore trembled. She hoped Adrian wouldn't notice.

"Mr. Adrian," Elinore said after a long silence, "may I ask you a question?"

"Anything, Miss Pruitt," replied Adrian.

"I was out at John Tisdale's house yesterday," Elinore began. She noticed Adrian tense. "I don't understand who shot him and why."

"Have those crazy homesteaders been putting ideas in your pretty head?" Adrian asked.

"I heard a lot of angry talk," Elinore said.

"Those men are thieves," Adrian said.

"Well, they are saying . . ." Elinore began.

"My lovely, never mind what they are saying," Adrian interrupted. "It is too beautiful a day to concern ourselves with those peasants. If you want my

opinion, I would simply advise you not to associate
with such commoners. They are hardly worthy of
your company."

Although Elinore was flattered by Adrian's remarks
she was still concerned about the death of John Tisdale. But she would forget it for now and enjoy this
gentleman's company. After an early marriage so
filled with love, Elinore thought she could never love
again but, now, perhaps . . .

"Shall we head back?" Adrian suggested, interrupting Elinore's thoughts.

Elinore thought she perceived a change in Adrian's manner but she dismissed this as being overly
sensitive.

"Why, yes, Mr. Adrian," Elinore said.

Adrian turned the carriage southward, back toward
the ranch. The sun was low in the westward sky.
Gorgeous colors were forming over the hills and already the little valley was beginning to turn the
blue-purple of sunset.

Finally, they approached the ranch house. Adrian
stopped the carriage a hundred yards from the house.
They sat for a moment in silence. Elinore began to
tremble again. She dared not look into that handsome
face.

Gently, Adrian took her face in his hands. Now
she could not help but look into his hazel eyes. He
stared down at her. Instinctively, she closed her eyes.
And softly, so softly, he touched his lips to hers,
playfully at first, and then forcefully. Elinore shivered
in his embrace. The sensation made her feel more
alive than she had in such a long while. One last
time, Adrian pulled her close to his chest and pressed
his firm lips to hers. She weakened and fully gave
in to his strength. When he pulled away, they looked
into each other's eyes for a moment. Then, without
a word, he drove her to the front door, gracefully
jumped from the surrey and helped her to the ground.

"May I come again next Wednesday, Miss Pruitt?"
Adrian asked.

"Yes, please do," Elinore replied, thinking herself
bold.

"Thank you. Next week then," he said, as he bent
to kiss her gloved hand.

Elinore turned and walked toward the house. It
was as though she were in a dream. She felt light,
and at once calm and yet excited. She turned to wave
a final goodbye to Adrian. He waved back. She was
so elated.

In her euphoria she failed to notice Stewart watching from the front door. But as she approached she
saw him quickly move inside the house. Her happiness withered as she thought of his inevitable reproach.

Elinore sat at the small oak desk in her room. By
candlelight she sent for the seeds and finished a
letter to Bette Iverson. This was the first letter she
had written to Bette and it was long overdue. She
had hesitated to write because of her feeling for
James Adrian and had finally decided to make no
mention of him. She pushed her chair back from the
desk for a moment and let her thoughts drift to his
handsome face, his strong arms.

The drone of Stewart's bagpipes interrupted her
thoughts. My God, would he never stop, she thought.

Elinore rose from the desk and went to her chest
of clothing. She had felt so good this afternoon dressing like a lady that she decided to continue the sensation into the night. She reached into the chest and
took out her finest dressing gown. She hadn't worn
it since Phillip's death and though she felt a bit guilty
wearing it, she knew it would make her feel feminine.

She undressed quickly and for an embarrassed moment she looked down to admire her full breasts and
narrow waist. Quickly, she reached for the white silk

gown and slipped it over her head. She rubbed her
hands over her breasts and down to her waist. Then
she buttoned the delicate lace cuffs.

Elinore undid her hair from the coronet braid and
brushed it thoroughly. Before climbing into bed she
went to the free-standing mirror to admire herself one
last time. She felt shameful but she enjoyed the contour of her buttocks, the roundness of her breasts,
and the lushness of her soft red hair as it fell to her
shoulders. Quite satisfied, she took the candle, put
it on the nightstand, and pulled the comforter over
her.

All the while she heard the bagpipes drone.

As she lay in bed, she realized for the first time that
all the finest things in the house were in her room—
the mirror, the featherbed, the pillow shams, the pos-
ter bed, even a small hand-woven rug. It was curious
she had never thought of it before. It was just another
of Stewart's peculiarities, she decided.

She could still hear that damnable bagpipe downstairs. Stewart played "Campbells are Coming" over
and over until she thought she would go mad.

Well, except for the bagpipes, it had been a lovely
day, she thought. Even the cowboys had gone off
to town for their weekly card game, so except for
Stewart, all was quiet.

Elinore opened her book of adventure tales and
read for an hour. When she became sleepy, she closed
the book, blew out the candle, then snuggled beneath
the covers.

In the dark, Elinore lay thinking of James Adrian
and the lovely afternoon they had spent together.
She retraced the entire afternoon, savoring every detail. In no time, she slipped off into sleep, hoping to
dream of her English gentleman.

With a start Elinore sat up in bed. In the dark
she could hear a whining noise. She was frightened
but soon realized it was Stewart still playing his bag-

pipes. She couldn't tell how long she had been asleep
and cursed him for waking her.

But in a moment she realized that there was something different about the familiar whine. She lay still
and listened. It seemed to drone longer than ever.
He must be drinking, she thought.

But there was something else different about the
dreaded song. It was louder than usual. The sound
seemed to be coming directly from the stairs now, no
longer muffled by the walls of the sitting room.

The sound grew louder. She heard him stumble on
the stairs. He must be drunk, she thought. He's coming up here!

Elinore wanted to scream but she knew no one
would hear her as all the cowhands were still in
town. She sat frozen with fear as the whining grew
louder.

Oh, I wish James were here, she thought. I must
find something to protect myself with. But the room
was dark. She dared not move from the bed. She
reached over and picked up the candlestick that lay
on the night table. It was brass and heavy, but it
would never be enough.

The sound grew closer. It seemed to be right outside her door. Suddenly the bagpipes were silent. She
held her breath and listened. She could hear Stewart
grumbling.

She gripped the candlestick tighter.

She heard his heavy footstep. But it was not getting closer. He must be going away!

The footsteps stopped. Elinore prayed he would
go downstairs. She held her breath and waited. Then
she heard it. He stumbled on the stairs. He was going
away!

Elinore got back under the covers. But it was a
long while before she could fall asleep.   ᕦᔕ

8

ELINORE ROSE early the next day though she had been awake most of the night. She attended to her morning chores quickly so she could start papering the sitting room.

She had found the wallpaper while cleaning out a storage room and decided to put it to use. The paper was a peach color with a striped background. Between the stripes were clusters of delicate rosebuds. Elinore thought it beautiful. She had discussed her plan with Stewart days ago and though she had not seen him today she decided to go ahead.

She mixed the paste in an old candy-bucket and brought a barrel from the barn to use as a ladder. Elinore had never papered a room before but that did not deter her. Besides, after last night's incident, she wanted to stay busy to keep from thinking.

She began with the ceiling and placed one long, sloppy strip up after the other. It was noon when she placed the last strip to the ceiling, all the while struggling to keep it from sticking to her. Suddenly she heard a noise behind her. It so startled her that she stepped off the barrel into the bucket of paste. She hesitated to turn around fearing Stewart would be standing there scowling.

But to her surprise when she turned she saw Mrs. O'Shaughnessy smiling. Mrs. O'Shaughnessy broke into a laugh when she saw Elinore's face. At first Elinore was offended but when she looked into Mrs. O'Shaughnessy's face she broke into a laugh, too. Mrs. O'Shaughnessy's eyes, she noticed, were the merriest blue.

"I'm sorry, Miss Pruitt," Mrs. O'Shaughnessy said, "but I couldn't help myself."

"Oh, that's fine," Elinore said, looking down at her foot in the bucket. "That's the best laugh I've had in a long while. Would you like some tea? I think I'm finished papering for the day."

Elinore took her paste-covered boot from the bucket. Both women broke into a laugh again. Mrs. O'Shaughnessy picked up the bucket and the rest of the tools and followed Elinore to the kitchen.

After cleaning herself and the tools, Elinore put each tool back where she'd found it, fearing Stewart's wrath. She filled the kettle and set out her favorite pair of matching cups and saucers from Stewart's potpourri.

Just as they were about to sit down to tea and some womanly conversation, Tucker, a newly employed cowboy, and Stewart came into the kitchen. Elinore tensed, as she didn't know how Stewart would react to her having tea in the afternoon with a friend.

"Miss Pruitt," Stewart began, "I was wondering if you would be so good as to take a look at this young man's thumb. He smashed the nail a few days back and has neglected to take care of it."

Tucker was lean, almost gaunt. Although he was tanned from his work his face was sickly. As he approached the women he tipped his head and laid his hand on the table for inspection.

Elinore looked at the thumb, and then at Mrs. O'Shaughnessy. They nodded in silent agreement. Immediately Elinore began various preparations with ingredients she took from the cabinet of medicines. Then she took the wooden chopping block from the wall and placed it on the table.

"Tucker, I fear there's a danger of blood poisoning," Elinore said. "If we place your thumb on this piece of wood and you look to the sun, I'll be able to see if there is any poison in it."

Mrs. O'Shaughnessy nodded to Tucker.

Trustingly, Tucker placed his thumb on the board and looked out the front hall to the afternoon sun. Before he could bat an eye, Elinore lifted the knife she held behind her back and chopped off the black, swollen thumb. It was so sudden and unexpected there seemed to be no pain.

"My God, woman," Stewart shouted, "what on earth do you think you're doing?"

Without answering, Elinore gave Tucker a dose of morphine and whiskey because she feared he would go into shock. Mrs. O'Shaughnessy then took Tucker's hand and turned it to expose a green streak starting up the arm.

"Mr. Stewart," Mrs. O'Shaughnessy said, "this man's thumb was gangrenous. Elinore did the only thing she could have."

As Mrs. O'Shaughnessy spoke Elinore took a razor and with one quick stroke she laid open the green streak in the man's arm and immersed the entire arm in a strong solution of bichloride of mercury. Elinore then immediately applied a cloth band around Tucker's arm to stop the bleeding.

"Tucker," Elinore said, "I'm sorry, but it was the only thing to do. You'll have to soak the arm for twenty minutes and then we'll have to get you to town to the doctor."

Stewart looked stunned.

"Mr. Stewart," Mrs. O'Shaughnessy said, "you'd better ready a team while Elinore and I dress the wound. This lady of yours is something. No one, not even me, could have done a better job."

She winked at Elinore.

"Elinore's quick thinking may have saved your life, young man," Mrs. O'Shaughnessy said to Tucker. "Now, don't just stand there, Stewart, you stubborn Scotsman! Get the team ready."

Stewart turned and left.

After twenty minutes of soaking, Elinore dressed the wound with absorbent cotton saturated with olive oil and carbolic acid. Then they bundled Tucker, who was now barely conscious from the effects of the whiskey and morphine, and helped him into the wagon. Stewart got up beside him and they started toward town.

"I may not be back tonight," Stewart said. "Mrs. O'Shaughnessy, I would be grateful if you could stay the night."

"Fine, Stewart," she said. "I hadn't any intention of leaving. Elinore and I haven't had a chance to chat."

Later that evening, after much preparation and a long nap, Elinore and Mrs. O'Shaughnessy sat down to a fine meal. Elinore had roasted a leg of lamb with potatoes. Mrs. O'Shaughnessy had brought some carrot jam in her mess box, along with some truly delicious rye bread she had made the day before. The food was such a treat, but the company was even better.

"Elinore," Mrs. O'Shaughnessy began. "You don't mind me calling you Elinore, do you? After the way you acted this afternoon I feel as though we are going to be good friends."

"No, of course not," Elinore replied. "It's a pleasure."

"Anyway, what I was about to say was this is the

finest lamb I've had since my mother roasted one for me in the old country," Mrs. O'Shaughnessy said.

"Thank you. I'm rather fond of it myself, particularly with fresh mint sauce."

"How are you getting along with that peculiar Scotsman?"

"Honestly, not very well. At times he even scares me."

"Little one, don't be scared of him," Mrs. O'Shaughnessy said. "His gruff exterior only covers up his softness. He's as harmless as a kitten."

"I'm not so sure. He seems to enjoy humiliating and even frightening me."

"Don't you remember when you were a little girl?" Mrs. O'Shaughnessy said. "And what the boys would do when they liked you?"

Elinore thought for a moment. Why, it had never occurred to her that Stewart might *like* her. But no, that was impossible! Stewart wasn't a mischievous little boy. He was a grown man.

"Mrs. O'Shaughnessy," Elinore replied. "That simply isn't the case. It seems to take all his energy to be civil to me. And last night . . ."

Elinore stopped. She didn't want to discuss it. Mrs. O'Shaughnessy must have guessed for she didn't ask Elinore to go on.

"Well, give it some time, girl, and we'll see," Mrs. O'Shaughnessy said. "What on God's good earth made you come out here in the first place?"

"Mrs. O'Shaughnessy, you're probably the only woman I know who might understand. I want to homestead my own place, so Jerrine and I will have a home of our own."

"Who's Jerrine?"

"Jerrine is my daughter. I was married but my husband was killed this winter," Elinore said, near tears. "I wanted to come and the Reverend Father Corrigan told me to put an ad in the Denver papers but then I met James Adrian and he fixed it up with Mr. Stewart."

Elinore got up and began clearing the table. She placed the dishes in the wash pan, careful to keep her back to Mrs. O'Shaughnessy. But it was no use. She felt Mrs. O'Shaughnessy put her arms around her.

"Go ahead and cry," Mrs. O'Shaughnessy said softly. "I know it feels good. You see, I'm a widow, too, and though I'm much older and my man has been gone a long while it still hurts. I was left alone to take over the ranch. Go ahead and have a good cry."

Elinore sobbed openly now. Mrs. O'Shaughnessy was right. It did feel good. But soon she stopped because though it felt good it was futile.

She wiped her eyes and said, "Shall we have tea in the sitting room?"

"That would be lovely," Mrs. O'Shaughnessy said. "Let's heat some water for the tea and the dishes and then I'll show you the last surprise in my mess box."

They set up a makeshift table from the barrel Elinore had used earlier as a ladder and put the two straight-backed chairs beside it. They sat down but as Elinore began to pour the tea Mrs. O'Shaughnessy jumped up saying, "I almost forgot."

She left the room and in a moment was back carrying two small plates and a small package. She placed the package on the table and unwrapped it. Inside was a large, lovely Irish soda bread. Elinore could smell the caraway seeds and the currants. This truly is a treat, Elinore thought.

"I bake these often and make enough to last for at least a week," Mrs. O'Shaughnessy said. "It's my mother's recipe. The secret is in the buttermilk."

Elinore bit into the small piece Mrs. O'Shaughnessy had put on her plate. It was wonderfully moist and slightly sweet. Thoroughly pleased, the women sipped their tea and enjoyed a moment of silence.

"You did a great job with the ceiling, Elinore,"

Mrs. O'Shaughnessy said, looking up. She finished her cake and cut another piece for each of them. "You'll have this place looking like a home in no time. That Scot is going to have to part with some of his money and get some furnishings though," she said with a laugh.

Elinore loved Mrs. O'Shaughnessy's wit, particularly when she chose to make fun of Stewart. She looked up at the ceiling and had to admit she had done a fine job. Then she suddenly thought of Tucker.

"I hope Tucker will be all right," she said.

"He's going to be just fine, but an hour or two would have make all the difference," Mrs. O'Shaughnessy said. "You saved that young man's life. Now, what of James Adrian? Do you know anything about him?"

"Nothing really," Elinore said, wanting to appear cool.

"Well, in that case, a bit of warning," Mrs. O'Shaughnessy said. "Stay away from him. He's trouble."

"What do you mean?" Elinore asked. She was indignant. "He's a gentleman."

She knew her tone of voice gave her away. She blushed from embarrassment. She remembered what Adrian had said about associating with commoners.

"I've known James Adrian a long while and he may be a thoroughbred, but he is no gentleman," Mrs. O'Shaughnessy said.

Elinore was angry. Who did this woman think she was, insulting James Adrian that way? But Elinore contained her anger, not wanting to make her emotions too obvious.

"Would you like more tea, Mrs. O'Shaughnessy?" she asked. "I'll boil a little more water."

Without waiting for a response, Elinore left the room.

She didn't understand why everyone was so disdainful of James Adrian. Well, she wouldn't listen. They're probably just jealous, Elinore decided as she refilled the kettle.   ☙

9

WEDNESDAY WAS a perfect spring day, brilliantly sunny and warm. James Adrian was up earlier than usual. He stood in front of the mirror, sprinkled tonic from a crystal bottle into his hands, and applied it to his hair. As he massaged it into his scalp the familiar musk rose to his nostrils. He wiped his hands on the linen cloth that hung from the brass ring on the table, straightened his tie, and reached for his well-polished black boots.

He paid extra attention to his toilet because he was to see Elinore that morning. But before he left there was some ugly business to attend to. He had asked all his cattle-owning hands to meet in the study. He had also ordered his stable boy to ready his fine new stallion, Noirceur, and its mate, Ma Femme.

The Association had informally decided that this was the most appropriate day to fire these men, as it was the end of the pay period and wouldn't complicate bookkeeping. Adrian reached for his long black coat, tucked a linen handkerchief into his pocket, and went downstairs.

As he entered the study the ten men were sitting

silently. What impertinence, Adrian thought. They hadn't even risen as he walked in. These cowservants would never learn their place.

"Good morning, men," Adrian said, as he took his place behind his oak desk.

"Please forgive me if I'm mistaken," Adrian continued, "but I believe all of you men own cattle of your own. Is that true?"

Each man nodded affirmatively.

"And that there are no other men in my employ who do?" Adrian asked.

They each nodded again. A few of them began to fidget like young boys in school. But not Jack Flagg. He looked steely-eyed at Adrian and would not look away. Adrian smiled.

"The Association has laid down a decree," Adrian said. "It has been passed unanimously by the membership and is therefore binding on all. Any man owning cattle of his own is prohibited from working for any member of the Association. Therefore, you're free to choose. Either sell your cattle or you won't work for us."

The men looked at Adrian with disbelief. Disbelief turned to anger. Jack Flagg rose.

"You mean to say that we are free to be slaves of the Association or starve," Flagg shouted. "You're denying any of us the right to prosper. We can't make a living just working for you a few months of the year and it's almost impossible to make a go of it independently. Some of us are family men, you know."

"And some of you are thieves," Adrian said calmly.

Flagg lurched toward Adrian. Several men grabbed him and held him back.

"I've never stolen anything in my life, Adrian," Flagg shouted. "Or killed anyone. That's more than you'll ever be able to claim."

"What are you saying?" Adrian asked. "Speak up."

"I'll speak up at the right time," Flagg said.

"I have no fear of an unemployed cowservant,"
Adrian said, as he turned to leave. "Good day."

Jack Flagg began to follow him but hesitated. "My
time will come," he shouted.

Elinore had planned to rise at dawn and work in her
garden before preparing for Adrian's visit. But instead
she had allowed herself to sleep late and simply to
attend to her toilette. She took a long, hot bath in
the kitchen, cautious to close the curtains she had just
made and lock the door. As she lay in the tub she
thought of the love that she and Phillip had shared.
Would she ever know that sensation again? she asked
herself. Her thoughts drifted to the long nights of
love-making that had only improved with the years of
their marriage.

Phillip had been so sensitive. She thought of his
hands, of his face beaded with sweat, of his strong
embrace so filled with love.

After a few minutes she told herself she must stop
this. Suddenly she thought of the time. She had to get
dressed.

What a wonderful life Jerrine would have if she
married James Adrian. My God, she thought, I mustn't
even allow myself to think of it. She stepped out of
the tub and patted herself dry. Wrapped in a towel,
she went up to her room.

Today she wore her green calico dress, with its
tight-fitting waist. It had the lowest cut neck of any of
her day dresses. She felt daring in it. She had made
a sunbonnet of the same material and now tucked her
French braid beneath it. She reached for her gloves
and started downstairs to wait for Mr. Adrian. She
thought of the beautiful stallion and carriage. She
hoped he would be here soon so they could be off before Stewart had a chance to see them.

As Elinore sat on the front porch she saw James
Adrian on the horizon. But instead of his carriage he

rode the black stallion and led a smaller horse by a rein. Elinore was disappointed. She had looked forward to riding again in the surrey with his arm around her waist, his body so close. He couldn't expect her to ride a horse, she thought. In minutes he was at the porch.

"Good morning, Miss Pruitt," Adrian called. "How do you like my surprise? I thought we could have a riding lesson."

"But . . . but I've never ridden a horse," Elinore stammered.

"This is the gentlest mare in Wyoming," Adrian said. "Besides, I'll be beside you all the time."

"Well . . . ," Elinore said.

"Come along now. Jump up next to me," Adrian said.

Elinore walked over to the stallion. It was taller than she was!

Adrian offered her his hand.

"Just put your foot in the stirrup, and lift," he said. "I'll do the rest."

She did as he said, slipping her boot into the stirrup, and lifted herself with one leg. Instinctively, she lifted her other leg over the horse. Suddenly she was sitting, her thighs wrapped around the horse, directly against Adrian. Her breasts rubbed against his coat. She sat back quickly.

"Now that wasn't bad at all, was it?" Adrian asked. "You did wonderfully. I can see you were meant to ride."

He clicked his heels into the horse's flank and they were off. In the excitement Elinore had forgotten about Stewart and now she saw him staring from the side of the barn.

"Hold on tight," Adrian said.

Elinore tightened her grasp around Adrian's waist. His back was so solid, just like the stallion.

They started out on a route Elinore had never taken

before. She sat snuggled up close to Adrian and couldn't have been more content. Dandelions spread in front of them like a carpet of gold. The larkspurs grew waist-high with their long spikes of blue. The service-bushes and the wild cherries were a mass of white beauty. Meadowlarks and robins and bluebirds seemed to twitter and sing from every branch. A sky of the tenderest blue bent over them and the fleecy clouds drifted lazily across the open plain.

Now they came to a wide open space. Elinore couldn't judge how long it had taken to get there.

"I thought this would be perfect," Adrian said. "There's nothing out here except Independence Rock."

He pointed to a rock that jutted out from a cliff in the distance. Elinore had heard of Independence Rock somewhere, but she could not remember where just now.

But the thought quickly slipped from her mind as James Adrian swung off the horse and stood, his hands raised to her. Cautiously she lifted her leg and swung around.

The next thing she knew she stood face to face with Mr. Adrian, his hands on her waist. She tilted her head upward and began to close her eyes. But to her surprise he let go of her waist and started toward the saddle bag on the mare.

"I thought we might have lunch and then begin your lessons," Adrian said. "I had my cook, Yup Mi, prepare us a picnic."

Elinore stood there feeling quite foolish. Quietly, she went to help Adrian with the wool plaid blanket and the fixings in the wicker basket. There was gooseberry jam, thick slices of ham, a big, crisp rye bread, fresh butter, and apples. They sat down and ate in silence. Elinore was surprised at her appetite.

"Do you know which tartan this is?" Adrian said, looking down at the red and green plaid with the white background.

"No, I haven't the slightest notion," Elinore said.

"Why, it's the tartan of your employer. It's Royal Stewart," Adrian said, with a laugh.

Elinore didn't laugh.

"Have I said something wrong?" Adrian asked. "I'm sorry. I shouldn't mention him at all. He must be very difficult to live with."

"Yes, at times even more than difficult," Elinore said.

"Well, are you ready for your first lesson?" Adrian asked.

"I suppose," she said with a smile.

They walked over to the horses. The mare was also black, but not nearly as large as Noirceur. Elinore looked at the stallion. It was huge, and so finely built. It had the essence of power, that particular kind that belongs exclusively to young males.

Elinore looked at Adrian. He seemed to possess all the characteristics of his horse. Young, powerful, and finely built.

"Shall I help you up?" Adrian said, interrupting Elinore's thoughts.

"Yes, please," Elinore said.

"First let me introduce you. Miss Pruitt, Ma Femme. Ma Femme, Miss Pruitt," Adrian said.

Again she put her boot in the stirrup and lifted herself onto the horse. Elinore was a little leery of the English saddle. It didn't look as secure as the Western ones she was accustomed to seeing.

"Now sit up as straight as possible, hold the reins firmly but not too tightly. The horse must know you are in control," Adrian said. "If you grip the horse's flank with your legs it will help you keep your balance. Now very gently touch the horse with your heels."

Elinore did just as he said and the horse began to move beneath her. It felt wonderful. She smiled at Adrian.

"You're going to be an excellent horsewoman. I can

tell," Adrian said. "Now click your heels again, very gently."

Again Elinore did as Adrian said.

"As she goes faster grip her flanks and go up with her, then relax your legs and come down," Adrian called. "Ride her as you feel her."

Ma Femme was in a trot now. As Elinore gripped the horse's flanks and then relaxed, she felt strangely aroused. Her legs were spread wide over Ma Femme's back and as she would come down each time her inner thighs would rub against the saddle over and over again. She felt her nipples grow rigid and press against her bodice. She blushed as she looked over to Adrian. Could he possibly know what she was experiencing?

"Miss Pruitt, you are a natural," Adrian said.

Elinore continued the trot. She felt the muscles in her buttocks tense, then relax. Again and again. It was maddening.

"Don't hold the reins too tightly," Adrian called.

Elinore realized that she had been gripping the reins so tightly her knuckles were white. She tried to dismiss her thoughts. But the rhythm, the tensing of her muscles, the slow continual rubbing of the inner leg continued to arouse her. She looked over her shoulder to the dark, handsome figure. She pulled on one side of the rein and headed back to Adrian.

"I think you've had enough for today," Adrian said. "You look a bit flushed. Are you certain you are all right?"

"Oh, yes. I'm fine," Elinore said, relieved that she would soon be off the horse.

"You did very well," Adrian said. "In no time you'll be riding on your own."

"Thank you," Elinore said.

She lifted herself off the horse. Again Adrian held her waist and looked down into her eyes. But this time he did not let go. He grabbed her tighter and pulled her against him. He pressed his lips to hers. She tensed, then relaxed and reached her arms around his strong shoulders and pulled herself up to him. He kissed her cheek and ran his lips down her neck. Chills ran through her. Suddenly his lips were on hers again, probing. He parted her lips with his own. Then he gently teased her mouth with his tongue.

"My sweet," he whispered.

He picked her up and carried her to the blanket. Her body ached and her lips trembled. Adrian kissed her harder, one hand firm around her waist and the other drawn to her half-exposed breast. Elinore wanted to pull away but his touch was so pleasing. Something that she thought had died was coming alive inside her.

She breathed deeply. His scent seemed to be everywhere. Slowly, he slipped her dress off one shoulder and exposed her breast. He licked at the dark pink nipple, bit into it and began to suck. He pressed against her thigh. She could feel he was aroused. She was frightened but so excited. She felt a surge of heat in her loins.

Adrian began to run his fingers up her calf, soothing her as he would a nervous colt. He stroked her white, soft skin. The sun was bright in her face.

"Oh, Mr. Adrian, you mustn't," Elinore said.

He pulled his hand away and rolled onto his back. He was silent. Elinore hadn't expected him to react so strongly. She almost regretted her words. He wouldn't look at her.

Elinore sat up and tucked her breast back into her dress.

Adrian turned to her. "I'm sorry, Miss Pruitt," he said. "Shall we be going?"

They packed up the picnic and in moments were back on the stallion. While they were gathering up their lunch Elinore had thought she had seen a man

staring down from Independence Rock. She had
thought for a moment it was Stewart. But now as she
looked back she saw no one.

"Noirceur is a remarkable animal," Elinore said,
wanting to end the silence.

"Yes, I've come to love him more every day," Adrian
said. "Soon I'll mate him with Ma Femme."

"What does Nwar-sir mean?" Elinore asked.

"It's not Nwar-sir but Nwar-ce-ur," Adrian said.
"Noir, like night, and ceur. It means blackness, darkness. It also connotes base action but I disregard that
aspect. I can't imagine this fine beast involved in anything base."

Elinore did not respond but she couldn't help but
compare Adrian and his horse, both fine and noble.

As they rode back to Stewart's the sun was hanging
like a great red ball in the blue haze of the West. Little
black squirrels chattered saucily as they passed. The
setting sun shot gold through the pines as Elinore held
on tightly to Adrian and his fine stallion. Just to smell
him was such a pleasure, she thought. The mare followed behind.

When they pulled up to the ranch a cowhand was at
work mending the railing of the front porch.

"Miss Pruitt, isn't that McPherren, Stewart's foreman?" Adrian asked.

"Yes," Elinore replied. "He does most of the handy
work around here."

"Does he own cattle?" Adrian asked.

"Yes, I think he owns a dozen or so," Elinore replied. "He's a mighty hard worker and plenty ambitious."

Elinore noticed concern in Adrian's voice.

"Is something troubling you?" she asked.

Adrian hesitated.

"No, I was just thinking," he said.

They rode to the front porch and Adrian dismounted, then helped Elinore down. She nodded to McPherren.

"Is your master at home?" Adrian called to McPherren.

"That man hasn't been born yet," McPherren replied. "But if you're talking about Mr. Stewart, he's not at home. He left this afternoon. Didn't say where he was going."

Elinore could tell McPherren's remark annoyed Adrian.

"Shall we have a lesson next week, Miss Pruitt?" Adrian asked.

"I'll look forward to it," Elinore said.

As he rode away Elinore couldn't help but think something was bothering him. She turned to wave a final good-bye but he did not look back.

By the time Adrian returned to the special stable he had built just for Ma Femme and Noirceur it was dark. The stable boy waited as he had been instructed.

"You take care of the mare," Adrian, still atop the stallion, said to the boy. "I'll brush Noirceur down."

Adrian dismounted. He took off the saddle and walked Noirceur to his stall. Once inside, he strapped the brush to his hand and rubbed Noirceur in long, firm strokes. He savored every inch of this fine beast, its long powerful legs, straight back and proud head. Adrian had never been so pleased with an animal. Noirceur was by far the finest horse in Powder River. Men would kill for a lesser horse.

Adrian's thoughts jolted to Stewart. I hope that fool doesn't intend to disobey the Association by keeping on his cattle-owning cowservants, he thought.

He turned back to Noirceur, who tossed his head and neighed.

"Good-night to you too, my friend," Adrian said.

He kissed Noirceur on the head, took the lantern and started towards the house.

He heard a rustling and stopped. Then he looked back at Noirceur.

The horse was still. He decided it must be the wind.

"Sleep well," he said. "We'll ride again tomorrow, just you and me." ৽৪

10

ADRIAN breakfasted on fresh biscuits, cured ham, and strong coffee. He planned on taking a long ride with Noirceur, eventually going into Buffalo for drinks at the Cheyenne Club. He had felt so good upon rising, looking forward to a solitary day with his horse that he had told the stable boy he would attend to Noirceur himself.

Before going to the stable Adrian went out to the barn to discuss the day's chores with his new foreman, Scott Davis, better known as "Quick Shot." Quick Shot was Adrian's only employee who decided to sell his cattle and keep his job.

Adrian walked over to Noirceur's stable. As he neared it he called out to the animal. He didn't hear the usual rustling. He opened the stable door and looked in, thinking Noirceur must be lying down.

Adrian walked down the corridor toward Noirceur's stall. It was unusually quiet. He couldn't see Ma Femme either. But as he approached her stall he saw her lying there. She picked her head up and rose to her feet.

Adrian felt uneasy as he took a few more steps and looked into Noirceur's stall. He saw the strong hind legs. One more step. Then Adrian looked at the horse full length.

"My God, what have they done to you?" Adrian screamed.

Noirceur lay there lifeless, decapitated. His eyes were open and expressed the terror he had felt. The fresh hay was soaked with blood.

Adrian screamed again as he fell to his knees and buried his face in his hands.

Luke Murrin's popular saloon was directly across the street from the Cheyenne Club. It was a dusty place, filled with an assortment of mismatched chairs and tables. In the back was a large, tiered room where cockfights were held. Tonight there was none of the familiar hooting, howling, card-playing and joviality. But there was plenty of drinking, even more than usual. Every blackballed cowboy in Powder River was there.

Jack Flagg had come to town with the rest, leaving his wife and child back home at the Red Fork of Powder River. Normally a sober man, he was drinking heavily. He was also talking freely about fearing for his life.

"They've killed Cattle Kate and John Tisdale," Flagg said. "What's to keep them from killing me?"

"We just won't let them," Nate Champion said. "They had the advantage of catching both Kate and Tisdale off guard. But we're ready for them now. The only way to beat them is to stick together."

"You're right, Nate," Flagg said. "This blacklist of the Association includes every cowboy in the county who owns a hoof of stock. There's nothing left to do except for all of us to take up a homestead and buy a brand. If you and me share in a brand it will be cheaper and easier to protect our herds."

"Sounds good to me," Nate said. "Nick Ray will want in, too."

"There's a guy, Hathaway, at the Powder River Crossing that's got a brand for sale," Jack said. "It's the Hat brand. I thought it would suit us just fine."

"We'll be duly registered with the county and respectable," Nate said with a laugh.

The two men smiled at each other.

"I got my government land, a string of horses, and a few head of cattle," Jack said. "The cattle I own are ranging Powder River and Johnson country. Whether the barons like it or not I'm goin' to take part in the roundup. It's sure to mean trouble."

They both took a swallow directly from the bottle that stood in front of them. Nate sipped it, but Flagg made the bottle bubble.

"You better take it easy, Jack," Nate said. "You ain't exactly a drinking man."

"You mean I wasn't a drinking man," Flagg replied. "It seems to me I'm becoming one mighty fast."

Just as Flagg finished his sentence the quiet din of Luke's turned to absolute quiet. Flagg looked up from his bottle to see James Adrian standing in the doorway, backed by two huge men who aimed their Winchesters at the cowpunchers. No one dared reach for their six-shooter.

Adrian's gaze was fixed on Jack Flagg. "You cowardly bastard!" Adrian said.

Jack Flagg was instantly sobered.

"What are you talkin' about, Adrian?" Flagg said.

"You know damn well what I'm talking about, Flagg."

"I know you're talking about cowardice when you got two guns behind you," Flagg said.

Adrian's nostrils flared. "You call chopping off my horse's head brave, you swine?"

Flagg was quiet. He was actually puzzled by what Adrian had said.

"You can't play ignorant, Flagg," Adrian said. "You aren't smart enough."

Flagg was still dumbfounded.

"You waited out at my ranch last night for me to return," Adrian continued. "And when I was asleep you took an axe to my defenseless horse."

"Adrian, you're crazy," Flagg said. "I think you're beginning to believe everybody's as cold-blooded as you are. Why, I was out at the Red Fork with my wife and kid trying to explain to them why you'd fired me."

"You expect me to believe that?" Adrian said. "You must think I'm a fool."

"I know you're a fool, Adrian," Flagg said.

Adrian lunged toward Flagg. Nate held on tight to Flagg's arms. The two men who accompanied Adrian grabbed him. After a moment Adrian shook them loose.

"Consider yourself a dead man, Flagg," Adrian said, as he turned and left the saloon. His two men followed.

"Did you really kill his horse, Jack?" Nate asked.

"No, but I wish I had," Flagg said. He turned to face the men in the room. "Well, it seems they officially declared war," he shouted. He took a long drink from the bottle.

"Here's to us," Nate said, lifting his glass to the cowboy-filled room.

Every man lifted his glass, nodded, and took a deep swallow. And with that gesture they were all silently united. ⨕

11

In her upstairs bedroom Elinore rested her arms on the small oak desk where she had arranged an inkwell, quill pen and writing paper. Bette had given her the fancy paper as a present when she left Denver, and made her promise to write. Elinore had just finished one of the promised letters, folded it, and slipped it into the matching envelope.

She addressed the envelope, put down her pen and rose to look out the window.

Her eyes sparkled at the thought of her anticipated guest, James Adrian. But she saw no sign of him.

It was another glorious day. As she stood at the window, she could hear the sound of the men working in the side yard. But it was James Adrian who was on her mind. Her longing to see him was acute and Elinore permitted herself a soft sigh to ease herself. She was half-ashamed of herself. For a moment she wondered if she were falling in love with him.

She looked up again to see the black surrey in the distance. Her heart began to pound faster. Quickly, she reached for her hat, peeked into the mirror one last time, and ran to greet him on the porch.

As he approached Elinore strained her eyes. The horse pulling the surrey was not Noirceur, nor was it Ma Femme. She wondered why he had chosen another horse for their outing.

Elinore stood on the porch in her low-cut, blue-striped dress and her sunbonnet. She waved to Adrian. He waved back but even from the distance Elinore sensed something was wrong.

"Hello, Mr. Adrian," Elinore called. "Where is your beautiful black friend?"

Adrian pulled up to the porch and lifted himself from the surrey.

"Hello, Miss Pruitt," he said, sullenly. "Noirceur is dead. He's been decapitated. Some cowservant's revenge."

Elinore was stunned. Brutality seemed to be everywhere. She held her hands to her face and began to cry.

"Oh, Mr. Adrian. Why would anyone do such a dreadful thing?"

"Those men are animals. They have no respect for a man's property. They are all thieves and murderers."

Elinore had to wonder what kind of men would kill an innocent animal.

"I'm sorry to bring this news," Adrian said. "Let's not let it spoil our day."

Adrian ran his lips gently across her gloved hand and then lifted her into the surrey.

As they rode across the plain Elinore sat close to Adrian. He somehow seemed a child, sullen and quiet. She felt so sorry for him. She wanted to take him and hold him against her breast.

Today they headed toward Powder River pass. There was no breeze and their carriage created only the smallest stirring of air. Larkspur, with its blue spikes, was interspersed with the goldenrod, making a carpet of blue and gold ahead of them. Soon they came to the pineries, which were filled with deep gorges and canyons. The sun shot arrows of gold through the pines. Adrian stopped the carriage and jumped down to gather an armful of the wildflowers. Elinore had never seen this particular flower before.

"Oh, they are lovely, thank you," she said.

"Yes, they are lovely. They're called columbines," Adrian said. "You see the five spurred petals? When you invert the flower it resembles a cluster of doves."

He took the flowers and turned them upside down. Elinore looked at them with delight, nodding her head in agreement.

Adrian handed Elinore the bouquet. She closed her eyes and lifted the flowers to her nose. The scent was sweet and filled her head. With her eyes still closed she felt Adrian gently move the flowers aside and press his lips against hers. A sharp, pleasant current shot through her. He moved away and she opened her eyes again.

Adrian clicked the reins and they were off. They drove through the pine trees and up and down the gorges, their fingers intertwined. All at once the pines ended and they were atop the same lush green hill she had practiced riding on last week.

Quietly they set up the picnic from the overfilled wicker basket and ate.

Adrian stroked Elinore's neck. Without warning, he said, "I think it important that you know how to shoot. This is untamed territory and you never know when you might have to defend yourself."

Elinore had wanted to ask him to teach her after Mrs. O'Shaughnessy's recommendation but had not thought it appropriate just yet. She was delighted that he was concerned.

"I have a six-shooter with me," Adrian said, "We'll have a lesson today. I'd rather put off our riding lessons."

"Yes, of course," Elinore said. "I've never shot a gun before, though."

"Come," he said, standing and offering her his hand.

He took the six-shooter from the carriage and checked the chambers.

"The first thing you should know about this type of gun is that it is a single-action revolver. It might go off at any time if it is dropped or if the hammer receives a sharp blow."

Elinore nodded.

"Therefore, you should always, without exception, leave the sixth chamber empty with the hammer resting on it," Adrian continued. "The other five chambers are, of course, loaded. There is a custom among cowpunchers to always keep a banknote rolled up in the empty chamber for burying money. Are you ready to give it a try?"

"All right," Elinore replied nervously.

Adrian stepped behind Elinore and reached his arms around her.

"Take the gun in your right hand," he said, "And look through the sights."

"Mr. Adrian, I'm left-handed," Elinore said.

"Fine, then take it in your left hand," he said and shifted to her left side. "Feel the weight of it."

Elinore did as he said. She was surprised at the gun's weight. She had to grip it firmly to keep it from falling out of her hand.

"That's right," Adrian said. "Now bring it up to eye-level. Squint your right eye and try to match up the sights with your left eye."

Elinore raised the gun.

"The sight is to help guide the eye," Adrian said. "Don't bend your arm. Now, try to set the sight on Independence Rock."

Elinore lifted the gun again, trying to keep her hand steady. She sighted the rock jutting out of the grass and took aim.

"Ready. Now pull back the trigger," Adrian said.

His arms were tight around her and the gun was heavy. She tried to concentrate but she kept thinking of his arms around her and his chest pressing against her. She squinted, steadied her left hand with her right, took aim, and pulled the trigger.

Her eyes were closed when the gun fired. The force of the explosion pulled the gun toward her. She opened her eyes.

"That was very good," Adrian said. "Only next time keep your eyes open."

He laughed. Elinore could not keep from smiling. She tried again. This time she hit the rock.

"Very good," Adrian said. "I'll give you this six-shooter to practice with."

"But what will you use?" Elinore asked.

"I have others at home," Adrian said. "And besides, I never travel without my Winchester. It's on the floor of the carriage at all times, or by my saddle."

Adrian glanced up at the sky. "Looks like a storm," he said. "We ought to be going."

Elinore looked up, too. She had been so intent on her lesson and James Adrian she hadn't noticed the sky turning dark grey. The wind had also picked up.

"We'll never make it back to Stewart's," Adrian said. "A friend of mine lives close by. We can go there and wait for the storm to blow by."

Quickly they gathered up their things and climbed into the surrey. As soon as they reached the other side of the hill Elinore could see a prosperous-looking ranch.

"Major Frank Wolcott's TA ranch," Adrian said. "I'd like to introduce you to him. He's a gentleman and a friend."

Elinore was flattered that Adrian would want her to meet his quality friends.

They rode down the steep incline. The sky was getting darker, the wind more and more turbulent. Elinore hoped they would make it to the ranch before it began to rain. She had seen the rain come these past few weeks, always suddenly and fiercely.

They approached the ranch but Elinore couldn't see anybody in the yard. They circled around to the front of the house and Adrian quickly helped Elinore down and put the blankets and provisions on the front porch. Elinore stood and watched. She attempted to tidy her hair.

Adrian took her arm and knocked at the door. Elinore felt so proud.

There was no answer. Adrian knocked again. The rain had begun by this time and the wind was sweeping it onto the porch.

Adrian picked up the tartan blanket and wrapped it around Elinore.

"There's a cellar with a trap door that leads into the house," Adrian said. "Wolcott uses it for a wine cellar. Originally it was the beginning of a secret tunnel that goes out to the hill beyond the house. A precaution of the old days in case of Indian attack. I'm certain Wolcott wouldn't mind our letting ourselves in under the circumstances."

Adrian put the blanket over Elinore's head and they went around the house. He led her to a set of doors and opened them. It was dark and the stairs were steep. Elinore was frightened as Adrian helped her down them.

"Let me see if I can find the latch," Adrian said, handing Elinore a handkerchief to dry herself with.

He lit a match and looked around the cellar. Finding the latch he reached up to unlock it but was not able to.

"I'm sorry, Miss Pruitt," he said. "It's locked. We'll have to wait here till the storm blows over. It shouldn't be long. Are you warm enough?"

"Yes, thank you," Elinore replied, and hesitantly returned the handkerchief.

"This is the only wine cellar in Powder River, other than the one at the Cheyenne Club," Adrian said. "Let's look for a candle."

He lit another match. Elinore glanced around the dusty cellar. She saw the opening to the tunnel behind a stack of wooden crates. Atop the crates was a candle in a holder.

"I've found one," she called to Adrian, who was at the other end of the cellar.

"Good work," he said, and walked back to her.

He lit a match and Elinore held the candle to it. Suddenly Elinore could see around the room. It was larger than she had realized.

Was all this necessary just to provide a passageway to a tunnel? Elinore thought.

"Let's put the blanket down and have a seat," Adrian said, disrupting Elinore's thoughts. "We might as well be comfortable."

He took the blanket from around Elinore and placed it on the floor.

"Come have a seat," he said.

They sat quietly for a while listening to the rain on the cellar door. Adrian's arm was around Elinore's waist.

"Elinore," Adrian said, lifting her face with his free hand.

He said nothing more but touched his lips softly to Elinore's. Her lips trembled beneath his. He pressed the kiss harder, gripping her waist firmly, then slid her down till she lay beneath him.

I must pull away, Elinore thought. But Adrian's embrace was so strong, so masculine, so soothing. She pushed at him with her last bit of strength. But he resisted. He took her hands and brought them to his lips, kissing each fingertip, one by one.

Then his lips were on her mouth again. Elinore shivered. Something was coming alive within her.

He ran his hand over the thin fabric of her bodice.

Elinore's tongue met his. A terrifying, pleasing sensation shot through her. He held her tighter and rubbed himself against her thigh.

"Mr. Adrian, no," she whispered.

He muffled the protest with kisses. She opened her eyes and looked into the dark, handsome face. She couldn't think, she was weak, and her body was so insistent.

Deftly he unbuttoned her bodice and exposed her round, full breasts. The nipples stood erect. He took one in his mouth, gently at first, then more forcefully. Elinore gasped. He opened his shirt and pressed his bare flesh to hers.

She threw her head back and gripped his shoulders. Adrian ran his fingers up her calves, soothing and exciting her. He parted her knees slightly, running his hand up her thigh. A surge of heat shot from her feet to her loins.

Elinore's hands ran through his thick, black hair and down his shoulders. He groaned and pushed himself against her.

He reached under her dress and in one motion lifted her buttocks and pulled off her petticoat. She was now naked underneath. The cool, moist air between her thighs was exhilarating. She thrust herself up to him.

Quickly, he unfastened his trousers, freeing himself. He slid his hands beneath her buttocks and raised her to meet his erection. He lifted Elinore to him and thrust himself inside. She held him firmly as he rocked within her.

My God, what am I doing? Elinore suddenly thought. But her doubts were soon overcome by her pleasure. In an instant, he groaned, surging violently, and collapsed atop her.

12

STEWART had not been to town in weeks. He came today using the excuse of pressing errands but what he really wanted was a few drinks. He stopped in on Robert Foote, a fellow Scotsman, and the leading merchant in Buffalo. Stewart knew there would be whiskey as well as intelligent conversation at Foote's.

Stewart entered the general store that afternoon to find Foote in his usual place behind the counter. Foote's eyes sparkled and, surprisingly, his red hair reminded Stewart of Elinore. Foote was helping a lady and her daughter decide on some fabric for a new summer dress.

"This calico is the best quality west of the Mississippi," Foote said to the mother. He glanced at Stewart and winked in reference to the difficult decision facing the ladies. Stewart smiled in return.

Stewart looked around the store. The wooden floors were swept clean and the shelves were packed with guns, ammunition, blankets, slickers, warm clothing, material, ribbons, thread, flour, bacon, nails, and tools. A small glass jar filled with hard candies sat on the counter. An entire corner displayed cowboy regalia—

the best Texan hats and boots money could buy, leather chaps, scarves, gloves, silver spurs, carved leather saddles—and every other conceivable accoutrement for a hard-working cowboy.

Although the store was well stocked, and Foote would order anything a customer wanted, there were none of the European delicacies or clothing found at the other stores in town. The cattle barons shopped elsewhere.

Stewart looked up from the boots to see Foote giving the ladies their change and bidding them goodbye.

"Hello, Clyde," Foote called. "Good to see you. Can I help you with something or is this a social visit?"

"Well, I'll be needing some things," Stewart said and handed Foote a list. "If you'll gather up these things and have a boy load my wagon I'll be grateful. I'm not feeling up to doing it myself today."

"No trouble, Clyde, is there?"

"No, no trouble, Robert. Just feeling a bit lazy."

"You seem troubled, Clyde. I've been saying you need a good woman to keep you company. You've been alone too long."

"You may be right but there are few women to be had out here."

"What about that new housekeeper of yours? I hear she's quite a looker."

Stewart glared at Foote. "She's come to keep my house and that's all," he said angrily.

"I didn't mean to get personal. I was just looking out for a fellow Scot and as good a man as lives in Powder River."

"I'm sorry, Robert. I'm just a bit irritable. You hear anything about the blacklist of that damnable Association?"

"I sure did. It's the talk of the town. All the wives are coming in asking for credit already. They were counting on their spring pay to help recover from this winter. Now they're left with no savings and no money coming in. Unfortunately, I have a family, too, and can only give credit so far. The Association is really asking for trouble. These men have little choice but to rustle a head or two of cattle to feed their families. If you call a man a thief long enough, soon he'll oblige you and become one. Have you fired your men?"

"No, how could I? My best men own cattle. Why, I gave a few of them a head or two last year as a bonus. Those men risked their lives this winter looking after my business."

"What are you going to do?"

"Haven't decided yet. Can't lay off the men, though, and live with myself. Looks like a confrontation with those pig-headed cattle barons. Got anything to drink, Robert?"

"As a matter of fact I keep this little bottle behind the counter for medicinal purposes," Foote said with a laugh.

He handed Stewart the bottle and Stewart took a long gulp. Foote then drained the bottle and opened another. They talked the afternoon away, wondering what was to be done.

At sunset Stewart sat in the oak-paneled sitting room of the Cheyenne Club. He had been drinking steadily all afternoon. He was hot and his appearance, normally neat, was now disheveled. He was sitting in a thickly padded leather chair, hunched over his whiskey and ale, when Major Frank Wolcott walked up. Wolcott was dressed in his usual costume of brown riding breeches, white collar and brown bowler. He held a riding crop in his hand.

"Ah, it's the 'Dude,'" Stewart said thickly.

"What did you say, Stewart?"

"I said, it's the 'Dude'! You must be aware that's what the cowboys call you. 'The Dude,' yes, it's very fitting."

"It's of no consequence to me what they find pleasure in calling me. Nor do I concern myself with the opinions of any member of this Association who refuses to abide by unanimous decisions reached by the group."

"Quit being evasive, Wolcott. Tell me what's on that small mind of yours now."

"You know perfectly well what's on my mind, Stewart." Wolcott squeezed the crop tighter. "It has come to my attention that you have not obeyed the decree of this Association to dismiss any employee who insists on owning cattle."

"And where, may I ask, do you get your information?"

"That is of no consequence. The issue is whether or not you're going to continue to ignore the Association and suffer the consequences, or whether you plan to abide by the group's decision."

Just then Adrian walked into the sitting room.

"Hello, Adrian," Stewart called. "I'm told that someone has been reporting upon my neglect of duty. Do you have any idea who that might be, my faithful friend?"

"Stewart, I . . ."

"Adrian, you're the only guest I've—excuse me—I or Miss Pruitt has had in weeks so there is no need to explain yourself. Your intention is clear. And don't try putting the blame on my 'ignorant' cowservants because they were all sworn to secrecy until I could come up with a decision."

"I did it for your own good. I thought that with the pressure of the Association you'd come to your senses. You can't go on defending those thieves."

"Adrian's right," Wolcott said. "If you continue to disobey the orders of this Association you may bring serious repercussions on yourself."

"Will someone shoot me in the back, too?" Stewart asked.

Wolcott and Adrian looked shocked.

"Just what are you saying?" Wolcott demanded.

"I'm saying that a perfectly honest man was killed— shot in the back—a few weeks ago and all evidence and logic point to the Association."

"I think you've lost your senses," Wolcott snapped.

"I think Adrian could clarify things for us as he was out at my place the day Tisdale was killed. They had an argument and Adrian left not far behind Tisdale. The hole in Tisdale's back could only have been caused by a Winchester, of the kind that Adrian carries at all times."

"Stewart, every man with enough money to buy a Winchester owns one," Adrian said. "You're drawing ridiculous conclusions from little evidence."

"I can't prove a thing just now, but for the time being keep off my land. You're no longer welcome," Stewart said.

"I think you're dreaming all this up. I think John Tisdale and those other peasants have little to do with your reasons for not wanting me around your place."

"Adrian, come to the point."

"If you insist. I think you're more concerned with my keeping company with Miss Pruitt than with your fantasies about my killing anybody."

"Miss Pruitt has nothing to do with my accusations."

"I saw it from the beginning. You've always been jealous of Miss Pruitt's affection for me and tried to conceal it. You were looking for a woman, not a house-keeper, when you hired her."

"My feelings toward Miss Pruitt are only honorable, Adrian."

"That may be your mistake. My intentions are not honorable in the least. I've already tasted the honey and will continue to do so. You understand what I mean?" Adrian smiled.

Stewart understood perfectly. He stood up and in one blow knocked Adrian to the floor.

"You're a blackguard and a murderer," Stewart said as he stood over Adrian.

Wolcott backed away, frightened.

"I wouldn't kick a dog, but you . . . ," Stewart jabbed his boot into Adrian's side.

Adrian clutched his stomach.

By this time every man in the club had gathered to see the altercation.

"Stand up and fight, you coward. Oh, I forgot. Shooting a man in the back or taking advantage of women is your style. Adrian, for all your pretensions, you're trash. Never, never cross me again."

Stewart tucked in his shirt, smoothed back his hair, turned and left.

But Stewart wasn't ready to go home yet. He stood outside the Cheyenne Club and looked onto the streets of Buffalo. Across the street Luke Murrin's saloon was crowded and seemed friendlier than the "gentlemen's" club he had just left. He hesitated a moment but his desire for another whiskey and ale overcame him. He walked through the swinging doors and took an empty seat at the bar. The saloon quieted for a moment but Stewart took no notice and ordered his ale.

I suspected that bastard of killing Tisdale but couldn't bring myself to admit it, Stewart thought. But now this thing with Elinore. . . . He took a long swallow from the ale the bartender had put in front of him and ordered a whiskey. The bartender nodded.

I knew Adrian was inconsiderate, but now. . . . Stewart thought. It surely means a confrontation with the Association and trouble for my business. But I did the right thing by standing up to that bastard. He took his whiskey in one swallow and ordered another. What will I tell Miss Pruitt? I'm certain she thought his intentions were honorable. Even I did, but now. . . . Well, I guess it will be up to her to find out. She's a grown woman and what right do I have . . . ?

Stewart's thoughts were interrupted by a tap on his shoulder. As he turned from the bar he saw a huge man he recognized but whose name he couldn't place. He was in no mood to talk.

"You're Clyde Stewart, aren't you?" the burly man asked, "One of the biggest cattle-owners in these parts?"

"That's right. Can I help you?" Stewart said, trying to be civil.

"Who says you're welcome to drink here?"

"Who says I'm not?"

"We do."

Stewart looked around the room. Everyone was looking at him. He was puzzled by the hostility but not in the mood to inquire.

"Look, all I want is a quiet ale to myself. I don't want conversation. So leave me alone or get to the point."

"The point is that you barons own this town, go anywhere, and do anything you like, but this place is ours and we don't want you here."

Stewart looked around the saloon again. The men stared at him. He didn't see any of his own men.

"Look," he said. "I don't care who owns what in this town. I want an ale and I want to be left alone."

"You're all so goddamn arrogant and we're sick of it. You lay off every man that owns a head of cattle and then don't even have the decency to leave them alone to drink away their troubles. I'm saying get."

Stewart understood the man's objections. In another mood he would have explained himself but not today.

"I'm staying," Stewart said as he rose from his seat.

The man was six inches taller than Stewart and his fist was a blur as it flashed toward him. Stewart tried to duck but the huge fist grazed his temple. He regained his balance and slammed his left fist into the cowboy's jaw, followed the blow with a quick jab to the side of his head and a kick in the stomach. The cowboy doubled over, but was up immediately with a roar, lunging at Stewart and ramming him against the bar. Stewart hoisted himself up on the bar and kicked the cowboy in the head with both feet. Before he could recover, Stewart hit him again. He fell to the floor.

As the cowboy got to his knees a voice called, "What's going on in here, Tommy? Stewart, what are you up to?"

Both Stewart and the cowboy turned to see Robert Foote in the doorway.

Tommy staggered to his feet. "We just don't want any of these lords in our saloon," he said to Foote. "Half of us here have families and now bein' laid off we don't even know how we're goin' to feed 'em. The least these lords can do is leave us alone to drink."

"Tommy, you've got it all wrong. This man is a big cattle-owner, but you don't see any of his men here drinking because he hasn't laid any of them off despite the Association decree. I think you owe Stewart an apology."

Tommy glanced at Stewart and stumbled silently to his table.

"Good to see you again, Robert," Stewart said. He tossed some coins on the bar and stormed through the swinging doors.

13

Elinore sat in her garden and looked up at the cloudless sky. Everything seemed perfect, almost too perfect. Her first attempt at gardening was going well. The potatoes had sprouted. Healthy green plants had appeared and she anticipated a fine crop come fall. Soon she would find some way to homestead and hopefully send for Jerrine. And then there was Adrian. She was in love and was confident that he was, too. If she could have her own land, her daughter at her side, and a good man, what more could she possibly ask for? She sighed with contentment.

Normally she would be doing other chores in the morning, but Stewart had not returned from town to give her her instructions for the day. So she decided to do the much-needed weeding in her garden after finishing her morning's work. She had thought it strange that Stewart had not returned from town and had not mentioned that he would be staying the night. But she was glad not to see him. Despite his warning about the dangers out here and the fact that all the hands were away, she felt safer with him gone.

The sun was now directly overhead. As Elinore

knelt in the garden she could feel the sun on her back and her head burned despite her bonnet. Weeding the garden was a big job but she enjoyed it thoroughly.

She jerked a weed from the parched ground. A strange rattling sound startled her. Then another sound at her back caused her to turn. Stewart was standing behind her. She gasped. His clothes were disheveled. He needed a shave, and his face was bruised. He had never looked so frightening.

Slowly, without a word, he lifted his gun from his holster. Elinore was stunned.

"No, no . . . Mr. Stewart," she murmured. "Please don't kill me."

"Just hold still, Miss Pruitt," he said. "Whatever you do, don't move."

Elinore did as he said. She was paralyzed with fear. She thought of Jerrine. He raised the gun slowly and took aim. Elinore covered her eyes with her hands. The gun exploded. She shrieked.

She waited for the next shot, her eyes still covered. There was no sound. Very slowly she took her hands from her eyes. Stewart had returned his gun to his holster.

"I'm sorry I frightened you, but . . . ," he said and pointed to the ground next to her.

Elinore looked around to see a snake at her feet. She glanced at Stewart and stumbled back from the snake.

"That's a rattlesnake," Stewart said. "They're deadly."

Suddenly, distinctly, Elinore remembered the rattling she had heard the moment before she turned to see Stewart.

She looked down at the snake again. Its diamond-patterned head was blown apart. Elinore was so relieved she ran over to Stewart and threw her arms around his neck. His arms stayed at his sides. Still trembling, she stepped back embarrassed.

"What happened to your face?" she asked. "Let me look at it."

"I ran into a few rough cowboys. No damage done," Stewart said, tilting his head down for Elinore to inspect.

"Come in the house and let me dress it."

"It's not necessary."

"Yes, it is. Don't argue, just come along," she said as she led him to the kitchen.

Elinore pointed to a chair and went to the medicine cabinet for her remedies.

She laid the bandages and the bichloride of mercury on the kitchen table and began to wash the bruise. Touching him made her nervous, but it also felt strangely satisfying. After all, she thought, he just saved my life. To Elinore he seemed somehow transformed. She admired his black, wavy hair for the first time as she brushed it back off his face. His skin was smooth and clear. Elinore sensed that he enjoyed her touch. It surprised her.

She lifted his chin and exposed the bruise to the light. He glanced up at her with his soft blue eyes but quickly looked away as their eyes met.

When she applied the bichloride of mercury he tensed. Elinore's instinct was to soothe him but she dared not. She cut the bandage to fit over his left eye.

"A bandage isn't necessary," he said.

"A bandage is necessary and so is a good long rest. I'm going to dress this and put you to bed for the day."

Elinore was amazed that he didn't put up more of a struggle. She bent down to apply the bandage, and suddenly she was aware of his man-smell. Elinore found she liked it.

"There, finished. I'll roll down your bed and cook you a good dinner when you wake up. I'll be quiet so you can sleep."

She led him to his bedroom behind the kitchen, rolled down the bed and started to leave.

"And, Mr. Stewart, thank you again. I'll always be grateful."

He nodded as she closed the door behind her.

Elinore took special pleasure in preparing Stewart's dinner this evening. It was her way of thanking him. She realized she wasn't frightened of him any longer.

She carefully chose the best T-bone steak in the storehouse and peeled the finest potatoes from the root cellar. She made biscuits for the gravy and mashed the potatoes, as she thought that was how he liked them best. She set out the big bowl of hominy with a chunk of butter melting in the middle and some freshly stewed prunes. Then she called him for dinner.

As he got ready she put the final touches on the table—a nice candle, napkins she had made from the spare curtain material, a sprig of wildflowers from the side yard—and set his place.

Stewart stretched as he entered the dining room. Elinore thought he looked much improved after his long nap and that a good meal would be the final touch to set him straight.

"I don't think I've slept in the daytime since I was a small boy and was made to take a nap," Stewart said.

His now clean-shaven face, rested from sleep, reminded Elinore of a schoolboy.

"Come and eat, then you can play your bagpipes," Elinore said.

Stewart was obviously pleased with Elinore's extra attention, but then a look of dismay crossed his face.

"What's the matter?" Elinore asked.

"Nothing, but I thought you would be eating with me."

"I assumed you liked to eat alone."

"Well . . . I . . . I think it's silly for us to both eat alone. Won't you join me?"

Elinore hesitated for a moment and then smiled.

"Certainly. I'll set another place."

Soon they were sitting at the table, both waiting for the other to begin. Elinore bowed her head and said a silent prayer.

They looked up at each other, smiled and began to eat. Elinore was nervous, but everything tasted particularly good. She had eaten alone since coming to Powder River and had forgotten the pleasures of a shared meal.

Stewart seemed pleased, too, and ate more than usual.

"Everything is so good, Miss Pruitt. You've done another fine job."

Another fine job? Elinore thought. She felt he hadn't noticed any of her efforts before but he obviously had. She was genuinely pleased.

After dinner she cleared the dishes, prepared coffee, and returned to the table.

"Do you still want to stay out here and homestead on your own after all you've seen?" Stewart asked.

"Yes, more than ever. I've written Jerrine many times. Together I think we'll do just fine."

"Who's Jerrine?"

"Mr. Stewart, Jerrine is my daughter. I'm sorry I didn't mention her before but I was afraid it might interfere with my getting the job."

"Nonsense. Where is she?"

"She's back East in St. Louis in a boarding school until I can send for her."

"How old is she?"

"She'll be eight, Mr. Stewart."

"She's welcome here anytime you like, except for all this trouble."

"That's very kind of you but I'll wait till I have a place of my own. I know it might take a while but . . . ."

"When the trouble ends, which for better or worse

will have to be soon, I think you should send for her.
A child should be with its mother."

Elinore was amazed at his sympathy for Jerrine.

"Yes, you're right. Her eighth birthday is coming up
and I feel terrible about not being with her. But I
have things to do yet."

"Next time I go to town you should come with me
and you can buy her something special. It will be my
treat."

"That's very generous of you but . . . ."

"Please, Miss Pruitt. It will be a pleasure for me."

"Why, thank you then. Would you like to see a picture of her?"

"Yes, if you have one."

Elinore rose from the table and went up to her
room. In a moment she was back holding a new
locket. She handed it to Stewart.

He unfastened the tiny gold hook and inside was a
dim, yet clear outline of a little girl's face as if she
were looking out from a mellow twilight. She had soft
abundant hair like her mother. The sweet elusive smile
came not only from her mouth but from her radiant
eyes. All that was visible of her dress was the Dutch
collar. She wore a large breast pin. Under the glass on
the other side was a strand of red hair, the color of
her mother's, and a slip of paper. On the paper was
written: "Jerrine Pruitt, age six, July 10, 1890."

"She's a beautiful child," Stewart said. "She looks
very happy."

"Yes, the picture was taken before her father died
and our troubles began. But we'll be together and
happy again soon."

"I'm certain it will be soon," Stewart said. His voice
was comforting. He glanced out the window for a
moment. "If you're serious about staying you must
have a horse. I have a mare that I rarely ride and
Chub could use more exercise than she gets. You're
welcome to ride her any time you like. Can you ride?"

"Well, not very well, but Mr. Adrian . . . ." She stopped, sensing she shouldn't discuss Adrian, but it was too late now. "Mr. Adrian has given me a lesson and thinks I'll be a good horsewoman in no time."

Stewart's mood quickly changed. All the good humor of the evening faded and he quickly reverted to his old self, quiet and forbidding.

After a long silence, he said, "Miss Pruitt, you're a responsible, grown woman but I feel it is my duty to warn you. Adrian has said things to me in public that hint that his intentions toward you are not thoroughly honorable. If you continue to see him it is your business, but as I said before, he is no longer welcome in my home."

Elinore couldn't believe what she was hearing. That fool, she thought, Mrs. O'Shaughnessy was right. Stewart was probably jealous but this was going too far. She could barely speak. She was hot and her face was flushed.

"You're a blackguard and a . . . ."

She couldn't finish the sentence. She burst into tears and fled to her room.   ঔৎ

14

When Elinore awoke the next day Stewart was gone. She finished her chores and decided, despite their row last night, to take Stewart up on his offer to lend her a mare.

She asked McPherren to have somebody saddle Chub. She waited till she was alone to mount the mare for fear of making a fool of herself, but to her surprise she mounted the horse effortlessly. She kicked the mare's sides and the horse started off gently, then progressed to a comfortable trot. She practiced riding in the yard for the rest of the morning.

By afternoon she felt restless and remembered Mrs. O'Shaughnessy's suggestion that she visit the Sioux Indian camp down by the river. They had moccasins and beadwork and perhaps she would find something to send Jerrine for her birthday. And it was only a mile away.

This was the first time Elinore had been off by herself and though she was a bit frightened it felt great to be alone and away from the house. The spring afternoon was warm and sunny. The Big Horn mountains were wrapped in a blue veil in the distance and the sparse gray-green sage, ugly in itself, completed the beautiful picture. Elinore found herself falling in love with the open spaces and beauty of Wyoming. Occasionally, she delighted in the glimpse of a shy, wild creature.

Off alone, and this day more than ever, Elinore knew that Powder River would be her home.

As she reached the top of the ridge she could see the Indian camp by the edge of the river. Squaws with their papooses were cooking the evening meal. When Elinore approached, a squaw went for the man who sold their wares. Elinore dismounted. Without a word, another woman led Chub to the river for a drink.

The trader was elderly, his leathered skin wrinkled but his countenance proud. His arms and chest were thin. A long, narrow braid hung down his back. He walked over to Elinore, smiled slightly, and gestured toward the river. Elinore followed him to a blanket that displayed his wares.

There were beaded moccasins in an assortment of colors, small leather pouches, beautifully colored necklaces of polished stone, and lovely trinkets of turquoise and silver. Elinore was reminded of Bette's ring and that Adrian had bought it from the Indians. A tinge of jealousy ran through her, but she dismissed it quickly. That was all before me, she thought. But she would like to get something special for Jerrine and though she probably couldn't afford such a grand ring she would ask anyway.

"I've seen a ring," Elinore said and gestured to her finger for clarity. "Heart-shaped turquoise stone in an engraved silver setting bought from the Sioux."

The old man thought for a moment. And though his English was limited he did understand the few words essential for his trade.

"Only one ring like that," he said. "It disappeared
and it is cursed. I sold it to my friend, Cattle Kate, the
day she was murdered."

Elinore was startled. She thought for a moment, but
not of Jerrine or her birthday present. How did James
get hold of the ring from a dead woman? she asked
herself.

Suddenly, the possible truth became too obvious to
ignore. Cattle Kate was murdered by unknown men
and John Tisdale the same. No, it couldn't be, Elinore
thought. But she must find out at once.

She nodded to the old man and ran to her horse.
Although she had never been to Adrian's house she
had to go. She had to know the truth.

Elinore rode off in the direction of Adrian's house.
Though she didn't know exactly where it was she was
determined to find it. She had to. The sun was setting
but she had only one thought in mind.

She rode for what seemed an interminable time. The
sun would soon be gone. In the dark she would have
no hope of finding her way to Adrian's. Her back
ached and she could sense the horse tiring. She passed
a few landmarks Adrian had described.

Finally, as the sun dropped behind the hills she saw
a grand house nestled in the valley below. She rode
directly up to it, tied the horse's reins to the porch's
bannister and knocked on the front door.

A servant, formally dressed, answered her knock.
His disdain for Elinore's appearance was apparent.

"Yes, may I help you?" he said. "If you are looking
for food please go around to the kitchen door." He
started to close the door.

"No, I've come to see Mr. Adrian," Elinore replied.
"My name is Elinore Pruitt. Please go and tell him I'm
waiting. I'm certain he'll see me."

"The master is not expecting you, Madame. He has
left orders that he is not to be disturbed."

"Go and tell him Elinore Pruitt is here," Elinore said defiantly.

The servant opened the door and gestured for her to enter. As she stepped into the foyer, he said, "Please wait here."

As Elinore stood in the hallway her eyes scanned the grandeur of the house. It was nothing like Stewart's. The great hall, paneled in solid walnut, extended through the length of the house. The wide staircase was also of walnut, and was intricately carved. There were thick wool Persian rugs everywhere, embroidered draperies, velvet upholstery, a small crystal chandelier in the living room, porcelain vases, huge paintings, and expensive trinkets everywhere. Elinore had never realized how wealthy Adrian was.

Mesmerized by the grandeur Elinore had forgotten for the moment why she had come. She had never seen such elegance. But when she heard James Adrian's footsteps all her horrible thoughts came back.

"Miss Pruitt, what a pleasure," Adrian said. "And to what do I owe this honor?"

"Mr. Adrian, there is something of great urgency I must discuss with you."

"Then let's go into the study," he said, leaning down to kiss her hand.

He led her along the dark-paneled hall past room after room until they reached the study. Adrian opened the door and followed Elinore inside.

Elinore smoothed back her hair and tried to tidy herself.

"Would you like a drink?" Adrian asked. "Some sherry perhaps?"

Normally Elinore did not drink, but in order to say what she had to say, she felt a drink might be helpful.

"Yes, thank you. Sherry, please."

Adrian went to the brass table before the fireplace and poured each a sherry in delicate crystal glasses.

Elinore sipped the sherry and began. "James, I hope you will forgive me, but something happened and I must discuss it with you."

"Fine. I think we should be able to discuss anything. Don't you?" He smiled.

"I've just come from the Sioux Indian camp. I asked about the ring you gave Bette. I wanted to price one for a gift."

"Yes, and?"

"Well, the old man said there was only one ring of that kind and that he sold it to Cattle Kate the day she was killed. How did you come to own it?"

"I got it from her, my little detective," Adrian said. His soft countenance was now harsh. "I don't expect a woman like you to understand, but she was a trouble-maker and a strumpet. I offered to buy her out and she refused. There was only one way left to deal with her."

"Yes, and what of John Tisdale? Was he a trouble-maker, too?"

"I'm sorry you had to be so inquisitive. You'd be better off if you had not discovered a thing. I'm a businessman, a successful businessman, and I didn't become that way by being sentimental. I like the life my success affords me, and I allow no one to interfere with my comforts."

Elinore couldn't believe what she was hearing. The man she'd thought she was in love with was telling her he was a cold-blooded murderer!

"You should have stayed the ignorant, pretty little thing you were," Adrian said coldly. "We would have had so much fun. And if you're thinking of going to the law with this information, you may as well forget it. The powerful people, the ones who count in this state, are all my friends. You'd only make a fool of yourself. Besides, who would take the word of a woman with a tarnished reputation against that of a prosperous, upright member of the community?"

"My reputation tarnished? But you wouldn't speak of the intimate things between us—" Suddenly she remembered Stewart's warning. "You're despicable, James Adrian. You're a scoundrel and a murderer. And even if I can't prove anything I'll make it my business to let everyone in this county know what you've done."

"I don't advise that, my dear. Have you forgotten so soon what I do with people who make my life uncomfortable?"

Elinore was seething. She was too angry to speak. She tossed the sherry in Adrian's face and threw the glass against the marble fireplace. She could hear Adrian laughing as she ran down the hall and out to her horse.

Now it was dark and she didn't know where to go or what to do. The mare could never make it home. She would have to stop at one of the houses she had passed.

As she mounted her horse and rode off Adrian's laugh rang in her ears. How she despised him!

Elinore started off in the direction in which she had come and decided she would travel till she sensed a house that would welcome her. She had passed two houses when she came upon one that looked hospitable. It was a low, rambling affair with a low porch and a red clay roof. It was situated among great red buttes with a lake in the back. In front of the house was a cottonwood with gnarled and storm-twisted branches. A hop-vine clung to the end of the porch.

Elinore tied up the horse and though she felt this was the right house, she hesitated for a moment. She was about to leave when a young girl came to the front door and seemed delighted to find Elinore there.

"Welcome. My name is Cora Belle."

"Hello, I'm Elinore Pruitt. I . . . I work for Clyde Stewart. I . . ."

Before Elinore could finish Cora Belle broke in.

"Oh, we're so glad to have company. Why, I just

finished spring cleaning today. Come in. Granny and Pa will be thrilled."

Elinore was relieved that she didn't have to explain herself. Her plight was evident, and this spirited young woman seemed happy to do whatever she could.

Her "Pa" hobbled over to the door to greet Elinore and then immediately went out to bed Chub down for the night. It was impossible for Elinore to feel as though she were intruding.

"Of course you're hungry and will stay the night," Cora Belle said. "Rest here and have a talk with Granny whilst I make supper. Actually, it's almost done. You came just in time."

Elinore took a seat next to Granny in the front room. Granny's wrinkled face glowed with love and pride in Cora Belle. In no time, she was talking every which way about every possible thing—adventures they had had, the occasional guests and her seemingly favorite topic, the various rheumatiz' medicines Cora Belle was always sending for to help both her and Pa with their pain.

In minutes, Cora Belle was calling them all to supper. Pa came in from the barn, assuring Elinore that the mare was comfortable and fed. They all sat down at the raw wood table in front of the fire. Cora Belle recited a prayer of thanks for the dinner and for the guest that the Lord had sent.

Cora Belle was really an excellent housekeeper and her cooking pleasantly surprised Elinore. Her bread was delicious and Elinore had never tasted anything better than the roasted leg of lamb. She was ashamed at how much carrot jam she ate.

Cora Belle was so animated and so straight-forward, so open in all her thoughts and actions, that Elinore felt she commanded love and respect at one and the same time. After supper Pa asked her to sing and play for them. Goodness only knows where they got the funny little organ that Cora Belle thought so much of.

It was spotted with medicine that had been spilled at different times and as Cora Belle said, "It's lost its voice in spots."

But that didn't set Cora Belle back at all. She played just as if the organ were all right. Some of the keys kept up a mournful whining and groaning, entirely outside the tune.

"They just play by themselves," Cora Belle said.

"Play my piece, Cory Belle," Pa said, after several pieces had been played.

So Cora Belle played and sang "Bingen on the Rhine."

Pa's face beamed with pride. Granny's squeaky, trembly voice trailed in after Cora Belle's, always a word or two behind.

Pa and Granny would have liked to sit up all night singing and telling of things that happened in the past, but Cora Belle began to nod, so they retired.

Cora Belle made up a bed for Elinore in front of the fire and as she lay there her thoughts returned to James Adrian. The company of such good folks had put him out of mind, but now as she lay there alone she began to seethe again. Soon, thankfully, her exhaustion overcame her anger and she fell asleep. ⋖§

15

NEXT MORNING Elinore was off early. Cora Belle packed her a mess box though she was sorry to see Elinore go. Elinore promised she would come again as soon as she could and that once she had her own place they all would be welcome any time. Finally, she waved goodbye to the threesome as they stood on the porch beneath the hop-vine.

On her way again, Elinore admired the Big Horn Mountains in the distance, the grey-green sage. Taken all together it was grandly beautiful. This is where she would stay. She would make it alone, just her and Jerrine.

She thought of Stewart. He must be wondering where she was. She wished she could have told him that she was going out to Adrian's, but that would have been impossible. And, in her heart she knew she had done the right thing. Thank God she had done it before she had more time to make a fool of herself. How she hated herself for her weakness! But she swore she would never indulge herself again. From now on her life would be simply Jerrine and herself.

* * *

It was noon before Stewart's ranch came in view. Elinore dreaded the confrontation ahead, particularly because Stewart had warned her about Adrian and she had not heeded his advice.

As she rode toward the house she saw Tucker run to the back. In a moment, Stewart appeared.

"Where on earth have you been, woman?" he called out in his Scottish accent.

Elinore dismounted. "I've been to see James Adrian."

Stewart's concern turned to fury.

"What the devil do you think you're doing?" he demanded, "taking my horse and staying away the night! You've gone too far this time."

"Mr. Stewart, please let me explain. It's not what you think."

"Miss Pruitt, I had half of my hands searching the plains for you. I think I deserve an explanation, but you've already said enough." He turned back to the house.

"I left yesterday to buy some things from the Sioux down by Powder River," Elinore called after him. "I asked about a ring that Adrian gave to my friend Bette back in Denver. The old Indian told me he had sold that ring to Cattle Kate the day she was hanged. It all came together suddenly and I rode to Adrian's house to confront him with what I had found out. He killed Cattle Kate and John Tisdale."

Stewart faced around. "I know that," he said. "Tucker here was with Cattle Kate the day she was hanged. He'd be a dead man himself, but Adrian thinks he's long gone, in another part of the country by now. Miss Pruitt, you were the only person in Powder River who didn't know about Adrian. When you mentioned the ring to Mrs. O'Shaughnessy she thought that if you went to the Indians yourself you would figure the whole thing out and come to your senses. She knew you were too stubborn to listen to any of us.

But I'd not have let her put you up to going to the Indians by yourself if I'd known about it. You could have been killed."

Elinore felt like such a fool. It was bad enough to find out these things for herself, but knowing everyone else knew of her stupidity and her resistance to the truth, she wanted to hide in shame.

"Come, I'll put the horse away," Stewart said. "Take the day off and rest. I've sent for Mrs. O'Shaughnessy. After your nap, we'll have dinner together."

He led Elinore to the house and gestured for her to go upstairs.

"If there is anything you need, call," he said. "Otherwise, I'll see to it that you're left alone."

Elinore went upstairs, threw herself on the bed and cried herself to sleep.

Elinore awoke from her nap to hear a strange voice downstairs. She couldn't place it at first but soon she recognized it to be Mrs. O'Shaughnessy's. Then everything came back to her—the Indian trader, her confrontation with Adrian and her return home. And now she would have to face them all. She didn't want to go downstairs but she knew she had to.

She pulled herself out of bed, went to the dresser, poured some water from the pitcher into the washbowl and washed her face. She rinsed it many times and took longer than usual to fix her hair. She reached for a clean dress and slipped it over her head. She was quiet because she didn't want them to know she was awake. She returned to the bed and sat down.

No, she told herself, this is silly. I must go downstairs. She dragged herself to the stairs. It was still light and from the stairs she could see Mrs. O'Shaughnessy in the sitting room with Stewart. When they noticed her they stopped their conversation.

"Hello, Miss Pruitt," Stewart said. "Are you rested?"

"Yes, thank you," Elinore said in a whisper. She

would have preferred for them to be cruel to her. Their kindness only made her feel worse.

"Come and have a seat, love," Mrs. O'Shaughnessy said, "and I'll pour you some tea."

Mrs. O'Shaughnessy went off to get a tea cup. Elinore and Stewart sat alone.

"We're both sincerely sorry for your troubles," Stewart said. "I feel as though I'm in part to blame for not warning you sooner or more forcefully."

"But, girl, you're just like me," Mrs. O'Shaughnessy said as she reentered the room. "You only believe what you find out for yourself about something you don't want to believe. I knew about the ring because Tucker had told us, and I took a gamble that you would ask the Indian about it, and hoped you were smart enough to put it all together. But going out to Adrian's, well I never figured on that. He could have killed you, too. You had us worried sick."

"I'm sorry, but once I found out, I didn't think of anything except going to Adrian's," Elinore said softly. "But now that I look back, it was pretty foolish."

Elinore was glad they were concerned, but they didn't know the whole of it. She prayed no one ever would.

"Dinner's ready," Mrs. O'Shaughnessy said.

They all got up and went to the dining room. Mrs. O'Shaughnessy had the table set with a feast, but Elinore was not hungry. Mrs. O'Shaughnessy had roasted a hen, and served a delicious gravy with a pyramid of flaky mashed potatoes, a big dish of new peas, and one of her Irish soda breads. The pieces of ice clinked pleasantly against their glasses of iced tea. Everyone was silent as the sun went down.

Elinore watched the last rays linger on Mrs. O'-Shaughnessy's abundant auburn hair and watched the orange, rose and violet creep up and fade into darker shades until the last dusk filled the room.

It wasn't till the sponge cake with a big blue jar of

grape marmalade and the coffee were set on the table that anyone spoke.

"Miss Pruitt, did you travel all night, or did you stay with someone?" Stewart asked.

"I left Adrian's house after dark and headed toward home. But I knew I couldn't make it all the way. I rode till I saw a house I felt right about and. . . ." Elinore realized she didn't even know their last names. "I stayed with Cora Belle and her Granny and Pa. They live among the great red buttes."

"I know the family," Mrs. O'Shaughnessy said. "They have to be the sweetest people."

"Where are Cora Belle's mother and father?" Elinore asked.

"Both dead," Mrs. O'Shaughnessy said. "It's one of the sorriest stories you'll hear out here."

Elinore listened as Mrs. O'Shaughnessy told the story.

"Cora Belle's mom and pop were kept in all winter with chores and were waiting for the spring to marry. Wyoming's winter being what it is, Cora Belle's mom found herself with child. Cora Belle's father set out right away for the marriage license and the preacher, but he died from exposure before he reached home. His last wish was that everyone would know what he'd tried to do and that he loved Cora Belle's mom and the little baby inside her. Granny and Pa were very unhappy about it all and Cora's mom went off alone and died in childbirth. When the child was brought to them, Granny and Pa couldn't keep their anger, and took her in. Now she runs that place single-handed."

"They take a lot of pride in her," Elinore said.

"Yeah, but do you know that there are some folks so righteous that they won't even visit them," Mrs. O'Shaughnessy said. "I guess they get pretty lonely out there."

Elinore realized now why they were so excited at having a guest and promised herself she would never forget their kindness. She was horrified that their shame had troubled them this long. It could be her so easily. She wanted to cry but instead changed the subject.

"What of Tucker?" she asked. "Is it safe for him to be here?"

"No," Stewart said. "I'm sending him home to his family in Texas. Not only was he around when Cattle Kate was hanged, but he told me he was the one who decapitated Adrian's horse. He said he had to take revenge for Cattle Kate, as she had always been good to him, and that he couldn't depend on the law."

"My God, what are we to do?" Elinore asked.

"The way I see it, we've got to stick together and defy the cattle barons," Stewart said. "Miss Pruitt, you'll have to learn to use a gun. Also, I think you and Mrs. O'Shaughnessy should do some visiting and talk to everyone. I've business in town and will spread the word there."

"That's a fine idea, Mr. Stewart," Mrs. O'Shaughnessy said. "I'll take good care of Elinore. We can start out tomorrow. It will also give Miss Pruitt a chance to meet the neighbors. Along the way I'll see to it that she practices shooting."

Elinore nodded, fearing that despite the danger and the killing the worst was yet to come.   ◄§

16

THAT same morning Adrian rode into Buffalo looking for a drink and some gentlemanly company. He walked through the town and realized how it had changed since he arrived seven years ago. Buffalo had two weekly papers, two banks, a sawmill, a flouring mill, and the saplings in front of the courthouse were finally beginning to look like trees. At the center of town Clear Creek rippled and purled under the Main Street bridge beside the Occidental Hotel. Up the hill to the north, past the scarlet iniquities of Laurel Avenue, with its bars and whorehouses, stood the modest Episcopal church.

All of this prosperity was due to the cattle industry and now these cowboys and farmers were revolting against the very thing that made all this possible. Fools! Adrian thought, as he walked quickly past Luke Murrin's saloon.

Once inside the Cheyenne Club, Adrian breathed in deeply the scent of the polished wood. He went to the study and waited for Stephan to appear. Stephan always sensed a member entering the club, and would appear instantly.

"Good day, sir," Stephan said, and waited for his orders.

"A large, cold gin and quinine, Stephan," Adrian said, thinking what a pleasure inferiors could be when they knew their place.

In moments, Stephan returned with the icy gin and placed it in front of Adrian. Adrian sipped at it and nodded his approval. Stephan dipped his head and left the room.

In moments Major Frank Wolcott entered the Club and followed Adrian's lead. He sat down, waited for Stephan and ordered a gin and quinine. Wolcott wore his brown bowler, riding breeches, and white collar, and Adrian wore his well-tailored black suit. Adrian was also much younger than Wolcott. Adrian ordered another drink.

"How's everything going, old chap?" Wolcott asked. He hadn't seen Adrian since the confrontation with Stewart.

"Barely tolerable," Adrian replied.

"If it's business, you shouldn't worry," Wolcott said. "The Association has everything under control. Have you gotten rid of all your cattle-owning cowservants?"

"Yes. All except one smart one, Scott Davis. You might know him as 'Quick Shot.' Anyway, he decided to sell his cattle and keep his job. I made him foreman."

"Sounds like a good man. None of mine were that smart. They all went off on their own to make a go of it. Ha! They'll starve."

"Not if this rustling continues. They'll just rob us blind and profit handsomely. I've given orders to shoot any man seen around my herds."

"That's a good idea, Adrian. I'll tell my foreman tomorrow."

"These cowboys are savages. They are all drunken and profane—except on the job where they are merely profane."

The two men nodded in agreement and took a long swallow from their drinks. Neither could understand the kind of man who would flounder through snowdrifts at forty below and stay with the herd in a stampede, but who would refuse to obey their masters. Centuries of being land-owning gentry had not conditioned either of them for this.

"And I don't suppose that this much business is done in any other place on earth as miserable as Buffalo," Adrian continued. "Insisting on our privileges here is the only thing that relieves the sense of utter desolation."

Wolcott agreed. They ordered another gin and quinine.

"Well, let's talk about something more pleasant. What of your affair with that pretty little housekeeper of Stewart's?"

"I've had my fill of her," Adrian replied.

"So soon?"

"Yes, but you know, ole chap, I've never thanked you for something."

"What is that?"

"Well, I know that you're always gone on Wednesdays. Off playing bridge here in the afternoons. So I took her for a picnic and told her I wanted her to meet my friend, the honorable Major Wolcott. All the while I knew that you wouldn't be in. She was flattered that I would want her to meet one of my distinguished friends. Anyway, you had locked the door, something I hadn't anticipated, but the rain saved me and we went off to your wine cellar till the rain stopped. . . ."

Wolcott smiled and Adrian returned the smile with a wink.

"Well, at least you had your pleasure. Besides, after this rift with that stubborn Scotsman Stewart, your relationship would have been made very difficult."

"Yes, quite right," Adrian said, wanting to appear cool, but his temper rose every time he thought of that bastard Stewart and the way he had insulted him. And Elinore! The impertinence to show up at his house and start making accusations! The little strumpet! He cursed himself for the stupidity of the ring, that he couldn't resist giving it to Bette as it was precisely what she had wanted; and it was somehow a final victory over Cattle Kate. How was he to know that Elinore would be a consideration? Anyway, he was immune from the law.

"I detest Stewart and his little strumpet," Adrian said, gritting his teeth. "And I also plan to avenge the killing of Noirceur."

"What are you going to do about Stewart?" Wolcott asked.

"I don't know yet."

"I have an idea. It's rather despicable but that is its beauty."

"Let's have a go at it."

"You've undoubtedly heard of Wyoming's strict laws governing cohabitation. Habitual cohabitation, as they choose to call it."

Adrian did not get Wolcott's drift.

"Buffalo periodically goes through a morality wave," Wolcott continued. "Couples that have been living together in open and unwedded bliss are hauled before the court. They can be fined or even put in jail. In any case, it would be humiliating to Stewart who rarely even visits Laurel Avenue. And if need be, you could be called on as a character witness to testify for the state against the woman."

"But Stewart and Elinore barely speak to each other."

"That's no mind. It will be hard to prove that all that occurs on those long nights alone in the wilderness is moral and chaste."

"Wolcott, that's brilliant," Adrian said. "It's the perfect revenge against the two of them. How do we go about it?"

"It's simple. You just go to the sheriff and file a complaint against them."

They smiled and raised their glasses in a toast. Adrian's mind raced gleefully as their glasses clinked.

"There's no rush, my friend," Adrian said and signaled to Stephan. "Let's have another round before we head over to see Red Angus."

They finished their drinks and went over to the sheriff's office. They entered to find Red Angus sitting behind his desk with his feet up on it.

Angus glanced up at the two men and said, "Afternoon, gentlemen. What can I do for you?"

Red Angus was twenty-nine years old, energetic, liked and feared. He had put several stage robbers out of business and, after a considerable display of courage arrested the notorious outlaw, Teton Jackson. Some disliked him because he was a man who had lived in saloons and houses of prostitution all his life. But it was said that he never seemed to sleep, and there had been a semblance of law and order since he had been elected sheriff.

"We've come to discuss a delicate matter with you, Red," Adrian began.

"Yeah," Red said, as he took his feet off the desk and sat up in his chair.

"It has to do with Clyde Stewart and his housekeeper," Wolcott added.

"Are they stealing your cattle, too?" Red asked, chuckling.

The two men didn't laugh.

"We have learned that there have been immoral things going on out at Stewart's ranch and we want the law to go in there."

"What kind of immoral things?"

"Stewart and his housekeeper are cohabitating."

"Are you gentlemen sure?" Angus asked. "And besides, since when are you two concerned with the immoral goings on around here?"

"We have proof. And we feel it's our duty to bring it to your attention," Wolcott said.

"What kind of proof?"

"They are out there every night alone and one of my hands heard and saw things one night when he was riding by," Adrian said.

"Even if he did, do you expect me to go out there and accuse Stewart?"

"Yes, as an officer of the law."

"Clyde Stewart is one of the most reputable men in this county and I can't believe what you say is true. Even if it were I wouldn't go out there harassin' him."

"I'm certain there are other members of this community equally reputable," Adrian said. "They would not want these things going on. The fine ladies of the community would be enraged if they were to find out."

"And the members of the Association wouldn't be glad to find a member of theirs engaged in such debauchery, but we feel our first duty is to the community, and so is yours, Sheriff," Wolcott said.

"Gentlemen, but. . . ."

"But nothing, Red," Adrian said, "I want to see this thing brought before a court of law. They can determine any wrongdoing. I needn't mention the fact that though you are elected there are certain personages in this town who could make your life pretty miserable if you failed to cooperate."

"All right. I'll see to it," Angus said reluctantly.

"We'll be back in a few days, once you've taken care of all the papers and such, and accompany you out to Stewart's ranch," Wolcott said, smiling under his brown bowler.

"Yes, that's a fine idea," Adrian said. "Please don't drag your heels, Red. I'm eager to have this thing resolved."

Red reluctantly shook the two men's hands as they left.

Back on the street Adrian and Wolcott were beaming.

"I'd like to buy a round or two to honor my great friend and his brilliant plan," Adrian said. "After they charge Stewart with cohabitation it will be just one step more to have him blackballed from the Association. Then we'll see how much he likes associating with those commoners he's always defending."

They laughed with great satisfaction as they walked back to the Cheyenne Club arm in arm. ❧

17

EARLY the next morning Stewart hitched his best team to the well-supplied wagon and Elinore and Mrs. O'Shaughnessy drove off. Elinore manned the reins and Mrs. O'Shaughnessy kept watch with her Winchester in hand. Their first stop would be the Mormon Bishop Beeler's house. The Bishop was widely respected and could help organize the people of Powder River. And they would certainly be welcome to spend the night there. Elinore had long been curious about the Mormons, and with Mrs. O'Shaughnessy so cheerful and confident, she left the ranch with no misgivings.

The evening sky was blazing crimson and gold and the mountains behind them were growing purple when they finally entered the little settlement where the Bishop lived. They drove briskly through the scattered, straggling village, past the store and the meeting-house, and drew up before the Bishop's dwelling.

The houses of the village were for the most part cabins of two or three rooms, but the Bishop's was more pretentious. It was a frame building that boasted paint and shutters. A tithing-office stood near, and back of the house they could see a large granary and long stacks of hay. A bunch of cattle was eating one stack, and Mrs. O'Shaughnessy remarked that the tallow from those cattle should be used when the olive oil for annointing gave out since the cows were eating consecrated hay.

Elinore and Mrs. O'Shaughnessy climbed from the buckboard and knocked on the Bishop's door, but no one answered. So they slipped a letter under the door explaining the reason for their visit and asking for the Bishop's help. After all, Mrs. O'Shaughnessy concluded, he should be willing to help as he was the preacher at John Tisdale's funeral.

They had just walked out the gate, wondering where they were going to spend the night, when a lanky boy of about fourteen drove up. The boy explained to them that the Bishop and Auntie Deb, his wife, were away.

"The next best house up the road is Maw's," he said.

Before they set off Mrs. O'Shaughnessy asked the boy, in her customary light-hearted fashion, "Are those cattle supposed to be eating that hay?"

"The Bishop said it wouldn't matter if they got into the hay but that I should knock off some poles on part of the stockyard fence so the horses could get in to eat, too," the boy said.

"But," Elinore said, "isn't that consecrated hay?—isn't it tithing?"

"Yes," the boy said. "But that won't hurt a bit, only that some always pays their tithe with foxtail hay and it almost ruins the horses' mouths."

"Is the Bishop's stock supposed to get the hay?" Elinore asked.

"No, I guess not," he said. "But they're always getting to it accidental-like."

Elinore and Mrs. O'Shaughnessy left the boy to make a hole in the stockyard fence "accidental-like," and drove the short distance to the "next best house" to see if the boy's "Maw" would accommodate them for the night.

There they were met at the door by a pleasant-faced woman who hurried them to the fire to ward off the evening chill.

"Why, certainly you must stay with me," she said when they told her of their plight. "I'm glad the Bishop and Deb are away. They keep all the company, and I so seldom have anyone come. You see, Deb has no children and can do so much better for anyone stopping than I can. But I like company, too, and I'm glad to keep you. You two can have my oldest girl, Maudie's, bed. She's gone to Ogden to visit, so we have plenty of room."

By now it was quite dark. The women bustled about, preparing supper and lighting the lamps. Elinore and Mrs. O'Shaughnessy sat by the stove and, as Mrs. O'Shaughnessy would say, "noticed."

Two little boys were getting wood for the night. They were eight years old, twins, and the youngest of the family. Two girls, ten and twelve years old, were assisting their mother. Then the boy, Orson, whom they had met at the Bishop's house, came home and they all had supper. Elinore wondered where the father was.

After supper the children gathered around the table to prepare the next day's lessons. They were bright, and they mingled a great deal of talk about family history with their studies.

"Mama," said Kittie, the twelve year old girl, "if Aunt Deb does buy a new coat and you get her old one, then can I have yours?"

"I don't know," her mother replied. "I would have to make it over if you did take it. Maybe we can have new ones."

"No, we can't have new ones, I know, for Aunt Deb said so," Kittie replied. "But she is going to give me her brown dress and you her gray one. She said so the day I helped her iron. We'll have to make those over."

For the first time Elinore noticed the discontented lines in her hostess's face, and it suddenly occurred to her that this was the Bishop's second wife! And these were all his children!

When Elinore had known she was to visit the Bishop, she'd had a dozen questions she wanted to ask about Mormonism, but she could never ask this careworn woman anything concerning her peculiar beliefs.

However, Elinore was spared the trouble of asking for the children soon retired and the conversation drifted to Mormonism and polygamy. Mrs. Beeler seemed to want to talk, and since Mrs. O'Shaughnessy rather liked to "argufy," Elinore left it to her to ask the questions.

It seemed that Mrs. Beeler had married the Bishop several years after he had married Deb and just before the law prohibiting polygamy. But Deb had no children, and all the money the Bishop had to start with had been Deb's. When it became necessary for him to discard a wife because of the law, it was a difficult decision because Mrs. Beeler was pregnant and he had nothing to support her with except Deb's money.

Deb said she would consent to his providing for the second wife if Mrs. Beeler filed for land and paid Deb a small sum every year until the debt was paid. So after formally renouncing Mrs. Beeler, Bishop Beeler helped her to file on the land she now lived on. He built her this small cabin, and now she lived as a "second."

"I would never consent to such a relationship," Mrs. O'Shaughnessy said.

"Oh yes you would if you had been raised a Mormon," Mrs. Beeler replied. "You see, we were all children of polygamous parents. We have been used to plural marriages all our lives. We believe that such experience fits us for our after-lives, as we are only preparing for the life beyond while here."

"Do you expect to go to heaven, and do you think a man who married you and then discarded you will go to heaven?" Mrs. O'Shaughnessy asked.

"Of course, I do," she replied.

"Well, if it had been myself and I believed that," Mrs. O'Shaughnessy said, "I would have been after a little more hell-raising here."

Mrs. Beeler was not offended, and there followed a long recital of earlier-day hard times. It seemed the first wife in such families was boss and, while they did not live in the same house, she could very materially affect the other's comfort.

"Did you ever marry again?" Mrs. O'Shaughnessy asked.

"No."

"Then whose children are these?"

"My own."

"Who is their father?" Mrs. O'Shaughnessy asked in her relentless fashion.

Elinore felt sorry for the woman as she stammered, "I . . . I don't know."

Then Mrs. Beeler said stoutly, "Well, of course I do know. And since I don't believe you're spying to try and stir up trouble for my husband, I'll say. Bishop Beeler is their father, as he is still my husband, although he had to cast me off to save himself and me. I love him and I see no wrong in him. 'Twas their foolish law that made him wrong the children and me, and not his wishes."

"But," Mrs. O'Shaughnessy said, "it places your children in such a plight. They can't inherit. They can't even claim his name. They have no legal status."

"Oh, but the Bishop will see to that," the woman answered.

Elinore admired her spunk and her devotion to her husband in such difficult circumstances.

"Do you have to work as hard as you used to?" Mrs. O'Shaughnessy asked.

"No, I don't believe I do. Since Mr. Beeler became the Bishop things come easier. He built this house with his own money, so Deb had nothing to do with it."

"Do you think you're as happy being the second as you would be as the first?"

"Oh, I don't know. Perhaps not. Deb and I don't always agree. She is jealous of the children and because I'm younger. And I get to feeling bad when I think she is perfectly safe as a wife and has no cares. She has everything she wants, and I have to take what I can get. And my children have to wait upon her. But it will all come right somewhere, some time," she ended cheerfully, wiping her eyes with her apron.

Elinore nudged Mrs. O'Shaughnessy to stop with the questions, and they all went off to bed.

The next morning no one would have known the woman's trials. She was cheerful as she bade Elinore and Mrs. O'Shaughnessy good-bye and urged them to stop with her every time they passed through. Both promised to return as they waved good-bye to her and the children from the moving wagon.   ᴥ§

18

Elinore and Mrs. O'Shaughnessy drove on through the fresh beauty of the morning, stopping from house to house telling people of the dangers and that they should all go and tell their friends. In this way the word was spread throughout Powder River in a matter of days. There was an adventure at every stop, and Elinore got to meet all her neighbors for miles around. She was also becoming adept with her gun.

When the sun was straight overhead, they came to the last good water they could expect before they reached Mrs. Louderer's so they stopped for lunch.

The road had crossed the creek, and they rested in the shade of a quaking-asp grove. After the half day's drive they were both hungry and sat down to an enormous picnic. For miles below lay the valley through which they had come. Farther on, the mountains with their dense forests were all wrapped in a blue haze. Soon they quit their grove of quivering, golden leaves and started on their way again.

About three o'clock they came out of the hills beneath which the Louderer ranch was situated. They

had just turned into the lane that led to the house
when a horseman galloped toward them.

Mrs. O'Shaughnessy leveled her Winchester at the
man and shouted, "Halt!"

The horseman slowed his pace and cautiously approached the two women with his arms raised. Elinore
reached for her six-shooter. She had never seen this
man before.

"Are you planning to go up to the Louderer ranch?"
he asked.

"We'll be spending the night there," Mrs. O'Shaughnessy said.

"Better not," the man said, his arms still raised.

Elinore and Mrs. O'Shaughnessy looked at each
other, fearing there had been some trouble.

"Is Mrs. Louderer all right?" Elinore asked.

"Yes, she's fine but she's not there," the man answered. "No one is there except Greasy Pete, her foreman. He's on a tear, been drunk for two days and he's
full of mischief. Ain't safe around old Greasy, ladies."

Mrs. O'Shaughnessy lowered her gun. Elinore returned hers to its holster.

"Thanks for the warning," Mrs. O'Shaughnessy
called as the man headed on his way.

As they drove westward past Mrs. Louderer's ranch
they could hear ominous sounds and wild yells coming
from the house. They made haste to get away, crossing
the great butte, and finally coming onto a broad,
grassy plateau.

That encouraged them as the horses could graze
and need not suffer. But they needed water and a
place to sleep so Elinore stood up in the wagon and
shaded her eyes against the sun's light to see what lay
ahead. She noticed that the plateau's farther side was
bounded by a cedar ridge, and better yet, smoke was
slowly rising column-like, against the horizon. That,
they reasoned, would be their destination. Even the

horses livened their paces, and in a short while they drove up to a roadhouse.

The roadhouse was presided over by a Mrs. Ferguson. Elinore and Mrs. O'Shaughnessy found her in the kitchen, having more trouble, she said, than a hen whose ducklings were in swimming.

"Can you accommodate Miss Pruitt and me?" Mrs. O'Shaughnessy asked.

"Yes," Mrs. Ferguson said. "I can give you a bed and grub, but I ain't got no time to inquire who you are or where you come from. There's one room left. You can have it but you'll have to look after yourselves."

Elinore and Mrs. O'Shaughnessy agreed. They went out to have the horses cared for and unload their things.

Leaning against the wagon was a man who made annual rounds of all the homes in the community each summer. His sole object was to see what kind of flowers succeeded, Mrs. O'Shaughnessy explained. Every woman knew Bishey Bennett, but she didn't think many would have recognized him that afternoon. Mrs. O'Shaughnessy said she had never seen him dressed in anything but blue denim overalls and overshirt to match. But today he proudly displayed what he said was his dove-colored suit.

Bishey was tall and thin. He wore top-boots under his trouser legs and, as the trousers were about as narrow as a sheath skirt, they kept slipping up and gave the appearance of being six inches too short. The coat was too small, his shirt was of a soft tan material, and he wore a blue tie. But whatever may have been amiss with his costume was easily forgotten when one saw his radiant face. He grasped Mrs. O'Shaughnessy's hand and wrung it as if it were a chicken's neck.

"What in the world is the matter with you?" she asked, as she rubbed her abused paw.

"Come here and I'll tell you," he answered.

He put his hand up to his mouth and whispered, "Miss Em'ly is coming on the afternoon stage."

"Who's Miss Em'ly?" Mrs. O'Shaughnessy asked.

"Well, just go in and set on the sofy and soon's I get your team took care of I'll come in and tell you."

Elinore and Mrs. O'Shaughnessy went to their room, and after rustling up some water to make themselves more presentable, went into the sitting room and sat on the "sofy." Presently Bishey sauntered in. He was so fidgety he couldn't sit down. But he did tell his story.

"Miss Em'ly and I were 'young uns' back in New York State and when we got older we planned to marry," he said. "But neither of us wanted to settle down to the humdrumness that we'd always known. We dreamed of the golden West. So I went to blaze a trail and Miss Em'ly was to follow. First one duty and then another kept her, until twenty-five years had slipped by since we'd seen each other, but now she's coming this very day. We'll be married this very evening."

Mrs. O'Shaughnessy and Elinore at once appointed themselves matrons of honor.

They immediately went out and gathered armfuls of asters and goldenrod-like rabbit brush. From the dump-pile they sorted cans and pails that would hold water, and they made the sitting room a perfect bower of purple and gold beauty.

Then they put on their last clean waist-shirts. When there was nothing else to be done, Bishey suggested that they walk up the road and meet the stage. But the day had been warm, and Elinore remembered her own appearance when she had come over that same stage route for the first time. And after twenty-five years, to be thrust into view covered with alkali dust and with one's hat awry, she knew would be too much for feminine endurance. She suggested that Bishey

clear out and let Miss Em'ly rest a bit before he
showed up. At last, he reluctantly agreed.

Elinore went to the kitchen to find what could be
expected in the way of hot water for Miss Em'ly when
she arrived. She found she could have all she liked if
she heated it herself. Mrs. Ferguson could not be both-
ered about it because a water company had met there
to vote on new canals, the sheep-men were holding a
convention, there were more than the usual run of
transients besides the regular boarders, and supper
was ordered for the whole bunch. All the help she had
was a girl who, she said, didn't have enough sense to
pound sand into a rat-hole. Elinore put the water on
to heat and then forgot about Miss Em'ly—she was
enjoying helping Mrs. Ferguson so much—until she
heard a door slam and saw the stage drive away toward the barn.

She hastened to the room she knew was reserved for
Miss Em'ly. She rapped on the door. It was only
opened a tiny crack.

"Miss Em'ly, I'm a neighbor-friend of Mr. Bennett,"
Elinore whispered through the crack in the door. "I've
brought lots of hot water for you and come to help if
I might."

Miss Em'ly opened the door and Elinore found a
very travel-stained little woman on whose dust-covered cheeks tears had left their sign. Her prettiness
was the kind that wins at once. She was a strange mixture of stiff reticence and childish trust.

After helping her all she could, and knowing that
Mrs. O'Shaughnessy was trying to hold Mr. Bennett
back, Elinore ran out to see about the wedding supper
that was to be served before the ceremony. She found
no special supper had been planned. It seemed a
shame to her to thrust the bride and groom down
among the water company, the convention, the reg-
ulars, and the transients. So she invited herself and

Mrs. O'Shaughnessy to the wedding supper and began to plan a little private party.

The carpenters were at work on a long room off the kitchen that was to be used as a storeroom and pantry. They were gone for the day, and their saw-horses and benches were still in the room. It was only the work of a minute for Elinore to sweep the sawdust away. There was only one window, but it was large and looked to the West. It took a little time to wash the window, but it paid to do it. When she placed a few asters and sprays of rabbit brush in a broken jar on the window sill, there was a picture worth seeing. Some planks were laid on the saw-horses, some paper over them, and a clean white cloth over all. Elinore sorted the dishes herself and rubbed the glassware till it shone.

By now Bishey could stay away no longer so he went to fetch Miss Em'ly and they came as Elinore was laying the table. They were beaming.

"Bishey," Miss Em'ly commanded, "do go at once to where my boxes are and bring the one marked 7. And bring me the jar you'll find in one corner of it."

Bishey went and came back and placed in the center of their improvised table a small willow basket heaped high with pears, apples, and grapes, all a little the worse for their long journey from New York State to Wyoming. But they were still things of beauty as long as they lasted to Wyoming eyes and appetites.

They had a perfectly roasted venison steak, hot biscuits, a big dish of new peas, and a pile of delicious mashed potatoes. They could all see the sunset. Its last rays lingered on Miss Em'ly's abundant auburn hair. They finished dinner and now all there was to do was to wait for the ceremony.

Elinore and Mrs. O'Shaughnessy went to the sitting room. There Bishey and Miss Em'ly were sitting on the "sofy." Miss Em'ly was telling him that the apples had come from the tree they had played under, the pears from the tree they had set out, the grapes from the vine over the well. She told him of things packed in her boxes, everything a part of the past they both knew.

Then he told her about the flowers he had planted for her. Mrs. O'Shaughnessy finally understood why he had acted so queerly about her flowers—the zinnias, marigolds, hollyhocks, and any others that would grow in this altitude. Many of these had been Miss Em'ly's favorites from childhood, but Bishey had forgotten their names, so he traveled from house to house and when he found a flower he remembered he asked the name and how it was grown, and then he would plant it for Miss Em'ly.

At last the white-haired old justice of the peace, Mr. Pearson, came and said the words that made Emily Wheeler the wife of Abisha Bennett. A noisy but truly friendly crowd wished them well.

It had been quite a day for Elinore, so she quietly slipped out to her room and was asleep in moments.

The next morning it was Bishey's cheerful voice that started Elinore's day. She had hoped to be up in time to see him and his bride off, but she wasn't. She peeked between the curtains, and saw Bishey's wagon piled high with boxes, and with Miss Em'ly. She heard the rattle of the wheels as the happy pair headed for their home which they had waited twenty-five years for. Elinore envied Miss Em'ly and the new life she would begin with such a fine man, and wondered if such a new life would ever be hers.

After breakfast and a big thanks from Mrs. Ferguson, Elinore and Mrs. O'Shaughnessy headed home, their job done.

19

Four days later Adrian, Wolcott, and other prominent citizens stood before the sheriff's office awaiting Red Angus. All the men present were only too glad to avenge themselves against Stewart for his growing insolence. Finally, Red Angus appeared. The men mounted and rode through town. The people who lined Main Street stopped to watch the procession and wonder what these men were up to.

As they rode, the sun got higher and higher overhead.

The men were hot under the blazing sun. The mountains lifted their blue heads above the dusty scene. The vista was of alfalfa fields, patches of emerald on the sunburnt grass.

To Adrian it was treeless and barren, with bad water and poor food. He detested the flat landscape, the muddy, rutted streets, and the mean buildings of the cowtowns. But today, despite his surroundings, he was ecstatic, for today he would have his revenge. If he pressed hard enough he might even get Stewart and Elinore jailed.

As Powder River was famous for its quicksands,

the men headed a bit eastward so they could cross at the spot where a hard limestone underlay the river bed. This was known as the Bozeman or Powder River crossing. A cluster of log shacks marked the spot.

It was getting on midday when they reached the last ridge before Stewart's house came into view. Adrian hadn't been this excited since he first came to Wyoming. He would have his revenge!

Red Angus seemed to hesitate on the last ridge, hoping to forestall his task. Adrian signaled him on.

The men rode up, tied their horses, and gathered on the porch. Adrian could barely contain his delight as Angus knocked on the door. No one answered. Angus knocked again.

In a moment Stewart came to the door. He was dressed in his Sunday suit. Adrian was puzzled.

"Come in, gentlemen," Stewart said, as he opened the porch door and indicated they should go into the sitting room.

The half dozen men sauntered in. There were only two chairs, and no one seemed to want to take them. Everyone remained standing.

"Good to see you, gentlemen," Stewart said. "What can I do for you?"

Just as Red Angus was about to speak Elinore walked into the room. The men nervously tipped their hats.

"Why, good afternoon, gentlemen," Elinore said. "Pleasure to see you all. Can I get anyone tea?"

All the men grumbled and shook their heads no.

"I'm sorry we can't offer you all seats," Elinore said, "but. . . ."

"Enough of this," Adrian said, impatiently. "On with it, Angus."

"Stewart, I apologize, but my hands were tied," Angus began. "I have a writ for the arrest of you and Miss Pruitt."

"On what grounds, Red?" Stewart asked, with amazing calm.

Adrian was getting impatient but there was a perceptible gleam in his eye.

"Well. . . ." Red said.

"The writ accuses you and Miss Pruitt of illegal and habitual cohabitation," Adrian shouted.

Stewart's demeanor did not change. Neither did Elinore's. The room was quiet.

"Well, Stewart, what do you have to say for yourself and this woman?" Adrian asked. "You know, of course, that this is a serious crime in our state, punishable by imprisonment."

"Yes, I know full well the penalties of such a heinous crime," Stewart replied calmly. "But I'm sorry to disappoint you. Nothing of that nature goes on in my home."

"I've witnesses willing to testify to the contrary," Adrian said.

"Someone on your payroll perhaps?"

"Sheriff, arrest this man," Adrian said. "I shouldn't have to endure his insolence any longer."

"I'm sorry, Stewart, but—" Angus started.

"Nothing to be sorry about, Angus," Stewart said. "There seems to be a grievous misunderstanding. You see, Miss Pruitt and I were married this morning."

Adrian's eyes widened. His face was red with fury.

"I don't believe a word you say. Show us the documents," he demanded.

Stewart calmly reached into the vest pocket of his suit and produced a piece of paper.

"Let me see that," Adrian shouted as he pulled the paper out of Stewart's hand.

He unfolded it quickly and read.

"My God!" Adrian mumbled.

Red Angus took the paper from Adrian's limp hand and read it. He looked relieved.

"I'm sorry, Stewart, and Miss . . . I mean Mrs. Stewart," he said.

"No harm done at all," Stewart said.

"You've not seen the end of me," Adrian threatened defiantly. "You and all your tricks and that strumpet!"

"Adrian, I've taken all I intend to take," Stewart said. "You and your little cubs get out of here. And if I ever see you on my property, or the property Elinore intends to file on, I will consider it a life threat, and it will give me great pleasure to shoot you on sight. Good day, gentlemen."

The men turned silently to leave.

But Elinore called out: "You'll have to forgive us, gentlemen, for ruining your inventive plan. We would have warned you but our engagement was very short, as we both agreed that the trend of events out here—something you all know plenty about—and the ranch work required that we marry in a hurry. You see, we had to wed between times, that is, between the planting of the oats and other work that must be done early or not at all. Why, you gentlemen should know that in Wyoming ranchers rarely have time to get married in the springtime."

"Red," Stewart called out. "Please wait a bit. We plan to have a celebration and would like so much if you would stay."

Red turned and looked at Stewart and nodded yes.

Adrian spat on the ground. He and the rest of his party rode off.

A moment after Adrian and his party left, people came out of the kitchen. Mrs. Tisdale was there with the children, Mrs. Louderer, Cora Belle, Granny and Pa, the indefatigable Mrs. O'Shaughnessy, McPherren and his wife.

Mrs. O'Shaughnessy said, "Red, it was a real nice thing you did warning me about Adrian's scheme, knowing I'd beat a fast trail out here to Stewart's. Well, we sat and thought and sat and thought, and then Clyde came up with the solution. They'd just get married!"

Red grinned, and said, "I would do twice as much to humiliate that pig Adrian. A truer pleasure I haven't known. But all I did was send out word. You all did the thinking."

"Well, it's no matter who did the thinking," Stewart said. "I don't get married every day, so I believe we should commence the celebrating."

Angus was a bit puzzled. Mrs. O'Shaughnessy could see it on his face. Elinore remained silent.

"I know what you must be thinking, Red," Mrs. O'Shaughnessy said. "That getting married was a pretty rash thing to do, but this is a true marriage of convenience. You see, Clyde had a considerable annuity from his family coming his way as soon as he was married, and Elinore wanted to file on her own homestead and send for her little girl. When they learned they might be arrested Clyde, in all his wisdom, proposed they get married. Then, he would get his annuity and help Elinore to get a start of her own. So you see, everyone is better off. And who knows, in time it might turn out to be a real marriage. . . ."

Elinore looked up at Mrs. O'Shaughnessy disapprovingly. She had turned bright scarlet.

Mrs. Louderer touched her shoulder and said, "Pay no mind to her. You know she likes to talk and tease."

Elinore forced a smile, and said, "I agree with Mr. Stewart. We don't have a marriage every day. We should commence the celebration."

Everyone got up and went to the kitchen to set out the meal. But Elinore stayed behind. She was glad to have outwitted Adrian and to be filing on land of her own, but the reality of being married to Stewart was troubling.

"Since I couldn't get here last night, could you tell

me about the wedding?" Mrs. Louderer asked, interrupting Elinore's thoughts as she returned to the sitting room.

"Why, I'd be pleased to," Elinore said.

She forgot her troubles as she told Mrs. Louderer how Mr. Stewart went into town for the license first thing yesterday. He returned in the morning and as soon as he came back they saddled up Chub and went down to the house of Mr. Pearson, the justice of the peace. There was no time for wedding clothes, so Elinore had to do with what she had. All she could remember distinctly was Mr. Stewart saying, "I will," and her chiming in that she would too. Then Mr. Pearson pronounced them man and wife. She explained that she had always wanted to homestead and that now she would have the chance. But before she filed on her land, Mr. Stewart insisted on going elk hunting for a holiday.

"It seems to me, child, you did good," Mrs. Louderer said as Elinore finished.

Elinore kissed Mrs. Louderer and went off to the kitchen. Dinner was almost ready and they all sat down around the makeshift table Stewart had improvised. Cora Belle beamed and said this was the first real party she had ever attended. McPherren stood and proposed a toast to a wonderful man and his new bride. Granny and Pa commented that the whiskey seemed to do a whole sight better than their rheumatism medicine had been doing. Everyone was so happy, but Elinore's thoughts began to trouble her again.

After dinner Cora Belle sang and Granny and Pa beamed with pride. Someone mentioned there were no musical instruments and that made dancing difficult. No more needed to be said. Stewart went directly to the closet and fetched his bagpipes. He played "Campbell's are Coming" over and over. No one seemed to mind except Elinore, who had heard it all night, every night, for the six weeks she had been in Powder River.

But suddenly it didn't sound so bad, now that she
wasn't frightened of Stewart. Everyone danced—Mrs.
O'Shaughnessy with Cora Belle, McPherren with Mrs.
Louderer, Mrs. Tisdale with her oldest boy, and even
Granny and Pa gave it a chance. Elinore stood behind
Stewart and watched.

The festivities went on till the sun started setting
when everyone, despite the fun, decided to start home
and leave the newlyweds alone.

Stewart and Elinore stood on the front porch and
waved good-bye as their guests set off. When all their
guests had disappeared in the distance Elinore and
Stewart returned to the dimly lit parlor.

Elinore was exhausted, Stewart half drunk.

"I think I'll go up to bed," Elinore said, suddenly
realizing that he was drunk and might expect some
intimacy from this marriage of convenience.

"Fine," Stewart replied. "I've got work to make up in
the morning."

Elinore was startled by his coolness.

They stood for an awkward moment at the foot of
the stairs and looked into each other's eyes. Then,
without speaking, Elinore ran up the stairs to her
room.   ◦§

20

Despite the spring chores and Elinore's fears, Stewart decided that they could use a holiday in the mountains. He hadn't had a holiday since coming to Powder River, he said, and he'd never have a better excuse than a honeymoon. Besides, the meat they brought back could be distributed among the unemployed cowboys and their families. McPherren assured him that all would be well taken care of in his absence.

But Elinore didn't want to go, particularly not alone with Stewart. She'd begged Mrs. O'Shaughnessy to come along, but she'd refused. Elinore felt doomed. But the afternoon before they were to leave Elinore was gladdened by the sight of Mrs. O'Shaughnessy, atop her buckboard, heading for the ranch.

"It's going with you, I am," Mrs. O'Shaughnessy shouted, once she was in earshot. "You'll need somebody to sew up the holes you'll be shooting in each other."

Elinore was so relieved that Mrs. O'Shaughnessy would be coming along and that she wouldn't have to be alone with Stewart that she didn't care about her reason.

* * *

Early the next morning they were all astir. The
wagons were outfitted before dawn, ready to begin
their journey into the Big Horns.

They set out in the dark to a great jangling of tin
campstoves. Elinore could not sit under the cover of
the wagon, as she would have been sick. So she and
Mrs. O'Shaughnessy, both armed, sat perched high on
the great rolls of bedding and tents while Stewart
drove, his Winchester at his feet.

All morning their way lay up the beautiful river,
past the great red cliffs, and through the tiny green
parks. By midday though, the sun was scorching and
the white alkali dust raisers came up making their
journey miserable. But they had to push on, for it was
thirty miles to where they could get water, and camp
for the night.

They finally reached their campsite just before sundown. In no time they had set up camp, eaten dinner
and were bedded down again for the night.

In the middle of the night Elinore was awakened
suddenly by deafening peals of thunder, followed by
flash after flash of blinding lightning. The thunder
echoed from mountain to mountain, creating a terrifying uproar. Before the echoes would die away
among the hills another booming report would set all
the tinware jangling. Elinore had always loved a storm
—the beat of hail and rain—but there was neither
wind nor rain that night. She was terribly frightened.

Amidst the fury of the storm, Elinore could hear
Mrs. O'Shaughnessy murmuring her prayers. The
storm lasted for hours, but at last the flashes grew
dimmer and the thunder turned to a mere rumbling.
The pines began to moan, and soon a light breeze
whistled by. Elinore finally lay down and went to
sleep.

Next morning the horses could not be found. The
storm had frightened them and they had tried to go

˙ıoot haphazard you may cripple an elk but not kill it.
So make sure of your aim when you fire."

It didn't seem a minute before Elinore heard the
beat of hoofs and a queer panting noise. First came a
beautiful creature with his head held high. His great
antlers seemed to lie half the length of his back. His
eyes were startled, and his shining black mane seemed
to bristle.

Elinore heard the report of the gun. The elk tumbled
in a heap. He tried to rise, but others coming after him
leaped over him and knocked him down. There were
more shots, and those behind him turned and went
back the way they'd come.

"Shoot, shoot," Stewart called. "Why don't you
shoot?"

So Elinore fired her gun. The next thing she knew
she found herself picking herself up and wondering
who had struck her and for what reason. She was so
dizzy she could scarcely move. But she got down to
where the others were excitedly admiring the two
dead elk that Stewart said were the victims of Mrs.
O'Shaughnessy's gun. Mrs. O'Shaughnessy was so excited.

"Sure, it's many a meal they'll make for little hungry
mouths," she said, rubbing her shoulder ruefully. "I
don't want to fire any more big guns. I thought I'd
been hit with a blackthorn shillelagh!"

Stewart turned to Elinore and said, "You're a dandy
hunter! You didn't even shoot at all until after the elk
were gone, and the way you held your gun it's a
wonder it didn't knock your head off instead of just
smashing your jaw."

Stewart worked as fast as he could with the elk. The
women helped as much as they could, but it was dark
before they reached the camp. Elinore went to bed at
once. Mrs. O'Shaughnessy and Stewart thought it was
because she was disappointed at not getting an elk, but
it was because she was so stiff and sore she could hardly

move. And now she was so tired she couldn't sleep.

Next morning her neck and jaw were so swollen she hated for anyone to see her, and her head ached for two days.

Stewart promised to take her hunting again. She didn't want to go, but she reckoned she had to. After coming so far and buying a license to kill elk, she couldn't go back empty-handed. And there were families that would need the meat.

So Stewart and Elinore took a long, beautiful ride. Mrs. O'Shaughnessy, since she had her limit, decided to stay behind and rest.

Elinore was hoping they would come to level ground so they could break into a sharp, invigorating canter, but the way was too rough. They headed for the cascades on Goose Creek in silence.

As they approached the cascades Elinore could not believe her eyes. She had never seen such a spectacle. There was a series of waterfalls running out of the mountains into a great, glistening pool. As the water flowed over the jagged rocks and the light moved through it, the entire mountainside appeared crystalline.

"I'd love to bathe," Elinore said. "Perhaps we could take turns."

"No, I'll not be going in, but if you like, go ahead," Stewart said. "But be careful. I'll watch the horses."

Excitedly, Elinore dismounted and crept along the edge of the lake to a place where she could go in unseen. She had never bathed in a fresh-water lake before and this one was so beautiful. She began to undress.

Stewart watched as Elinore walked away. He tied the horses securely to a pine tree and sat down to wait for her return. He thought of her white skin and beautiful red hair. Then he thought of her undressing, and though he hated himself for it, he could not resist.

He got up from the carpet of pine needles and followed her.

He made a wide arc through the heavy woods to avoid discovery, then hid himself behind the bushes that marked the lake's edge. Luckily the rushing water created a loud din and she had not heard him.

Elinore had already removed all her clothing except her slip and petticoat. She waded into the water, her skirts held high. The water dripped from her thighs. Stewart sank into the bushes and stared at Elinore's white flesh. She started out of the pool. Stewart was afraid she had changed her mind.

Elinore now stood but a few feet from him. She looked around once and then slid the petticoat off from beneath her slip. Then she pulled the white slip up over her head and stood naked before him. Stewart knew he should turn away, but he couldn't. She excited him so. Her nipples stood erect and were rosy against her white flesh. She ran her palms over them, across her belly, and down to her hips. Stewart felt his manhood rising unbidden.

Elinore went back to the lake and tensed as her toes touched the cool water. Slowly, she slipped into the pool. Her breasts heaved as she braced herself against the cold. Suddenly, she was swimming. Stewart lay tensed, watching as she stroked the water.

In a moment she climbed from the lake, shivering, and again stood before him. To him, she was perfect, everything that he could want. He fantasized holding her, having her. Oh God, he was making himself mad!

He turned away, crouched lower, and crept off unseen as Elinore dressed.

Elinore returned from her bath to find Stewart on his horse anxious to be on the way.

"I'm sorry, did I take too long?" Elinore asked.

"No, but if you're going to get your elk we'd better get going," Stewart said.

His sudden coolness reminded Elinore of the way he had been when she had first arrived. He was frightening.

Elinore mounted her horse quickly, wondering what was troubling Stewart.

They started homeward through the heavy woods, where they were compelled to go slowly. They had dismounted and were gathering piñon cones from a fallen tree when, almost without a sound, a band of elk came trailing down a little draw. They watched them file along, evidently making for lower ground on which to bed. Elinore's horse snorted and a large female stopped and looked in their direction. Elinore knew the elk had no calf, because she was light in color and cows with suckling calves were of a darker shade.

A loud report rent the forest, and the beauty dropped. The remaining elk disappeared so suddenly that if the fine specimen weren't lying before Elinore, it would have almost seemed a dream. Elinore had shot the cow elk her license called for.

Stewart quickly took the head off and removed the entrails, then covered the game with pine boughs, to which they tied a red bandana so as to make it easy to find the next day. Stewart would come back in the morning to divide it down the back with a saw and pack it in.

When they returned to camp there was an imposing row of sage hens hanging in the pines back of the tent. Mrs. O'Shaughnessy had done some hunting of her own and had dinner ready, too.

They would start back home tomorrow. Elinore was glad, for she had been uneasy about being away during the trouble. Also, she was expecting a letter from Jerrine and was eager to get home to see if it had arrived. The camp stove was glowing when Elinore went off to sleep to rest herself for the journey home.

21

THE WEEKLY meeting of the Cattlemen's Association was better attended than usual. The members were all properly dressed in their "Herefords." The meeting had not yet been called to order and the members were having their after-dinner brandies and cigars, and enjoying convivial conversation. But there was an underlying gravity in the air. Adrian stood in a corner and watched.

Thomas Sturgis, a Harvard man and secretary of the Association, pounded the gavel and called the meeting to order. There was a flurry of men finding seats and ordering another drink from Stephan, the butler. Sturgis was so short he could barely look over the podium, and so squat that his bulk extended beyond the sides of it.

"Cattle are selling for a lower figure than ever before in the history of the range," Sturgis began, "and we have an overabundance of the poorer grades. The grass seems depleted and the animals are feeding on such poor nutrients as sagebrush and greasewood. Poisonous weeds, normally choked out by the healthy grass stems, are springing up on the half-bare plains. The cattle are eating it and dying."

There was a sigh from the group. The men looked around at each other nodding gravely, their brows creased.

"Something must be done to protect our investments and profits for this season," Sturgis continued. "The executive committee has met and come up with several ideas I wish to present here this evening." He took a swallow from his water glass. "Firstly," he began, "I—"

He stopped his speech and was staring at the doorway. The men in the room turned to see what had happened.

A big powerful man, well-built, with piercing deep blue eyes stood in the doorway. Clyde Stewart. He was not in his "Hereford" but in his cowboy regalia—boots, spurs, chaps, and a big Texas hat. He walked through the room, took a seat and signaled to Stephan for a drink.

Sturgis stood for a moment in disbelief. Then, not knowing what else to do, he cleared his throat and went on.

"We are forced to make the most painful of economies. At least six of our stock inspectors must go, and the others have to take a cut."

Adrian was very displeased with this. These were the men who kept order on the range.

"And furthermore," Sturgis continued, "we must ask our cowboys to agree to a cut in wages by at least five dollars a month from the prevailing forty dollars a month. We're also forced to abolish the free board and hospitality of the grubline for wandering men."

Adrian was pleased with this news—anything to take from those low-life cowservants.

Stewart rose.

Adrian sneered at Stewart, deriding the sentimentality he was certain would follow.

"Gentlemen, excuse me, but I would like a moment of your time," Stewart said, his blue eyes glancing about the room. "Winter unemployment is now becoming permanent unemployment, and this free board system condemned by the Association is many a man's way of getting by. You can't possibly expect to cut a man's wage and ask him to start paying for his meals at the same time. You'll be asking for trouble. The spring round-up is just a week away." Stewart paused.

"I would like to list the things I feel are responsible for the disastrous year we . . . or rather you, are about to have," he went on. "First, the practice of buying cattle by book count instead of going to the trouble of rounding them up and counting them. Buying cattle by looking over another company's book is madness. It is my calculated guess that not half of the cattle represented in these books ever existed, and now only a fraction of these exist after the long winter."

"Are you accusing us of cheating each other?" Adrian stood up and shouted.

"No, not at all. Just bad management."

The gentlemen looked at Stewart in horror.

"Secondly," Stewart continued. "The range is half-bare from overstocking, and the earth in every direction has been trampled into powder. Every gust of wind is laden with dust and sand, but I expect few of you men have been out there yet to see. Well, these lowly cowpunchers of yours whose wages you want to cut are out there every day with their neckerchiefs tied over their noses and mouths to keep from choking."

Stewart could tell the men were getting restless, like little boys being chastised and hating it.

"Third, this maverick obsession amounts to a madness on your part, gentlemen, especially since your losses from mavericking is only a drop in the bucket compared to your winter losses. Why do you think the

Montana Cattlemen's Association dropped their maverick laws right after they were adopted?"

The men were squirming in their chairs by now, but not one said a word.

"Fourth and last, you've blacklisted every man in the state who owns a hoof of stock. And by abolishing the grubline and cutting wages in one stroke, many of the men who would just as soon stay honest are virtually going to be driven into killing cattle and selling beef in order to get through the winter."

"Are you threatening us again?" Adrian shouted, red-faced, his hands clenched.

"Not at all."

"Well, just remember what happened to Tisdale and Cattle Kate."

"It seems you're the one doing the threatening now, Adrian," Stewart said calmly. "Too bad your last little scheme didn't work. But I'm warning you. I'm not John Tisdale nor Cattle Kate. Don't threaten me, Adrian."

Adrian lunged toward Stewart. The other men moved away. Adrian swung at Stewart but missed. With one blow Stewart knocked Adrian to the floor.

"It wasn't enough that I humiliated you in front of that viper Wolcott," Stewart said. "You wanted me to do it again in front of the entire Association."

Adrian stood quickly. He swung at Stewart. Stewart moved aside, then the fist grazed his temple. Stewart shook his head, feigned a punch with his right and shoved his left fist into Adrian's gut. He kept hitting him until Adrian fell in a heap on the carpet. No one came to his defense.

"You think you had opposition in Cattle Kate and John Tisdale, but you have yet to meet your nemesis, Mr. Adrian," Stewart said. "I'll kill you the next time you cross my path." He turned and left.

Once Stewart was gone, the men went over to Adrian and offered him assistance. Stephan brought him a fresh cognac and began to wash his bruises. Adrian pushed him away and stood.

"Gentlemen," Adrian said. "I believe we should vote on the wage cut, the abolishment of board for our servants, and for the discontinuation of the grubline hospitality. But I would also like to propose that we bar any man from the round-up except members of the Association and their employees."

The vote was passed by a unanimous show of hands.

"And now, one last item," Adrian called. "I propose that we blackball Clyde Stewart from our gentlemen's Association."

Again there was a unanimous show of hands. Adrian grinned with great satisfaction and took a long swallow from his cognac. ᴥ§

22

STEWART DIDN'T want to lose any time warning the cowboys of the cattle barons' newest plan to use them as scapegoats. He walked directly over to Luke Murrin's saloon and banged on the bar.

"Excuse me, boys," he began.

Suddenly there was silence. Not a drink was lifted.

"I've just come from a meeting of the Cattlemen's Association."

Several men cursed aloud.

"I've come to tell you of their newest scheme. With some warning, there may be something we can do."

The men looked at one another and shook their heads, knowing nothing was beyond the barons.

"They plan to cut all wages at least five dollars a month. The free board system is going to be abolished, and so is the tradition of riding the grubline."

"Those bastards," a burly black haired cowboy stood and yelled. "Next they'll be asking for our first-born sons."

"Listen men," Stewart shouted. "We're going to have to come up with a solution. Let's meet tomorrow night, but not in town. At my place."

"Who appointed you in charge?" a man shouted.

"No one. And if you can find anybody better suited I'll be glad to step aside. But for now, like it or not, you need a forceful voice if you plan to fight those men. They may be despicable, but they're not stupid."

There was a muttering among the men. Jack Flagg, who had been sitting in the back of the saloon near the cock-fighting arena, came forward.

"He's right, men," Flagg said. "Alone we're just sitting ducks, but maybe together we have a chance. I recommend that you all make it your business to get yourselves and the others not here now out to Stewart's tomorrow. And don't take any unnecessary chances."

He walked over to Stewart.

"Thanks a lot, Stewart," he said. "I'll be at your place before the sun goes down tomorrow. Can I buy you a drink?"

"I'll have one, but then I must be going. I'm a little concerned, now that I've thoroughly antagonized the Association, about leaving Miss Pruitt, I mean Mrs. Stewart, alone out at the house."

"Yes, I heard. With all the commotion I forgot to congratulate you. She's mighty pretty, and smart too."

Stewart just shrugged uneasily and lifted his glass. He emptied it in one gulp and was out the door.

23

By MID-AFTERNOON the next day Stewart's place was filling up with what seemed to be all the men in the state. There were Texans who had come north with the longhorned herds; west-coast men who had come eastward over the mountains with the heavier, better-bred Oregon cattle; and all sorts of tenderfeet who had fallen in love with the cowboy life—farm boys from Iowa and Missouri, college-bred Easterners, penniless younger sons from England and Scotland determined that cowboys they would be. All had lasted out the initial period of hard times and hard falls until they had become so adept at their new calling that only an expert could tell an outsider from a native.

There were also the settlers who had by now figured out that their lot was cast with the small ranchers and independent cowboys against the powerful barons. They were anybody from everywhere—migrants from the East, mustered-out soldiers, freighters, prospectors, railroad-builders, and townsmen—all the drifters of a frontier economy who were filing on homesteads and turning their small bunches of cattle onto the open range to mingle with the big herds.

Elinore was in the kitchen all day cooking, knowing full well there would be men who had left home hurriedly without provisions and who would have traveled all day. There were also pitchers and pitchers of tea, Elinore knowing that any man wanting a more spirited drink would be carrying it with him.

She put out platters of cold meat, cold boiled potatoes, fresh beans Mrs. O'Shaughnessy had brought over a few days before for canning, and all the fresh bread she could bake in a day. She had emptied the cupboard.

She was in such a state of excitement. Somehow she knew tonight was the beginning. Of what, she wasn't quite sure, but she felt it coming. Stewart had been preoccupied all day, but had thanked her profusely for her efforts when he saw what she had done.

Once the hungry men had eaten everyone who could fit gathered in the sitting room. Other men sat on the stairs looking through the bannister; others filled the hallway. Late arrivals listened from the porch.

Stewart stood and called the meeting to order. A hush went through the room.

"We're all well aware of what brought us here today," he said. "Hopefully, by daybreak we'll have come up with a plan."

Jack Flagg rose in turn.

"We just can't let the barons get away with what they're doing. They've got to be stopped somewhere 'cause they'll just keep pressing. The time's come for us to make a stand!"

An angry "Yeah!" came from the crowded room.

Nick Ray and Nate Champion, the most notorious and most able of the Texans, sat quietly.

"The cattle barons have to be reminded that they are not the only citizens of Wyoming," Jack Flagg said. "In fact, most of them aren't even citizens!"

"Yeah!" from the crowd again.

"They accuse us of rustling," Nate called angrily.

"When they're caught branding or rebranding a cow, they say it was improperly branded, but if we do it, they call it rustling. Men, this is no longer a minor disagreement, but a war of classes!"

The men shouted in agreement.

"Now they want to go even further by cutting every honest working man's pay because they themselves are losing heavily," Flagg said. "They're going to charge board and make us refuse a hungry man a meal if he rides up to the chuckwagon. That's denying the first law of the West—hospitality. It's rough country and if we can't offer a hungry man a meal there'll be no living with ourselves! It's time for action!"

The room roared with approval. Men were all talking to their neighbors and nodding their heads furiously.

"Listen, men," Stewart called. "You must not resort to thievery. Thievery will bring bloodshed. We're here today to come up with a solution, not to start a war."

The room fell silent. No one wanted a bloodbath, but some didn't see how it could be avoided.

"I think it is a case of every man helping himself to cattle on open range," Nick Ray said.

"You can't be serious," Stewart warned. "That just gives them a reason to shoot you, Nick, and there are men here with wives and children to think of."

Again the room was silent. Elinore, who had been listening from the kitchen, made her way through the men and into the living room. Every man turned his head as she entered.

"Excuse me, gentlemen," Elinore began. She was so nervous she was shaking. "I'm a newcomer out here and feel quite forward standing up and giving advice to men, but I think my idea might work."

The men looked at her in disbelief, but were willing to indulge a pretty woman's whim for the moment.

"It seems to me there's only one way to hurt the cattle barons," Elinore continued. "And that is in their

pockets." She remembered Adrian's speech that night
she had ridden out to his ranch.

The men were polite, but obviously not over-
whelmed by Elinore's revelation.

"A lot of these barons, or at least their families, are
industrialists back East or in Europe. They're greedy
in their dealings with their workers there too. From
what I've read, the workers work under deplorable
conditions, but they seem to have found a way to get
these 'lords' to listen."

Elinore paused. Some of the men were getting restless.

"The spring round-up is only a week away and the
barons count on your work to bring in their stock so
they can sell the cattle and get their profit. I know this
sounds farfetched, but I think it just might work. I propose that all the cowboys strike. The timing is perfect."

The men looked at her in amazement. Some even
laughed. A cowboy *strike*? She had to be joking!

"Mrs. Stewart, we appreciate your concern, but
we're not factory workers," Nate Champion said with
a touch of condescension in his voice.

There was a rumbling across the room. Elinore
wished she hadn't spoken up. Who was she to think
she could solve these men's problems? She turned to
see Stewart looking at her. She wanted to avoid his
eyes, but it was too late. He began to smile.

Oh, God, she thought, I can stand anything but his
laughing at me too!

Stewart rose.

"Gentlemen," he said. "I must admit that Miss
Pruitt—I mean Mrs. Stewart's idea does appear farfetched at first. But the longer I think of it the more
nearly perfect I think it is. It's amazing that none of
us thought of it before."

The men around the room appeared baffled.

"It's the showdown we've been waiting for and it
requires no bloodshed," Stewart continued. "The bar-

ons can't leave their stock out on the range. It's been such a bad year that most of them will be out of business altogether if they don't get their stock to market. It's playing against their weakness instead of against their strength."

"I've got to agree with Stewart," Flagg said. "At first the idea sounded, excuse me, Mrs. Stewart, crazy. But I think that's what makes it sound. They'll never expect it. By the time they know what we're up to it will be too late for them to do anything about it, and we'll be sitting on their profits."

Elinore was silent now but she glowed with pleasure at Stewart's and Flagg's acceptance of her idea. Now it was for the majority of the men to decide.

"I think we should take a vote in half an hour," Stewart said. "That will give you all a chance to think it out. But if we decide to go ahead it has to be unanimous. Take a walk, get a drink. We'll vote in half an hour."

The men got up, stretched, and sauntered into the kitchen and out to the front yard.

In a short time Elinore watched them congregate in the living room again. There was complete silence.

"We're ready to vote, men," Stewart called from the center of the room. "Remember, whatever the group decides must be adhered to by all. This thing will be useless unless we're all together on it. All in favor of a strike before the spring round-up, say yea."

Elinore closed her eyes to listen. There was a great roar of "Yea!"

"All those not in favor say nay."

Silence.

Then, all at once, hats were flying and all the men were hooting and howling. Elinore was thrilled.

She looked around the room and everyone was smiling. Elinore had never seen this usually grave bunch so elated.

Once the commotion died down they agreed to meet

on the range to organize the strike. The men began to file out and head home. As they left every man stopped to thank Elinore for her hospitality and for her idea and the courage to suggest it. She had won the respect of so many men in one night!

When everyone had gone, she and Stewart straightened up the house without a word exchanged between them. Finally, Elinore said, "I'm tired. I'm going up to bed. Good-night, Mr. Stewart." She was too tired to confront him now with her eagerness to homestead as soon as possible.

Stewart looked up from what he was doing and followed her to the staircase. She stood on the first step. He stood on the floor. They were eye to eye.

"Miss Pruitt, you did a fine job today cooking and everything for all those men," Stewart said. He paused. "And I want to tell you how proud I was of you for the idea you had, and for not being too shy to stand up and tell it, as most women would have been."

He leaned over and kissed her cheek.

"Good night, Miss Pruitt. Sleep well."

Elinore stood where she was for a moment, dazzled. He had never kissed her before. Then suddenly, she picked up her skirt and turned and ran up the stairs to her room.

24

THE men had agreed unanimously to wait until the day before the round-up to announce the strike. With no time to make alternative arrangements, the barons would be the most vulnerable then. So, for a few days, work went on as usual with nothing perceptibly different. But inwardly the cowpunchers had the satisfaction that at last they were to make their stand.

Successful or not, the cowboy strike would be the first in the history of the United States. In any case, it was the best kept secret ever in Powder River.

But below the surface there were things to do and plans to make. Elinore had suggested to Stewart that if the strike lasted for a long time the striking men would have to be sheltered and fed, and she took it on herself to organize the women of Powder River. In every house extra bread was being baked, spring vegetables were being put up early in case they might be needed, attics were searched for extra bedding and clothing. Powder River was abuzz, and its people had never felt so united or so good.

With everything finally in order, Elinore began to feel restless and was thinking more and more about staking her claim. She was hesitant about doing it, but she approached Stewart.

"Certainly, woman," he said. "That was our agreement. You've done a lot for Powder River and it's time you had a piece of it for yourself. The round-up is not for a few days and you've done all you can, so be off and file your claim before someone gets the property adjacent to mine. It's prime grazing land. McPherren and his daughter Samantha are going to Casper on business. I've been meaning to suggest you go along."

Elinore was surprised and pleased. Not only was she going to file, she was going to have a trip to Casper!

She was on air. Her dream was about to be realized. Land of her own!

Elinore, McPherren and Samantha set off the next morning at daybreak.

About noon on the first day of their journey the threesome came upon a sheep-wagon. Stalking alongside of it was a lanky fellow, a sheep-herder, going home for his midday meal.

Many cattlemen despised the sheepmen, but McPherren was not that narrow-minded, so Elinore called out a hello to him. The man was clearly glad to have company, especially since they weren't antagonistic cattlemen. He invited them to stop and have a bite with him. Elinore and little Samantha, both starved, implored McPherren to accept the invitation. McPherren, unable to withstand two determined females, gave in, and they stopped for a bite with the sheepherder.

The meal consisted simply of coffee and biscuits. But Elinore had never tasted such coffee.

They stayed only a moment longer than it took to eat, for McPherren was anxious to get to water before nightfall so they could camp.

They drove all afternoon over level desert. At sundown they came to a canyon. It was beautiful to look at, but they had to follow the edge for several miles before they came to a place where they could attempt to cross it. Once inside the canyon, they found themselves in shadow, but when they looked up they could see the last shafts of sunlight on the tops of the great bare buttes. Suddenly a great wolf loped along the edge of the canyon, his silhouette black against the setting sun. He stopped when he saw the wagon, and stood watching it approach. Elinore held onto Samantha, but the wolf only howled dismally as they neared it, and disappeared beyond the rim of the canyon.

After they left the canyon Elinore saw the most beautiful sight. It seemed as if they were driving through a golden haze. The violet shadows were creeping up between the hills, while back of them the snow-capped peaks were catching the sun's last rays. On every side of them stretched the desert, the sage grim and determined to live in spite of being starved by the arid soil, and the great bare, desolate buttes. The beautiful colors turned to amber and rose, and then to a dull gray.

They stopped to camp and hurried to gather brush for the fire and to get supper ready. Everything tasted so good and little Samantha ate like a man. She was a good little girl, with long red braids, and plenty of freckles, which her father loved to tease her about. This was the first trip her mother had let her go on and she was so excited. She was the eldest of the McPherren's three children.

After supper they raised the wagon tongue and spread the wagon sheet over it and made a bedroom for Elinore and Samantha. They made their beds on the warm soft sand and crawled into them.

But it was too beautiful a night to sleep, so Elinore put her head out to look and to think. She saw the

moon come up and hang over the mountain, and saw
the big white stars beyond the hills.

A coyote came trotting along. Elinore felt sorry for
him, having to hunt for food in such a barren place.
But presently she heard the whirr of wings and then
she felt sorry for the sage chickens he had disturbed.

A cloud came up obscuring Elinore's view, and her
thoughts turned to the upcoming strike. She prayed
she had done the right thing suggesting something so
radical. What if it didn't work? She would be in part
to blame for the misery that would follow. But she
wouldn't let herself think of failure. The strike had to
work!

And tomorrow she would file on her own land. Once
that was done, Stewart had promised to help build her
a modest house. And then she could send for Jerrine.

But what about Stewart? What would their life together be like? Would they ever share the intimacy
and love of a real marriage?

It was all too much to think about at once. She
would file on her land and make a life for Jerrine and
herself and worry about Stewart later. There seemed
nothing else to be done, she thought. She lay her head
down, determined to sleep.

But thoughts kept her awake. Did Stewart even
want her?

Oh, this is madness, Elinore told herself, and rolled
over and nestled beneath the covers. Soon her exhaustion overcame her and she was asleep.

The next morning Elinore awoke to see several inches of snow. Though it would be gone by midmorning,
she cursed it under her breath as she struggled with
her corset and shoes. Why, it was almost summer!

It was in the night before they reached Casper.
They went immediately to the hotel for a late dinner,
and to sleep, for tomorrow was a big day and there
was much to get done.

Elinore was up at daybreak and after breakfast went directly to the land office where she would file. When she arrived, the door was open. A taciturn old man sat behind a desk. Elinore hesitated at the door, then stepped inside and coughed. But the old man didn't look up nor seem aware of her presence. She kicked a chair, meaning just to make a scraping noise across the floor, but she kicked too hard and the chair toppled over.

The old man was as startled as if she'd shot him.

"Well?" he asked. "I thought you was sick the way you been standing there. What can I do for you?"

"I came to file a claim," Elinore said.

The old man looked baffled.

"Under whose name are you filing, young lady?"

"Elinore Pruitt Stewart."

"Is that your own name?"

"Yes."

There was a pause. Then the old man said, "I'm sorry, Miss, it's just that I ain't never known a woman to file a claim on her own. But there ain't no law against it, so let's get on with it."

He pulled two sheets of paper from the desk drawer.

"Miss, you're entitled to one hundred and sixty acres. The law requires a cash payment of twenty-five cents per acre at the filing and one dollar more per acre when final proof is made."

Elinore had done the arithmetic dozens of times in her head. She had the forty dollars from her savings in an envelope ready to give the man.

"Now, you have five years to prove up on your land, and after two years more you can get a deed for it. Are you married?"

"Yes."

"Is your husband still proving up on his land? If so, you won't be able to keep a homestead of your own."

"My husband, Clyde Stewart, proved up years ago and has his deed."

Elinore showed the man the plot of land she wanted on the huge map that hung on the wall. It adjoined Stewart's, as she and Stewart had agreed when they married.

Elinore signed the papers, paid the money, and went to the hotel for a rest.

After all their business was taken care of, McPherren and Samantha met Elinore back at the hotel for a fine dinner. Elinore brought her papers to the table to show McPherren. She was so proud. She couldn't believe her dream, which had seemed so remote just two months ago, was now a reality. There was a lot of hard work ahead, but Stewart had promised to help with building the house, which would be the greatest chore.

Directly after dinner they all went up to bed for they would be up before dawn. Samantha shared the room with Elinore and before long both were contentedly asleep. Elinore held Samantha and dreamt of Jerrine.

The wagons were hitched and supplied in the dark of early morning and they were off toward home. Samantha, though she said she was a big girl repeatedly, was eager to go home to her mother. Elinore was also eager to get home to see Mr. Stewart and tell him of her success.

Two days later McPherren dropped her at the ranch. The day had been incredibly long, but Elinore's excitement overcame her exhaustion. She and Stewart sat in the living room for over an hour while she described every detail. He sat and listened patiently, obviously enjoying her enthusiasm.

When Elinore finally went upstairs to get cleaned up and go to bed, she thought, *that Scot was glad to see me!* He even held off playing his bagpipes, which he usually got from the closet directly after dinner. It's not often anyone is appreciated so much, she thought with a laugh and went to bed a contented woman. But she lay awake wondering once again about the future she and Stewart would share.

25

WEDNESDAY all the barons, as they had previously agreed, sent for their foremen and announced their "fair but reduced scale of wages" for all cowhands. They went on to announce the abolition of free board and the hospitality of the range. Without exception, the foremen left quietly and without protest. The barons thought they had scored another great victory over their contemptible cowpunchers. Immediately, signs went up at every ranch—MEALS 50 CENTS—and the barons headed for town to toast their success. The cowboys headed quietly back to the range, not to seethe, but to organize their strike.

The round-up outfits met on the south fork of Powder River the next day and the men agreed to strike for forty dollars a month all around. This was done by men who would still be receiving forty dollars a month or more as foremen, but who disapproved of men working at their sides for as low as thirty dollars a month. They agreed that not a wheel would move until a representative submitted their terms of forty dollars a month to the barons. The representative would be Clyde Stewart, for he was the natural leader.

Friday night Stewart and Elinore headed into town in their wagon. Elinore had begged to come along, promising not to say a word. Stewart relented for he feared leaving her alone at the ranch. They went straight to the Cheyenne Club and entered. Stephan greeted them at the door.

"I'm sorry, Mr. Stewart, but you are no . . ."

Before Stephan had a chance to finish Stewart pushed him aside and, taking Elinore by the hand, stormed into the sitting room.

Elinore could hear Stephan calling, "But, Mr. Stewart, a woman . . . a woman has never entered this gentlemen's club!"

"Excuse me, gentlemen," Stewart said. "Mrs. Stewart and I have come as spokesmen for the cowboys in your employ. We'll only take a minute of your time."

Adrian was there. He stood immediately, enraged.

"Stewart, you are no longer a member of this Club. You were unanimously blackballed. And you know that no women are allowed here. What is the meaning of this impertinence?"

"If you'll calm down, I'll be glad to tell you. Firstly, I want no part of this Club as a member or otherwise. And since I'm no longer a member, as you were so kind to point out, I'm not bound by your rules."

The men squirmed nervously in their seats, not knowing what to expect from their former colleague, whose belligerence frightened them.

"There has been a unanimous decision," Stewart began, "on the part of the cowboys of Powder River to boycott the spring round-up unless all men working it are given forty dollars a month, without exception. They also insist that you rescind your decree abolishing free board and the open hospitality of the range. Until that time not one head of cattle will be rounded up and brought in to be sold."

"That's impossible. These men can't strike. It's unheard of," Adrian said, obviously shaken.

"Until now," Elinore said staunchly.

Adrian looked at her. Murder was in his eyes.

Stewart touched Elinore's arm to silence her.

"When you gentlemen come to an agreement you can notify your foremen," he said. "Good evening."

Stewart hurried Elinore out of the Cheyenne Club and helped her up into the wagon. Elinore knew he was very angry.

"Why did you speak up in there? You promised you wouldn't. Miss Pruitt, those men are murderers not to be trifled with. I should never have let you come with me."

"Mr. Stewart, I know I promised, but those men made me so mad—"

"I don't want to alarm you, but if those men think you're part of this scheme, they will also consider you easy prey. I should never have given in to you. Now, you'll really have to learn to handle a gun, and never, never travel alone. Do you understand?"

"Yes," Elinore replied, and though she knew Stewart was right, she felt defiant at his chastising her. At the same time, she was glad that he cared. She wanted to change the conversation before it became an argument.

"Mr. Stewart, I understand what's going on now, but I don't know how it got so out of hand."

"Well, Miss Pruitt, the big industrialists of England, Scotland, and the American East invested millions in the cattle industry. The men they needed to look after their cattle came mostly from Texas, calling themselves 'Texians'. They came up the trail with a big herd and elected to stay on in Wyoming because of the higher wages, despite the cold climate."

"Men like Nate Champion and Nick Ray?"

"Yes, and men like McPherren and John Tisdale. The weather wasn't the only thing they had to get used to. Most of the Texians were merely kids when they came up the trail and the others called them 'rawhides' because they mended anything that broke down or fell apart on the trail with strips of rawhide. Some of these boys were really green. I remember one time I passed a kid some sugar for his coffee on the round-up and he said, 'No thanks, I don't take salt in my coffee." The kid had never seen sugar before, only sorghum! But these Texians were no greenhorns and were top hands, quick with a rope and a gun. While the good times lasted these men were content to work, and work mighty hard, for wages. They sat so tall in the saddle it was easy to forget how young they were. They spent their money on gambling, whiskey and women. The only possessions they wanted were some fancy boots, a Stetson hat, and silver-mounted horse finery."

Elinore stared at Stewart in amazement. He had never spoken so much at one time, nor demonstrated such empathy for these men. She sat closer to him on the wagon and put her arm through his. The night was getting cooler.

"But then came the tightening of the belt," Stewart continued. "They were getting a little older now and started sending home for women if they couldn't find them out here. They set up homesteads on the choicest spots along the streams. None of this was regarded with favor by the big cattle owners. They met head-on over the maverick question, the unbranded calf of unprovable ownership. You know the rest."

Elinore nodded.

"To a rich man, one head one way or another couldn't matter," she said.

"No, but to a penny-scraping homesteader with a wife and kids it could make the difference between making a go of it or not."

Elinore's answer was to snuggle closer to Stewart and rest her head on his shoulder. She shivered, thinking of the violence that was certain to come.

* * *

The "Lords" of the Cheyenne Club were left baffled by Stewart's announcement, but soon their bewilderment turned to rage. Cognacs were ordered all around. There was a din of grumbling at the impertinence of their cowhands.

"We can't yield to their demands," Adrian stood up and shouted. "If we give in now they'll only ask for more."

"Adrian, I'm not so certain that we'll be able to buck them," Frewen answered. "Now that the reports of our winter losses have been reviewed it looks as though many of us are dependent on getting our cattle to market in order to survive."

There were angry murmurings around the room. The men were enraged at the prospect of giving in to the demands of the lowly servant class, but no one could come up with a solution.

"I have to agree with Frewen," Secretary Sturgis said. "If we can't get in our cattle, many companies will not be able to recover financially. I hate to admit it, but as good businessmen we must also know when to yield, even if it is disagreeable to us. We'll make them pay in the long run. But for now—"

"Now nothing, Sturgis," Adrian said. "If we give in there'll be more blackmail the next week. We must stand firm. And as for Stewart! If any of you are thinking he's acting out of altruism, you're mistaken. He's not looking out for the cowboys, he's looking out for his own interests. If none of our cattle get to market, his winter-fed cattle will be the only ones available this spring. He'll have a monopoly and see a pretty profit."

"All the more reason not to allow the cowpunchers to strike," Sturgis said. "I would rather give them a few dollars more a month than to see that scoundrel profit from this."

"Gentlemen, we can wait a week at least," Adrian suggested. "Let's let them worry a while at least. In the meantime, perhaps we can come up with an alternative plan."

The "Lords" agreed with Adrian, cursing as they ordered another round of cognacs. ᵛᵉᔓ

26

ELINORE sat up in bed. It was early in the morning, still dark, but there was a commotion in the front yard. She grabbed her dressing gown and ran to the window. There were at least twenty men on horseback in the yard! She couldn't make out any faces. She was terrified. She remembered Stewart's warning the night before. What should she do? She had no gun. How could she defend herself? Perhaps she could sneak quietly down to Stewart's room.

Slowly she opened her bedroom door and listened. She could hear voices but couldn't make out what the men were saying. She crept to the top of the stairs and looked down. She could see the men on their horses, but from the angle where she was standing their faces weren't visible. Perhaps if she slid along the wall down the stairs they wouldn't see her.

She had no choice. She started cautiously down.

She was halfway down the stairs when someone yelled, "Mrs. Stewart!"

Elinore froze.

But just then Stewart's head appeared in the front door.

"Come and see," he called.

Elinore was puzzled and hesitant, but Stewart waved his arm, indicating she should come down. She descended the stairs and went out onto the porch.

All the men on horseback were cowboys who had decided to strike.

"The men have a surprise for you," Stewart said.

The men all nodded.

"Go ahead and tell her, Stewart," a man called from the darkness.

"Well, Miss . . . I mean, Mrs. Stewart," Stewart said. "The men really appreciate your idea to strike, and they would like to do something real nice for you so . . . well, since they won't be working anyway till this strike thing is settled, they decided that—"

"Spit it out, Stewart!" someone called.

"Well," Stewart went on. "They heard that you went to Casper and put in your claim, and that you wanted to build a house next to mine for yourself and Jerrine. Well, since they weren't working otherwise they thought with all these hands they could put up a respectable house in no time."

Elinore was stunned. She couldn't believe these men could be so kind. She stood there in her dressing gown forgetting everything except the vision of her house. She knew just what it would look like! She ran to Stewart and buried her head against his chest to hide her embarrassment and her tears. He stroked her head for a moment and then pushed her away.

"Don't you think the least you could do is fix these men a cup of coffee and a working man's breakfast?" he asked, smiling down at her.

"Of course. How could I . . . Oh, how will I ever thank you . . . I mean . . . I'm so happy . . . Oh, I'll have breakfast for you all in no time!" She ran to get dressed.

She lit the stove and put water on to boil. She had one of the men gather up a basket of eggs from the chicken coop and got a huge smoked ham out of the storehouse. Thank goodness she had baked plenty of bread a few days back!

The sun was coming up when the men gathered around the kitchen for their breakfast. Elinore was spooning out scrambled eggs and pouring coffee when Stewart pulled her aside.

"Miss Pruitt," he whispered. "I think you'd better go get those plans for the house you told me you were working on, so these men can get an idea what's ahead of them."

"Oh yes, of course," Elinore said as she put down the coffee pot and wiped her hands on her apron. She ran up the stairs. She was elated as she pulled the plans out of her desk drawer.

From the time she had known she was coming to Powder River she had worked and reworked these plans. Now they would be a reality! She wished she could tell Jerrine that very minute!

Stewart was waiting for her at the bottom of the stairs.

"You'd better slow down, young lady," he said with a smile. "You're liable to hurt yourself."

Elinore nodded excitedly and handed him the plans. He took them into the kitchen where the men were finishing their coffee.

Stewart laid the plans on the table and the men gathered around.

"Well, someone may as well get started cutting some logs," Stewart said. "Make 'em the longest and the straightest you can find."

The plans called for two rooms, each fifteen by fifteen. The house would face east and would be built against a hillside. They would have to excavate, and Elinore wanted the dirt laid out in front of the house and terraced smoothly. Later she would sow it with California poppies, and around the porch, which would be six feet wide and thirty feet long, she was going to grow wild cucumbers. Each room had a door and a window on the east side, and the south room had two windows with a space between for a fireplace.

Elinore stayed behind in the kitchen as the men went out to begin their task. She buzzed about the kitchen humming "The Old Gray Hoss Come A-Tearin' Out the Wilderness" as she cleaned up. Goodness, she thought, could she be any happier?

All day long she heard the cutting and sawing, the digging and the groaning. She almost felt guilty watching these men work so hard. She made them big pitchers of tea and readied the noon meal.

She would peek out to the side yard every once in a while and would be amazed at the men's progress. There must be close to fifty men by now. More had been coming in all day. It seemed they had met the night before and decided on this surprise while she and Stewart were at the Cheyenne Club.

She sat now and looked out on her land adjoining Stewart's. There was a grove of twelve swamp pines that would circle the house. Elinore thought how lovely and romantic it would be to live among the whispering pines. There was a small stream that ran right through the center of her land and there were plenty of trees nearby. She would always have plenty of water and wood. It was a choice spot right in the middle of the valley, good for ranching and farming, too.

Elinore stood up finally and called out, "Come and get it!"

The men looked up, dropped their tools, and headed for the house for lunch.

For days there was no news of the barons' decision and the men came daily to Stewart's. There were more men at some times than at others, as some had other chores to attend to at their own ranches or elsewhere.

The house was coming along fine. Elinore was exhausted, feeling as though she hadn't left the kitchen in days. Stewart had agreed to provide the food since Elinore was doing the cooking. He even neglected his own chores to work alongside the men who had volunteered. He was an excellent carpenter, and acted as supervisor.

Every log in the house was as straight as a pine can grow. The logs were left unhewed outside because Elinore liked the rough finish, but inside the walls were perfectly smooth and square. The cracks in the walls were snugly filled with daubing and then the walls were covered with a heavy gray building-paper, which made the rooms very insulated. Elinore liked the appearance, too. The woodwork would be stained walnut brown, oil finished, and the floor would be stained and oiled the same.

Saturday was the roof-raising, and some of the men brought their women along to see their work and to give Elinore some help in the kitchen.

There had been no word from the barons yet. The men tried not to show it, but Elinore knew they must be worrying by now. She was beginning to feel badly about her suggestion, but there was nothing to do now except wait and see.

The women milled around the kitchen helping to prepare the vegetables and the meat for the afternoon meal. And although Stewart's house was sparsely done Elinore could tell many of these women admired the "luxury" in which she and Stewart lived. This made Elinore feel doubly bad, for if the strike kept the men out of work, they would be without an income and some of these families just couldn't make it through the next winter.

The men came in again to eat, but the enthusiasm of the first days was diminishing. There was far less joviality and general talk. Everyone was worried. Elinore was the only one who had benefited from the strike so far. She knew some of these women, as good as they were, must be thinking that very same thing.

Just then a young man burst into the house. He was sweating and out of breath. Everyone turned to him.

"I've just come from town. The strike is over! The barons have agreed to all our terms!"

A great yell came from the men. Hats flew. Everyone knew now that work was finished for the day and a celebration was sparked spontaneously. Some of the men jumped on their horses to spread the news and tell of a party at the Stewarts that very night.

By sundown a grand banquet was set in the front yard on makeshift tables. Every delicacy known to Powder River was displayed. There were roasted chickens, geese, turkeys, pigs, beef, lamb, and even goat. Bowls overflowed with potatoes, carrots, fresh peas, tomatoes, and splendid pickles. There were preserved green tomatoes and pickled beets. Every woman brought her favorite bread and lots of butter. There were carrots, onions, parsnips, and lots and lots of cabbage. They had venison served in half a dozen ways, antelope, and porcupine—hedgehog. There was beaver-tail and a barrel of trout prepared like mackerel, only these were more delicious than mackerel because they were finer-grained. Elinore had never seen such a country feast. They ate well into the night.

Everyone Elinore knew was there: bright-eyed Mrs. O'Shaughnessy, Mrs. Tisdale and her children, Nate Champion and Nick Ray, Mrs. Louderer, Jack Flagg and his family, Cora Belle and her grandparents, Mc-Pherren and his family, all of Stewart's other hands, and, seemingly, every working man in Powder River and his family.

With the eating finally coming to an end, dancing was in order. Elinore didn't know where they came from but suddenly there were a fiddler, a guitarist, two people on the harmonica; there were triangles, tambourines, and thimbles tapping on glass. She had never seen anything like it. Everyone was dancing.

The moon was so new that its light was very dim, but the stars were bright. Everyone was singing and laughing, but when the noise let up for a moment Elinore could hear the subdued roar of the creek and the crooning wind in the pines. She sat off from the crowd, wishing a moment of solitude, and looked out over her land.

Suddenly she heard a shout from the crowd and before she knew it she was being carried to the center of the throng. Stewart stood on the other side of the circle of people.

"We want to see the newlyweds dance," Mrs. O'Shaughnessy called. "Stewart, you lead off the reel. It's a Scot dance and we need a Scotsman to show us the way!"

Elinore stood unmoving. She didn't want to dance. Why was Mrs. O'Shaughnessy doing this? Stewart seemed hesitant as he walked toward her. He was tall and so well-built. Elinore feared his touch. His deep blue eyes compelled her. Without a word, he took her in his arms, as if he had done it many times before. He was handsome, and so close now. There was a strength and purpose in him as he led her to the center of the circle. Elinore was frightened.

The fiddler began and the other musicians followed. Before Elinore knew what had happened Stewart was leading her gracefully around the circle. She need only hold him firmly and follow. As they reeled in larger circles she could hear the neighbors applauding them. The kerosene lanterns, which dotted the yard, whirled by like earthbound stars. It was all so wonderful.

Stewart's hair was thick, dark and wavy. Elinore held his shoulder, which was firm beneath her fingers. She dared not look into his eyes.

The reel became faster and they quickened their pace. It was dizzying but Stewart held her firmly. And that was the best of all, that she was confident he would hold her and keep her from falling. His arms conveyed a strength Elinore had never felt in any other man. It was wonderful, yet terribly frightening.

Elinore didn't know how much longer she could keep it up. She felt weak and dizzy. It had been a long time since she had danced. She depended more and more on Stewart's strength. Finally the music stopped. Everyone applauded wildly. Stewart steadied Elinore, holding her tightly with his arm around her waist. He bowed, and led her from the crowd.

"Shall we walk and cool down?" he asked.

Elinore did not answer, but again followed his lead. They walked around to the back of the house. It was quieter there, and dark except for the starlight.

"You dance very well," he said.

"Thank you, Mr. Stewart. But it's you who dances well," she said, and laughed. "Honestly, I was surprised. I never heard you mention dancing, and you do it so well!"

"There hadn't been much opportunity for dancing until. . . ."

There was an awkward silence.

"I guess you'll be making Powder River your home now, at least for a while," Stewart said.

"Yes, everything has worked out so well and so quickly."

"This piece of land that we share is one of the best in Powder River. You know, the three main forks of the river come together here, so there's always plenty of water. The South Fork reaches into the center of Wyoming. Surprises you to come across it here if you've seen it first in Montana. You see, it's a long river, five hundred miles long. And do you know that there are sixty thousand people in this state according to the 1890 census?"

Elinore nodded, sensing he wasn't really thinking about the river or the population of the state.

"Miss Pruitt, you know so little about me," he said. "I mean, you didn't even know I could dance. It's a bit strange, don't you think?"

"Yes, Mr. Stewart, very."

"Well, to give you a few facts about me, I was reared in Scotland." He went on, not needing encouragement. "After my formal education I started out on a trip around the world. Sons of gentlemen were expected to do that, to finish their educations. Well, I started out originally to go to Australia, but when I came to Wyoming I loved it, and I haven't left it since."

"Don't you miss your family?"

"My parents are dead. There are only my older brother and myself. Since he's the oldest he inherited the land and the responsibility. I was free to leave and make a go of it on my own. I've gotten money from the family estate every year and invested it in my business here, and now with our . . . the marriage, I'll be getting the whole of my inheritance. I shouldn't have to work any longer."

At this Elinore became a little concerned.

"Do you mean you would leave Wyoming? Would you travel?"

"No, I think not. That's not the life for me. I traveled enough before coming out here. I love Powder River. The people are sincere, and the living honest. I would just like to fix up the house more and try to. . . ."

He stopped and looked down at Elinore. His arm tightened on her waist. Gently, he pulled her toward him. Elinore did not look up. With his free hand he lifted her chin. Now she couldn't help but look into his deep blue eyes. Slowly, he bent down to her and pressed his lips to hers. She resisted, not knowing what else to do, but a wondrous sensation ran through her and she gave way to it. She kissed him back, pressing herself close to him.

"Enough of this newlywed stuff," they heard behind them. It was Nate Champion and Jack Flagg. Both were very drunk by now.

"Come and join the party. You can do your courting and sparking later." They were boisterous and laughing.

Elinore was embarrassed. Stewart seemed annoyed. But how could anyone know that was their first kiss? They had been married for weeks now.

"Mr. Stewart," Elinore said, "I think I'll go up to bed, if you think it's all right. I'm tired."

"Might as well. These cowboys will be going strong till dawn. I hope they won't keep you awake."

"They won't. But you should get some sleep, too. You've been working so hard these last days."

"No. I think it's a drink I'll be needing. Good night, Miss Pruitt."

He turned and headed for the front of the house. Elinore wanted to call him back, but what would she say? Slowly she walked up to her room. She threw herself on her bed and wept. She didn't cry from fear or hatred, as in the past, but because of uncertainty about her future. Could her marriage to Clyde Stewart ever be a real marriage?

27

So the spring round-up of 1892 began. While the
dawn was only a hint of things to come, the wranglers
were bringing in the horses and penning them in a
rope corral. In a minute or two, they were roping their
mounts out of the remuda—the herd of horses from
which the ranch hands selected their mounts—and
saddling up in the half-light. While the first pink and
gold clouds tinted the sky, impromptu rodeos broke
out as half-wild horses took to bucking their riders.

Shouts of laughter would be heard when some
tenderfoot was thrown.

"Stay with him!"

"Jump off!"

"Spur him in the eye!" would be yelled at some poor
fellow who was trying tooth and nail to stay on his
unmanageable steed.

The cowboys vied with each other in the splendor
of their regalia: silver-mounted bridles and spurs;
handmade boots with designs of scrolls, butterflies or
the Texas star worked into the tops of the colored
leather; gaily colored scarves; and the finest hats
money could buy.

By the time the sun appeared the men had been divided into small groups. They would drive every creek and watershed within half a day's ride and bring in the cattle.

By nine o'clock the sun was high and the day half over as the drives began coming in from every direction, each under its own cloud of dust. Soon as many as seven thousand head of cattle would be gathered on the round-up ground.

Every day or two the camp would move to a new location, and the process would be repeated. It went on for weeks, until the whole vast area of the roundup district had been worked.

The spring of 1892, its cloudless days and silvered nights, was what the old-time people called a weather breeder. It was too perfect. Work on the round-up was hot under the blazing sun, but the sweat evaporated in the dry air and the men's faces shone like oiled wood. The mountains lifted their great blue heads above the dusty scene. The alfalfa fields, more of them every year now, were patches of emerald on the golden earth. The grass was getting richer every year, and each new generation of cattle finally getting fatter. Despite all the to-do about rustling, there were thousands of head of cattle in. Some were even turned back out on the no-longer overstocked range.

But many tally sheets showed a loss of about eighty per cent. The estimates varied wildly, depending on local conditions and the class of cattle. Losses in the Big Horn Basin were tragically large, but lucky owners who had moved their herds to the sheltered ranges in the foothills that winter weren't hurt.

A big outfit in Crook County, northeastern Wyoming, lost 11,090 cattle out of one herd of twelve thousand, and wrote off twenty-two thousand head out of a total of thirty thousand. Skepticism was expressed over some of these hard-luck stories. Many managers of the big companies, it was pointed out, for years had systematically overstated the size of their herds, at the same time understating the normal annual loss. Now the accumulation of lies was written off at once and blamed on the hard winter, which, said the cynics, saved many a reputation.

While the round-up went on the cattle barons seethed. They were determined not to let these cow-servants get away with their victory, so they got together and issued still another decree.

The round-up was followed by the usual shipping. The Association issued an order to the inspectors at all the market points to seize all cattle shipped by certain men, "known to be rustlers," and hold up the proceeds of the sale. This was not a question of strays; the cattle were clearly branded and their owners known. In cases where a second party had bought the cattle in good faith from a person whom the livestock commission regarded as a rustler, the bill of sale was disregarded and the proceeds held up anyway. Any shipper of seized cattle was privileged to come to Cheyenne and submit proof of ownership to an "*ex-parte*" board—which had already decided against him.

Although charges of rustling were leveled against men in six counties, it was noticeable that only Powder River residents' cattle were seized.

According to the Association, the incriminating information was furnished by the "northern protective association," which was the Cattlemen's Association, so it was the perfect triangle, and every suspected man the Association wanted to come down on was certain to be a loser.

The outcome was not slow to appear. There was more rustling done in one week after the seizure went into effect than had been done in any six month period before. The stolen cattle were being driven out to Idaho, Utah, and Montana. It was said that one herd of two hundred fifty head and another of three hundred had been driven openly across half of Wyoming without even the bother of changing the brands, an exploit worthy of Robin Hood and his men. Like Robin Hood, these outlaws were getting popular support.

A group of Johnson County citizens, including men who had never before aligned themselves with the rustler faction, sent the Association a petition requesting that body, in no very humble terms, to return the impounded money withheld from "good and reputable citizens and taxpayers of said county." Johnson County was closing ranks like never before.

And the Cheyenne *Leader*, which up to that time had been a vociferous supporter of the cattle barons, did the kind of about-face that was not unknown in the frontier press. It came out with an editorial headlined, "Time to Call a Halt," in which it denounced the policy of seizing cattle and called on the Association to return the impounded funds. Never tolerant of opposition, the strongmen of the Association were furious, and Secretary Sturgis was heard to declare publicly that "the only thing left for us now is to knock out that damned outfit." An advertising boycott of the *Leader* was declared.

Nothing could have played better into the hands of the editor, John Carroll, who retaliated by flaunting a patchwork of blank spaces on his pages to show where advertising had been withdrawn. Public opinion was sizzling. Carroll was inundated with letters reading: "I believe in free speech. Double my space." The advertising boycott and the seizures were abandoned. The Association was humiliated once again.

The vicious circle went round and round. First men were shut out of work for wages, either because work no longer existed or because they were accused of some real or suspected crime. Next these men took up homesteads and started raising cattle on their own in order to live. Then they were barred from the big round-ups, and when they took their cattle to market, the cattle were seized and the funds impounded. Conceivably, some of these men were no longer particular whether the cattle they drove were theirs or not. It was a system that would have made outlaws out of angels, and there were very few angels on Powder River. ⌯

28

STEWART AND Elinore headed into town late in the afternoon the day before the Fourth of July. Although both were excited, as the Fourth of July parade was the grandest celebration of the year for Buffalo, each feared the violence that could erupt at any moment. Sheriff Angus was taking no unnecessary chances. He had recruited extra deputies and had made it clear that no guns of any sort would be allowed into town during the holiday. This law was always in effect, as it was in many western towns, but honoring it was up to each individual. The sheriff was determined that today would be different.

Stewart was the first to sight the group of men stationed outside Buffalo as they approached. These were the newly deputized men, and they would collect the guns as people entered town.

"Miss Pruitt, I see Red Angus means to be as good as his word," Stewart said.

Elinore was frightened. She said nothing, but looked at Stewart.

"I'm usually a law-abiding citizen," he went on, "but I don't relish going into town without a gun. I know the men of the Association will be armed. They consider themselves above the law."

"Mr. Stewart," Elinore suggested, "perhaps I could carry your small six-shooter under my skirt."

"Well, you could," Stewart said after a moment's thought. "But I wouldn't want to offend the Sheriff."

"You won't be able to sleep tonight if you're not armed. You know that Adrian and the others will stop at nothing."

"Are you certain you're willing to do this? The Sheriff has threatened to jail anybody trying to smuggle a gun into town."

"I don't think we have a choice."

Stewart slowed the horses and removed the small revolver from his shoulder sling. He unfastened the sling and tucked it under a blanket in the back of the wagon and handed the gun to Elinore. He turned his head as she slipped the gun into her petticoat.

He clicked the reins and in a moment they were stopped by the group of deputies.

"Hello, Stewart," a man called in greeting.

Elinore did not recognize him. She was suddenly frightened. "Hello, McNeill," Stewart called back. "I don't think you've met my wife. Mrs. Stewart, Mr. McNeill."

Elinore nodded down at the man from the seat of the wagon.

"Pleasure, Mrs. Stewart," he said. "I've heard a lot about you. Wish you both much happiness."

"Thank you, Mr. McNeill. That's very kind of you," Elinore replied, and smiled timidly trying to mask her nervousness.

"Well, McNeill," Stewart said, handing him his Winchester and undoing his six-shooter from around his hip. "Take good care of my guns will you?"

"Certainly, Stewart," McNeil said, handing the guns to a man who stood behind him. The other man began to tag the guns.

Elinore was relieved, and anxious to be going.

"You'll have to come down from the wagon, Stewart. I have to frisk everybody, the Mrs. too," McNeill said. "Sorry, but Red gave me strict orders."

Elinore froze. She hadn't anticipated this, and didn't know whether the gun, which she was holding between her thighs, would stay in place if she stood up. Quickly, Stewart jumped down and raised his arms to her.

"Gently, Mrs. Stewart," he said, looking her directly in the eye.

She held out her arms. He lifted her as though she were made of china and placed her on the ground. Elinore felt the gun slip a bit and gripped her thighs together to try to prevent it from slipping any farther. McNeill stepped toward them. Another man picked through their things in the wagon.

Stewart spread his arms voluntarily and McNeill frisked his upper body thoroughly.

"Spread your legs, Stewart," McNeill said.

Elinore blushed and gripped her thighs tighter.

McNeill knelt and ran his hands up and down Stewart's thighs.

He nodded and turned to Elinore. Elinore forced a smile and raised her arms. Cautiously, he ran his hands down her sides.

He nodded again. Elinore was relieved.

"Please lift your skirt a bit. I need to check to see if you're carrying anything in your boots."

Elinore pressed her thighs so tightly it hurt her knees and tried to separate her feet slightly. She looked up at Stewart. Slowly, she began to lift her skirt. McNeill twisted his head back and forth looking to see if anything were bulging in her stockings. Elinore could feel the gun warmed and hard between her thighs.

McNeill looked up. Elinore prayed he would ask nothing else.

"Well, enjoy your holiday. I apologize for the thoroughness but I wouldn't want to be in town this Fourth unarmed and I know most other people feel the same. In fact, that's partly why I volunteered to be a deputy. But you'll have no worries. Sheriff Angus will have an armed man posted on every block. He wants no trouble. See you in town."

Stewart and McNeill shook hands. Stewart turned to Elinore, and gave her a slight smile.

He took her by the waist and lifted her into the wagon. She felt the gun slip and gripped it with her knees and sat down quickly. Stewart climbed in. They nodded to the men and were off. Buffalo was only a hundred yards ahead.

"You were wonderful, Miss Pruitt," Stewart said, smiling.

"It was you who was wonderful, Mr. Stewart," Elinore said. "If you had let me down any less gracefully the gun would have surely dropped from under my petticoat."

Stewart nodded and reached for his shoulder sling. Elinore took the gun from between her knees while he looked the other way again. Stealthily, Stewart fastened the holster beneath his jacket and replaced the gun.

The sun was setting when Stewart and Elinore arrived in town. All the other guests at the Occidental Hotel had eaten by that time and the help were having their supper when they walked into the dining room. Those still eating quickly finished their meals and Stewart and Elinore were served.

One of the help interested Elinore particularly. She was a small person. Elinor couldn't decide whether she was a woman or a child. Before the meal was over it came out that she was the dishwasher. The others had gone, but she had to stay and wash Elinore and Stewart's dishes.

Since Elinore felt responsible for the woman's having to stay late she offered to help her carry the dishes out to the kitchen, and as it was only the work of a minute to dry them, offered to do that too.

The woman introduced herself. Her name was Connie Willis. She was so small she had to stand on a box in order to wash the cups and plates.

"This wash table was made for real folks," Connie said. "I have to use this box to stand on, or else the water runs back down my sleeves."

She talked non-stop as she washed. Elinore thought she had a splendid voice. It turned out she was the eldest of her "Ma's" children. When her ma died she left a baby only a few hours old. Connie's face lit up when she spoke of little Lennie.

"Lennie's eight years old now," she said, "and she's just as smart as the smartest, and as pretty as a doll. All the children are pretty, and smart too. I'm the only homely child Ma had."

Connie's clothes were clean, but they were odds and ends that had served other possessors. Her shoes were not mates, one being larger than the other. Elinore couldn't help noticing, and Connie saw her looking at them.

"These shoes, they're hand-me-downs from two different pairs," Connie said, "but they saved me from having to buy any for myself and I was able to buy Lennie a pair of patent leather slippers to wear on the Fourth of July."

Elinore knew what it was like to want to do something special for a child.

"Can't your father help take care of the children?" Elinore asked.

"Oh," Connie said, "Pa's a good man. He has a good heart, but there's so many children that it's all he can do to rustle up what has to be had. What I'm doing for Lennie is as much for Ma as for her. Ma always wanted to see me dressed up real pretty just once, but we were too poor, and now I'm too old. But I can fix Lennie up, and tomorrow on the Fourth of July I'm going to put all the beauty on her that Ma would have liked to see on me. Then, if Ma is where she can watch, she'll finally see one of her girls dressed up."

Watching Connie work Elinore thought of her days at the Windsor in Denver and of the endless hard work there. She left Connie in the kitchen and went out to find Stewart.

But he was gone. He'd left a note saying he was at Luke Murrin's saloon.

Elinore was disappointed. She had wanted to ask him if there were some way they could help Connie.

I doubt if Connie would accept any help from us anyway, Elinore thought, and if she did, every cent we put in would take that much away from her pleasure. She's obviously a proud woman.

So Elinore went back to her room to write Bette.

At the small oak desk she began the dreaded task. She had to tell Bette what she had found out and, to be truly fair, what she had done. She felt so disgraced. Bette had been a good friend to her when she needed a friend. But now, with Connie Willis's courage as an example, Elinore put pen to paper. She told Bette everything—the affair, the ring, the evidence of Adrian's being a murderer, his attempt at revenging himself against her and her subsequent marriage. She began to cry as she folded the fine writing paper Bette had given her and slipped the letter into the matching envelope. She would post it tomorrow.

Elinore lay in bed a long while thinking of Connie Willis, Bette, and Jerrine. She would not admit to herself that she couldn't sleep from wondering about Stewart. Where could he be? It was hours since he had left. She thought about the cowboys and what they did when they came to town. They would drink, gamble, and evenually find their way up to the women on Laurel Avenue. Elinore's stomach turned when she thought Stewart might be up there with a woman.

He wouldn't, she thought. He's just not the type. Oh, what am I thinking? Any man is the type. And I haven't been a wife to him. He's a healthy young man. He has his needs.

Her thoughts were interrupted by a sound in the hallway. It must be Stewart! But as she listened the footsteps continued past Stewart's adjoining room. Her heart sank. Yes, he must be up there with those women. I hate him, she thought, and buried her face into the pillow and began to cry. What have I gotten myself into?

She cried until she exhausted herself and finally fell asleep.

Elinore awoke to a beautiful, cloudless blue sky. She took special care with her toilette as the Fourth of July was the day everyone turned out in their best. And though she hated herself for it, she wanted to impress Stewart this morning. Those women on Laurel Avenue weren't the only pretty things in town. She was still angry with him, and now with herself for wanting to please him.

Well, he is my husband after all, she thought.

Elinore wore the sheer blue calico she had made herself. Its full gored skirt emphasized her delicate waist. Her sash was designed with a pattern of forget-me-nots. She hadn't forgotten, she would never forget, that the last time she wore this dress she had gone riding with James Adrian.

But she quickly dismissed the thought and reached for her patent leather slippers. She looked down at the white stockings that she used only for dress, enjoying the feeling, as she always did, that they made her legs look smooth and refined. As she headed downstairs she reached for her white crocheted gloves and her sunbonnet with the narrow edging of lace. They would provide the finishing touches.

When she entered the dining room Stewart was there waiting, just as she had hoped. When he saw her he smiled and stood up as she crossed the room. He seated her and then sat down again.

"You look a celebration all in yourself," he said. "Did you sleep well? I suspect you were fast asleep by the time I returned."

Elinore just nodded. She didn't want Stewart to think she had given him a single thought last night. She was so angry, though she had no right to be. She looked up at him. He didn't look well. She was glad.

"And how was your evening, Mr. Stewart?"

"Great fun, but I'm feeling it today."

Elinore blushed. She couldn't reply. She was silent until the waiter took their order for breakfast.

They ate well—delicious coffee, fresh eggs, spiced sausage, buttermilk biscuits—and Elinore hadn't had to prepare one morsel of it. It was such a treat, and only a short while ago she herself had been the employee of a hotel. She hadn't dreamed she would be eating in a hotel dining room, particularly with a new husband, by the Fourth of July.

Though it was still morning when Stewart and Elinore left the hotel the streets were astir. Everyone was there—the merchants, the officials, the preachers, the saloon men, the housewives, the children, the cowboys, and the girls from Laurel Avenue with their silks and velvets and nodding plumes—filling the sidewalks or driving out in buggies to await the parade. Interspersed with the revelers were the newly deputized men armed with Winchesters.

Elinore looked up the street toward Laurel Avenue. She thought she saw a dark-haired, voluptuous woman nod familiarly to Stewart. Stewart tipped his hat slightly. Elinore felt a hot sensation of jealousy run through her. So that was the woman he was with last night!

Without thinking, Elinore tucked her hand into Stewart's arm and led him away from the dark beauty. I won't let this spoil my holiday, she thought.

She looked around at the attractive people promenading. Everyone was dressed in his finest and carried gaudy boxes of candy. Among the children friendships were proved by invitations to share lemons. Elinore heard children cordially invite their friends to "come get a suck o' my lemon." She loved to watch the children, but they made her miss her own Jerrine terribly.

There were contests of every sort being held before the parade, but Elinore wasn't interested. She was too busy watching the faces.

She noticed a blond-headed man heading for her, but she didn't know him. As he approached, Stewart nodded to him.

"Hello, Foote," he said in greeting. "Haven't forgiven you for last night."

"Forgiven me, you old Scot?" the man replied. "My wife said this morning that you must be in town. You're the only man who keeps me out drinking till dawn. The woman's right."

Elinore listened intently. Could Stewart have been with this man all night? She was gratified at the thought.

"Well, Foote," Stewart said, "you best be quiet now or you'll have me in trouble with my own wife. You two haven't met, have you? Mrs. Stewart, I'd like you to meet Robert Foote, the best merchant and Scotsman in Buffalo. But also the worst influence."

"Pleasure, Mrs. Stewart, but if you'll be excusing me the Mrs. is expecting me and after last night I don't want to keep her waiting." Foote tipped his hat and left.

Elinore was so relieved, but before she could fully appreciate the feeling she saw Connie Willis making her way toward her. Pride lighted her every feature.

She led by the hand the most beautiful child Elinore
had ever seen. The child was younger than Jerrine
and much smaller. She had an elusive beauty that
Elinore couldn't describe. One not acquainted with her
story might have thought her dress out of place among
the sand dunes and sagebrush in the hot sun. But Elinore knew, and felt a thrill at the sight of the sheer
blue silk, the dainty patent leather slippers and the
big blue hat loaded with pink rosebuds.

"This is my Lennie," Connie said proudly.

Elinore introduced Stewart.

Elinore saw Connie's whole family before she left
—the weak-faced, discouraged-looking father and the
lovely little girls. Connie was neat in a pretty dress,
cheap but becoming, and her shoes were mates. The
others were comparably dressed. But Lennie was the
center of the family pride. She represented the ful-
fillment of all their longings.

Connie came closer to Elinore as she was leaving
and whispered, "You see, all the work is worth it."

Elinore gave her a hug and Connie and her family
were off.

Elinore looked down the Main Street. It was draped
with flags, the Protection Hose Company had dec-
orated its cart, and the Hook and Ladder boys had
done the same.

At 11:30 A.M. bugle calls from both ends of town
gave the signal that the Sixth Cavalry had been
sighted in the Red Hills east of Buffalo. Kids and cowboys galloped around on their ponies and horses. The
sun sparkled down on the snow-topped Big Horns. At
last the Cavalry trotted into view, sunburnt and handsome in their natty blue uniforms. Cheer after cheer
filled the air, all amid the strains of the Buffalo band.
The people of the town were proud to have Fort Mc-
Kinney nearby.

Elinore looked from the soldiers to Stewart. She
could tell he was proud of them too. As she squeezed

his arm he looked down at her and smiled. But suddenly the smile faded. He was looking past her.

Elinore looked up to see James Adrian coming toward them. He was accompanied by Mike Shaunsey, the Association detective.

Stewart unbuttoned his jacket and slid his hand under it to the gun strapped beneath his arm. After checking it he let his hand drop to his side. He was ready for anything.

Shaunsey made a gesture toward Elinore, but Adrian held him back, whispering something in his ear. Shaunsey nodded. He laughed as he and Adrian continued past Stewart and Elinore.

Elinore looked up at Stewart, frightened and near tears.

"Don't let them scare you, Miss Pruitt," Stewart said. "I won't let anything happen to the prettiest lady at the Fourth of July parade."

Elinore wished she could feel reassured. Stewart was only one against so many.   ✌§

29

ELINORE sat in her new front room cutting out roses of red, yellow and pink to make a border to brighten up the wall of gray paper. She felt contented.

She put down the scissors and wondered at the miracle of having her own home and the cruel irony of not being able to live in it. What torture it was to sit at her bedroom window in Stewart's house and look out at her own empty house. But Mr. Stewart was probably right. It would be safe enough in the daytime, but dangerous to spend the night there.

The sun was going down when she heard horses approaching. She was worried a moment, but the horses galloped past.

It was the cowboys returning from the range, she told herself. She knew she should go back to Stewart's house and fix dinner. But she continued to sit on the wooden crate, her chin cupped in her hand.

Suddenly there was another noise outside the house. She sat up and listened. It was definitely footsteps. They were getting louder but she could not tell the direction from which they were coming. Now she was frightened. Without moving, she listened. It was getting dark, and there were no lamps lit.

The footsteps were coming from the other side of the house, toward the door. She held her breath.

She heard the footsteps stop at the door. Slowly, the door was pushed open. She was about to scream, though she knew no one would hear. Suddenly McPherren spoke up.

"Mrs. Stewart? Are you in there?" he called.

"Yes, Mr. McPherren, I'm here."

He opened the door and stepped in.

"Mr. Stewart was worried about you and sent me to find you."

"I'll be at his house in a moment," she said, picking herself up from the box and looking out the window one last time.

McPherren turned and headed home to his family. Elinore walked back to Stewart's house.

Elinore prepared dinner disinterestedly and set the table. Stewart's bagpipe droned from the sitting room. She went into the room silently and nodded, indicating that dinner was ready. She returned to the dinner table and took her seat. Stewart followed.

Elinore mumbled a prayer and Stewart began to eat.

"Fine meal, Miss Pruitt," he said.

Elinore just nodded. Silence followed.

"How was your day?" Stewart asked finally.

"Fine."

Silence followed again.

"What's the matter with you, woman?" Stewart asked, his voice suddenly angry.

Elinore looked up from the plate where she had been pushing her food around, never lifting the fork to her mouth.

"Nothing," she said.

"Don't be telling me 'nothing'. You've been pouting

all day, and now you haven't touched your dinner. I won't be standing for it. Tell me what's on your mind."

"All right. If you insist. You promised that if we married you would help me with my house, which you have. But now that it's finished you won't allow me to live there. It's cruel!"

"Cruel nothing, woman! I told you it was too dangerous now. When things calm down—"

"When things calm down! When will that be? A month? A year? I came out here to homestead and have my own home and now you won't let me!" She added, looking around, "This isn't my home!"

"I'll hear no more of these hysterics. I have no compulsion to keep you here except for your safety. Stop acting like a child!"

"A child!" Elinore rose from the table. "I'll show you who is a child. I can take care of myself, Mr. Stewart. I never asked for your protection!"

Elinore turned from the table and ran out into the yard, across the distance that separated her house from Stewart's. She was crying as she lit the gasoline lantern. Then she sat on her wooden crate and buried her face in her hands.

After a long cry Elinore began to feel a chill. She scolded herself for leaving the house in such a hurry and forgetting a blanket. She couldn't go back now, not after she had said she could take care of herself. She crouched into the corner, shivering.

A few minutes later she heard a noise outside the house. She tried to look out, but with the lantern lit she couldn't see.

It must be Stewart come to get me, she thought. She hated to admit it but she would be glad to go back to the big house where it was warm. And if he asked her to go back, it wouldn't be nearly as humiliating as going back on her own.

She sat back contentedly waiting for him to enter

the house. But after a minute he still had not appeared.

He's hesitating, but he'll come in, she told herself. He won't let me stay out here all night by myself. I'll even apologize for the things I said.

The door was eased open.

"Come in, Mr. Stewart. I'm sorry for the things...."

But when Elinore looked up at the door it was not Stewart. A strange man stood in the doorway. She screamed.

He lurched toward her and grabbed her, covering her mouth with his hand. She bit into his palm. He jerked his hand away. Elinore screamed again. He pulled the bandana from around his neck and gagged her with it. She struggled, but it was useless against his strength. He pushed her into the corner.

"Look, you little heifer," he said, tying her hands with a rawhide thong, "you can make this easy or hard on yourself. We've got a meeting to attend out on Independence Rock. One of your favorites will be there waiting for us, James Adrian. And he promised that if I got you out there without complications I could have a little pleasure of my own. You see, I've always been partial to red-heads."

Elinore struggled to her feet. He laughed and pushed her back into the corner. She prayed someone had heard her screams, but it was unlikely. Stewart couldn't hear a thing over those bagpipes, and most of the help would be bedded down by now.

Elinore looked at the man. He needed a shave and was filthy. The gleam in his eye was frightening. He was actually enjoying this. She sat huddled in the corner. She kicked at him as he came at her, and tore her hands free from the rawhide.

"Adrian said you were feisty," he said, with a smile. "But I'm warning you, they don't call me 'Quick Shot' for nothing."

He grabbed her hands. She knocked over the crate

and kicked at the wall, ripping the gray wall paper, in her struggle to get away. He gave her right arm a yank, throwing her to the floor onto her belly. A pain shot through her arm. He grabbed her other arm from under her belly and tied her hands together behind her back and jerked her to her feet. Her right arm was on fire with pain. She had to fight back tears.

God, they plan to kill me, she thought frantically as she bit into the filthy bandana.

He lifted her over his shoulder. Elinore kicked furiously. He gasped and dropped her, holding his groin. She started for the door but he grabbed her hair. He smacked her hard with the back of his hand. Elinore fell to the floor. Blood dripped from her mouth. Quick Shot tied her ankles with another strip of rawhide.

"I'll have to hang you over the saddle if you can't behave," he said. "I was going to let you ride on the saddle with me, but now . . . It's going to be a painful ride all the way out to Independence Rock. You'll regret kicking me before long."

He hefted her over his shoulder and kicked over the lamp, putting it out. Once outside he threw Elinore over the back of his saddle. The impact knocked the wind out of her. She struggled for air.

Quick Shot led the horse away on foot, to avoid any noise. Elinore bumped along on its back. When they were a few hundred feet from her house, Quick Shot jumped on the horse and gave it a kick. As the horse galloped Elinore bounced unmercifully on its hind quarters. Quick Shot held her wrists to keep her from falling off. Her right arm was numb with pain.

Elinore was terrified. He's going to rape me and then they'll kill me! Why did I ever come to Powder River? What ever made me think I could homestead in this wilderness? What will happen to Jerrine?

Hot tears stung her eyes. Jerrine will end up in an orphanage or in some factory. Oh God, I've failed so miserably!

* * *

Stewart sat in his usual chair in the sitting room, his bagpipe in his lap, but he did not play. He got up and headed for the front door, then hesitated.

"That woman is so strong-headed! Damn!" he cursed aloud. "I thought she'd be back by now. Why, she didn't even take a blanket when she stormed out. Wilful and proud! I'll let her sit!"

He returned to his chair and picked up his bagpipe from the floor. He sipped at his whiskey and started to blow into the instrument. But before he produced the first note, the bagpipe was on the floor again and he was headed for Elinore's house.

As he strode across the yard that separated their houses he noticed that there was no lantern lit, but the full moon provided plenty of light for his walk.

My God, she's asleep already, he thought. That woman!

As he approached the house he peered in the window but he couldn't see Elinore. He walked to the door and entered.

"Elinore?" he whispered. He found the overturned lantern in the corner and lit it.

He looked around the room and saw the ripped gray wall paper, the toppled crate, and the spots of blood on the floor.

"My God, they've come and got her!"

He ran from the house and shouted for his men. He looked down on the ground and saw the tracks of a single horse. They headed southwest. He ran to the bunkhouse.

"Men, get up! I need your help! Mrs. Stewart has been kidnapped!"

In no time the cowboys were dressed and saddling their horses.

"Bring your rifles and pistols. This may be bloody," Stewart called.

He ran to the house and got his Winchester and

pistol. The men had readied his best horse and in minutes they were off in the direction of the fresh tracks, Stewart leading.

Thank God we have a moon, Stewart thought, otherwise we'd be in a sorry position. God, I wish McPherren hadn't gone home. He's my best man.

"Stewart, there's only one thing out in this direction," a young Texan called. "Independence Rock."

Stewart thought about it. The boy was right. They would have to gamble, for if they took the time to watch the tracks all might be lost.

"Right!" he called. "Six of you men come with me and, just in case, two of you stay behind and follow the tracks. Good luck!" he shouted as he spurred his horse.

His head was low. He rode the horse as hard as it would go. The men followed.

They plan on hanging her, he thought. Adrian, if she's harmed I'll kill you straight out and ask questions later. There'll be a bloodbath that will shock even the West! I'll have every head of that damnable Association!

They rode hard, praying their horses would hold out.

Elinore bounced on the back of Quick Shot's horse. He had quit the gallop, as he could barely hold her on the horse at that pace, and had slowed to a canter. Still, the thumping up and down was torture for her. Elinore almost prayed they would get to Independence Rock and end her suffering, though she knew death awaited her there.

After what seemed an eternity Quick Shot stopped the horse and dismounted. He stood her on her feet and cut the rawhide that bound her. He pointed up the ridge with his knife.

Five men waited there. Elinore remembered the last time she had been out here. It was the day James

Adrian had taken her riding and taught her to shoot a pistol. She remembered the rock that jutted out from the cliff, but she had forgotten its significance. Now it was all too clear. This was where Cattle Kate had been hanged!

Over the far ridge she could see the roof of the TA ranch. Oh how she hated herself for what that reminded her of! How could she ever have believed James Adrian's intentions were honorable? She was such a fool! And now she would die!

She looked up on the ridge behind them, hoping to see a miracle, some help, but no one was there. As her eyes moved around the rim of the ridge she saw a man sitting on his horse, watching.

It's James Adrian, Elinore thought, come to oversee.

Suddenly Quick Shot grabbed her arm and jerked her up the ridge to the rock. A noose was tied to the limb of a stunted pine.

Stewart rode hard. He could feel the horse tiring beneath him but he would not relent. He pushed on. The full moon stood in place as they rode. So, seemingly, did time.

He spurred his horse again and gripped its flanks harder with his legs.

I love that woman, Stewart thought. And I've never told her. If nothing else, I must tell her. I'll kill them all if they deny me that chance.

The five men, heavily armed, watched Elinore carefully. She stumbled as she approached the stunted pine. Quick Shot pushed her on.

"Get going now," he said, pulling the gag from her mouth. "There are people in this town, important people, who don't like what you've been doing. The easiest solution, seein' as you're not the reasonable type, is just to get rid of you. You went and suggested that the cowboys strike. You must have expected this. But what really got them mad was when you filed on that property next to Stewart's. That's some of the best grazing land in Powder River. You should've known they wouldn't stand for that. No damn *woman* is going to homestead that property. Right, boys?" he said, turning to the armed men.

Elinore looked around. There was no escape. If she tried to run she would be shot before she got ten feet. The memory of what she had said to Stewart about not asking for nor wanting his protection came back to her. What a fool she was! He was the only protection she had, and she'd thrown it away out of spite. Now they were going to kill her! Jerrine would be an orphan. Elinore began to cry.

"No sense crying, little lady," Quick Shot said. "You ain't gonna die. Not yet anyhow."

Elinore looked up at him.

Quick Shot chuckled.

"I mean to have my pleasure while there's still life in that pretty body," he said, staring at her.

Elinore screamed.

"No sense screaming, either. There's nobody to hear you out here excepting those men up there, and they ain't gonna help you. But if it makes you feel better. . . ."

The others were all laughing at Elinore now. Quick Shot shoved her. She fell to the ground. Her arms were still tied. Searing pain shot through her right arm.

"We're goin' to put on a little show for the guys," Quick Shot said. "You don't have any objections, do you now?"

Elinore lay on the ground and looked up at him. All was certainly lost now. To die was frightening, but for this man to have her first! She wished she were dead already and spared the humiliation.

"I told you before I liked red-heads," he said. "After I get finished maybe the others would like a taste."

The other men were silent now, but each face wore a malevolent sneer.

Quick Shot pushed Elinore's shoulder with his foot, making her lie flat. He bent over and grabbed her bodice with both hands and ripped it open, exposing her breasts. With her hands tied, she could do nothing to cover herself.

Why didn't I listen to Stewart? Elinore moaned inwardly. He's been only good to me. Why was I so stubborn? She closed her eyes and pictured his face. Oh, if I had another chance, I would be such a good wife to. . . .

Quick Shot laughed obscenely. She opened her eyes to see him unbuttoning his dungarees. She turned her head away. Over her shoulder she could see the mounted man on the ridge, watching. How she despised James Adrian!

"I'm going to make you do something for me that even my fancy lady in town won't do." Quick Shot knelt on the ground close to Elinore's face. "I'm going to put this in your mouth."

Elinore turned her face as far away as she could. He jerked her head back, forcing her to look. Elinore gagged.

"Quick Shot, I wouldn't if I were you," one of the men called. "If she's as smart as they say, it'll be gone in one bite!"

The men all laughed. But not Quick Shot. Suddenly he looked angry.

"You all can just look somewhere else if you find it funny. And the first one that looks this way I'll shoot dead. Now turn around like I said."

Elinore watched as all the men quit laughing and turned obediently away. They looked out toward the opposite direction from which they'd come, toward the TA ranch.

Quick Shot pulled Elinore's skirt up and tore her petticoat from her. Then he straddled her. His face was dirty and unshaven. Just the idea of being touched by him was sickening.

"I'm going to give it to you like you never had it. Nothing like that strange Scotsman of a husband you got. I ain't gonna be gentle. I'm gonna pound you till you break in two."

Elinore wanted to die. Why couldn't they kill her and be done with it?

He pulled his dungarees to his knees and separated her legs. He looked up at the men once more. They were all looking out over the far ridge.

He took her legs, one in each hand, and pushed them violently apart. Elinore screamed. She closed her eyes, bracing herself. Her whole body was tensed. She could hear Quick Shot's breathing.

Suddenly a volley of shots rang out and she heard a thud beside her. She lay frozen, eyes still closed, paralyzed with fear. The shots continued. She dared not look up.

After what seemed an eternity, there was silence. She still could not move.

Then she heard it! Could it be true?

"Elinore, are you all right?"

She opened her eyes to see Stewart kneeling next to her. Quick Shot lay crumpled beside her, dead. His wide-open eyes were staring blankly.

Gently, Stewart rolled her over and cut the rawhide that bound her wrists. She tried to lift her arms but she could not.

"Clyde, I . . ."

"Sh-h-h," he whispered. He wrapped a blanket around her and picked her up. "You have nothing to worry about now. All those men are dead, and I'll never leave you alone again. Elinore, I love you."

He bent his head and kissed her so very gently.

"Let's go home, my love," he said.

Elinore cried softly as he held her in his arms. ⋞§

30

Later that night James Adrian stood at the window of the Cheyenne Club, clutching a glass of gin and looking out onto the dark streets of Buffalo. He was consumed by murderous rage. Stewart and Elinore had thwarted his revenge once again!

He finished the glass of gin in one long swallow and replenished it from the bottle that sat on the table beside him. He was trying to drink down his frustration, but it wasn't working. The gin was only inflaming him. Something must be done.

Others had known of his plan to deal with Elinore, and now he would have to tell them of his failure and be humiliated once again. Wolcott, Frewen and Sturgis would be arriving soon, as they had planned to meet and celebrate their victory. Adrian took another long swallow of gin. It burned his throat and heated his chest.

Damn, he thought, it's almost midnight. They'll all be here any minute.

The gin bottle was half-empty by the time they had all assembled. No one needed to ask the outcome of Adrian's plan. The outcome was evident on his face.

"What happened, Adrian?" Wolcott asked. "It seemed a simple plan."

"I watched from the ridge," Adrian began. "The men waited as instructed for Quick Shot to return. The noose was ready. But then when Quick Shot got there with the woman he got an idea into his head."

The men looked puzzled. Adrian explained.

"I guess he just couldn't resist taking a little masculine pleasure before seeing her hanged," he said, not wanting the others to know that he had been the one who had wanted Elinore to suffer the shame of being raped in front of the other men and himself.

He felt safe in saying whatever he wanted to say. Dead men couldn't defend themselves.

"Well," he went on, "of course I couldn't hear from up on the ridge, and I thought he would have her quickly and be done with it and then get on with the hanging. For some reason he made the men turn their backs before he straddled her. While their backs were turned Stewart and a posse of his men came up from behind. I saw them, but if I had shot to warn Quick Shot and the others, I'd have been seen. Stewart and his posse got up the ridge before my men knew what was happening, and they gunned down all my men. I hid behind some sagebrush until they left and then headed directly to town."

"You did the right thing, Adrian," Frewen said. "If you had given warning you would have involved yourself. A gentleman of your stature should never dirty his hands, no matter how dirty the business he is forced to become involved in."

"Are you certain all the men are dead?" Sturgis asked.

"They were all wounded, and by the time they're found they will surely be dead," Adrian answered.

"Good," Sturgis said. "Dead men can't talk. It could be sticky if our part in this thing got back to the Association."

They all sipped at their drinks.

"The question is, what do we do now?" Wolcott said. "We can't allow this setback to defeat us. We must think of another strategy."

There was general agreement among the men.

"It seems to me that the measures we've taken so far have one major drawback," Wolcott began. "They're on too small a scale to ever be truly effective. Killing one or two rustlers only arouses the sympathy of the other citizens. Our tactics to date have played into the hands of the rustler faction. We must do something far broader. We must wipe out the entire opposition in one stroke."

The men looked at Wolcott, baffled, but very much interested.

They ordered another round of drinks and sat back, waiting for him to explain.

"We need an expedition of some kind," Wolcott said after a long silence. "Northern Wyoming is the hub of our troubles. We must concentrate our efforts there."

"What are you suggesting, Wolcott?" Adrian asked.

"Well, I haven't quite formed the idea," Wolcott admitted, "but I propose that we organize an expeditionary force and simply march through Powder River County, eliminating all who oppose us. The fervor of the citizenry will die quickly once they see what they're up against. I'm certain that with the influence this Club commands we can get the Governor to back us up."

"Yes," Frewen joined in. "We have all heard of the problem of poachers back home in England and the means they have of dealing with them. The Lords simply hire tough characters from London's roughest areas to search out and destroy the poachers. Any who are missed in the process are so intimidated they never poach again. Wolcott, it's brilliant!"

"It must be kept in total secrecy if the plan is to be effective," Wolcott warned. "And we must hire the best possible men. I think we should do our recruiting out of state, of both men and horses, thereby not arousing any suspicion. I think Texans would be our best choice for hired guns."

"Yes, I agree," Sturgis said. "But how will we convince them to come?"

"Money," Wolcott said with a knowing smile. "We'll pay them five dollars a day and fifty dollars a head for every dead man."

"Won't that get expensive?" Frewen objected.

"Not compared to the losses we've suffered so far," Wolcott replied. "Or considering the possibility of being forced out of business if this unlawfulness continues."

The men nodded in approval.

"Do you think any of the hired guns will object to the quasi-legal character of this expedition?" Adrian asked.

"No, I can't imagine that would be a problem," Wolcott said. "We all know, too well, that Texans are the most independent and irreverent group of men on earth. And they will sympathize with our difficulties with rustling, seeing they are in the same business we are."

"If they do raise the question of legality," Frewen said, "we can just tell them we have warrants and that it's their duty to serve them. They'll be deputized of course."

"Yes," Adrian agreed. "The idea of warrants is a good one. Makes it all nice and legal-looking."

"We can go to Colorado for horses and supplies," Sturgis said. "I've numerous business connections there. I'll also see to it that the Governor knows of our intentions, and get his blessing. It will be good for the State to be finished with this problem once and for all. That will be his view, the same as it's ours."

"We'll have to draw up a wanted list, in order of priority," Wolcott said.

"I think we should start with the most notorious of the rustlers," Frewen suggested. "The Hat Brand—Nate Champion, Nick Ray and Jack Flagg—and then work north."

"Moreton," Adrian said, turning to Frewen. "Have you forgotten who's responsible for turning this situation into war, and who's the cause of our being together this evening? I propose that we give top priority to the death of Elinore Pruitt Stewart and her loving husband, Clyde Stewart!"

The men raised their glasses in agreement. Adrian drank long and deeply, with great satisfaction.

He would have his revenge yet!

31

ELINORE slept all day. It was late in the afternoon when she rolled over, still half asleep. An acute pain shot up her arm. She sat up in bed, at first unaware of the events of the night before, but in a moment it all came back to her—the argument with Stewart, the kidnapping, the attempted rape and, thankfully, Stewart's rescue. She slipped down under the covers again, wanting to hide herself. She was glad to be alive, but so humiliated!

She felt a soreness in the left side of her face, which was resting against the pillow. She got up from the bed to go to the free-standing mirror. Every muscle ached when she stood up. When she saw herself in the mirror she gasped.

"My God," she said aloud.

The left side of her face was swollen and bruised. She now remembered Quick Shot hitting her before he kidnapped her.

Her red hair was a mass of tangles. She reached for the brush on the dresser and began brushing. It was an effort even to lift her arm. And she was too weak to stand any longer. She returned to the bed.

She sat up in the bed, adjusting the pillows and trying to make herself comfortable. It was impossible. She looked at the sun slanting in through the windows, and realized it was late in the afternoon. She had slept all day. She looked around the room and tried to recall her first impressions of this room the day she arrived. If she had known then all that was going to happen to her she probably would have turned right around and gone back to Denver.

She remembered her first impression of Stewart, how quiet and forbidding he had been. And how frightened she had been. She smiled when she remembered him approaching her at the stage stop at Buffalo. She had thought he was one of her new employer's hands, never dreaming that he was Mr. Stewart himself. And now she was married to him!

A wistful hope filled her. I wonder, she thought, if it's too late to have a real. . . .

Her thought was interrupted by a knock on the door.

"Miss Pruitt, may I come in?"

It was Stewart. She longed to see him, to have him hold her as he had the night before, but she was embarrassed now, and anxious. What must he think of her after last night? Could he ever forgive her?

"Yes, Mr. Stewart, come in," she said hesitantly.

He pushed open the door with his foot and appeared, carrying a tray.

"I was waiting to hear you moving around," he said, "I thought you might like some tea and biscuits. You must be hungry by now."

His kindness to her made her want to cry. She had to blink back tears, looking up at his concerned face. His deep blue eyes were grave now.

He set the tray down on the table next to the bed and sat down on the edge of the bed and poured tea for her. He added sugar and cream, then handed the cup and saucer to her. He had even brought her favorite cup, Elinore noticed.

She could feel him watching her intently as she sipped her tea. She was embarrassed by the bruise on her cheek.

"I've sent for a doctor," Stewart said. "He should be here shortly."

"I don't want to see a doctor," Elinore protested, blushing with embarrassment.

"Elinore . . . I mean, Miss Pruitt, someone must look at you. You've been through a bad ordeal and you really should let the doctor examine you."

"You don't understand. I—"

"I understand perfectly. You don't want what happened last night known. It won't be. I've told my men they're not to talk about it, not even among themselves. The doctor is an old friend of mine, and a man I trust. He won't talk. It's best for everyone concerned that this thing be kept secret. Have you forgotten that there were six men killed last night? You and I, and my men, are the only witnesses."

"Mr. Stewart, there may be another witness. I saw a man watching from the top of the ridge. I think it was James Adrian."

"That won't be a problem. Adrian would never speak up. He has far more to lose than you or I if this thing gets out. Quick Shot was his foreman. He'd be implicated."

"Stewart, the doctor is headed toward the ranch," someone called from the base of the stairs. Elinore recognized McPherren's voice.

Stewart touched Elinore's arm gently. "It'll be all right," he said. He called down to McPherren, "Tell him to come on up when he gets here."

Elinore was thankful to Stewart for taking care of everything, especially for making sure that what happened to her would be kept secret. She couldn't bear to have everyone in Powder River know of her humiliation.

She heard McPherren speak to the doctor on the porch, and then heard the doctor climbing the stairs to her room. His steps were slow and heavy. When he walked through the door Stewart stood up.

"Hello, Doc," he said. "Thanks for coming out right away. I'm a bit worried about Mrs. Stewart."

Elinore thought how strange it was that when they were alone Stewart called her Miss Pruitt, but in the company of others referred to her as Mrs. Stewart. At first she had minded, but now she found she liked being regarded as Mrs. Stewart.

"Had a rough night last night, did you, Mrs. Stewart?" the doctor said, turning to Elinore in the bed.

Elinore nodded without speaking.

"Stewart," the doctor said. "Why don't you go fix me a tea and whiskey. I'll call you when we're through here."

Stewart hesitated a moment and then said, "Fine, just call me if you need me."

He turned and left the room.

Elinore was left alone with the doctor. He was an elderly, gray-haired man. His manner was paternal, and she felt confident in his care.

He looked at her face and examined her arm and shoulder.

"No bones are broken," he said, "but I think you tore up that shoulder pretty bad. You'll have to take it easy for a few weeks.

"I can't," Elinore said. "How am I supposed to do my chores?"

"Never mind about those chores. Just be thankful you're still alive."

He replaced his instruments and closed the black bag he had brought with him, then turned his attention back to Elinore.

"I'm sorry we had to meet under these circum-

stances," he said, "especially since I suppose I would
have seen you soon enough anyway."

Elinore was puzzled.

The doctor, seeing her expression, explained. "What
I mean is, you being a newlywed and all, there'll be
children coming. You don't suspect that you're pregnant now, do you? All that bouncing around you had
yesterday wouldn't be any good for you or the baby."

Elinore shook her head. How could she tell this kindly old man that she was certain she was not pregnant
because she had never made love to her husband?

"You know, young lady, I consider you a mighty
lucky woman, and I don't mean about just last night
either. I mean marrying a man like Stewart. He's as
fine a man as you'll find. If I had a daughter I'd like
her to marry a man like him." He chuckled. "Unfortunately, I never married myself, so I have no
daughters to marry off."

Elinore wondered if her marriage to Stewart could
ever be a real marriage. Oh how she wanted it to be!
She had been so blind and so stubborn. And now it
might be too late.

The doctor called down to Stewart and in seconds
Stewart was bounding up the stairs and into the
room, asking as he came through the door, "Is everything all right, doctor?"

"Well, those bruises on her face will take a while
to clear, and her left arm and shoulder are in bad
shape. She'll have to take it easy till they heal," the
doctor said, smiling at Stewart's anxiety. "But other
than that, I think you can rest easy about her."

Stewart looked uncomfortable under the doctor's
knowing smile.

"Your drink is ready, Doc," he said.

"Thanks, Stewart. Now, young lady, remember not
to overwork yourself—and be a good wife to this
man," the doctor said, and winked at Stewart.

Elinore was silent. She would follow the doctor's

advice, all of it, if Stewart would let her. She would make everything up to him if he would give her the chance. She looked up at him, so strong and so good, and wished she could tell him her thoughts.

"I'll be back after the doctor leaves," Stewart said.

"Thank you, doctor," Elinore called as the two men headed down the stairs.

Elinore relaxed now that the ordeal of the doctor's visit was over, and was asleep in no time. When she awoke it was nearly dark and Stewart sat at her bedside. He had brought back the tray, only this time it held a lovely decanter and two crystal glasses.

"How long have you been there?" Elinore asked.

"About fifteen minutes. I was enjoying watching you sleep. You look so beautiful."

Elinore smiled, thinking that impossible with her bruised face and her aching arm held stiffly across her chest.

"I thought perhaps you'd like a glass of port," Stewart said. "I brought this bottle with me when I came from Scotland. I've been saving it for a special occasion." He smiled at her. "I've waited a long time for that special occasion."

"In that case, how could I refuse? I would love to have some port."

"I also had this decanter and these glasses hidden away," he said, pouring their drinks.

"I would like to propose a toast,' he said, as he handed Elinore a glass. "I would like to drink to never losing you, Elinore. I didn't know how much I loved you until last night."

Elinore couldn't believe what she was hearing. She sat up and lifted her face to look at him. He leaned down and ever so gently kissed her lips.

"Can you ever forgive me for all I've done?" Elinore whispered.

"Sh-h-h."

"But I've been so stupid, so stubborn, and even mistrustful of you. And all the while you were so good, and only concerned for me. And James Adrian. . . . Can you ever forgive me?"

"Elinore, I want you to forget all that. I feel as responsible as you do for all the terrible things that have happened. Can you forgive me, and be my wife, really my wife?"

"Clyde, how can you even ask? I love you. And I want nothing more than to be your wife."

Stewart moved to sit on the bed beside her. He took her glass and put it with his on the tray, then put his arm softly around her.

"I'll make a good life for you," he promised. "We'll fix up your house and send for Jerrine as soon as the trouble dies down. I'll love her like my own, and if we're fortunate we'll have others to keep her company. You'll never want for anything. Oh Elinore, how I've longed to tell you I love you!"

He pressed his lips to hers. A warm, wonderful sensation ran through her. She pressed herself to him urgently, wanting desperately to feel him respond to the love they shared.

"When I thought yesterday that I might lose you I felt I might have lost my last chance to tell you I loved you. I was waiting for the right moment, which never seemed to come. I love you, Elinore," he whispered, "I love you."

Elinore's lips trembled beneath his. Stewart kissed her harder now, one hand firm around her waist, the other drawn to her exposed breasts that had slipped from her dressing gown. Elinore shivered when his strong fingers found her nipples. His touch thrilled her. She breathed in deeply and let out a sigh. Something was coming alive within her.

"My lovely, my wife," Stewart whispered, lifting his mouth from hers.

Elinore opened her eyes to see him above her, so handsome, so strong. Oh, how she loved him! All her emotion and desire seemed to be welling up at once. She caressed his dark hair. How thick and shiny it was. Her fingers touched his ear, and slid along the hard cords of his neck onto his thick shoulders.

He stood and removed his shirt, then leaned over her body and kissed a path from her throat down to her breasts. Elinore lay back against the pillows, feeling a surge of heat in her loins.

Stewart stroked Elinore through the thin fabric of her gown, arousing her even more. Then he sat her up and gently began to remove her dressing gown.

"Don't be frightened. I'll be very gentle," he said and bent down to kiss her throat.

As he slid the gown over her arm he took care not to hurt her. He looked down at her and smiled. As his eyes followed the lines of her body, reveling in every contour, all Elinore's pain seemed to vanish.

Stewart caressed her bare breasts, then took one in his mouth and sucked tenderly. A tremor shot through Elinore.

He pressed himself to her and Elinore could feel his rigid penis pressing against his pants. His hands shook now as he stroked her, sensing her fright and desire. He rolled his tongue around each breast, then nibbled at them, taking up the skin in tiny bites.

Elinore whimpered, intensely aroused, her eyes on Stewart's naked body. It was brown and muscular, softened only by the dim light of dusk. Suddenly he looked strange to her. Strange and powerful.

Her attention, emboldened, fixed on his penis. It was thrust up at her, taut and stretched. She held it and felt its life. Stewart let out a loud, visceral groan. He knelt over her.

Gently, he slid between her thighs, stroking and petting them. Then, as though he had suddenly lost control, he gripped her buttocks and lifted her to his penis. Gently he began to probe, but soon forgot himself again and thrust himself inside her. Elinore writhed in ecstasy.

"I love you," she whispered. "I love you. I'll always . . ."

Just then Stewart thrust himself powerfully. Elinore arched up to squeeze his penis tighter and draw him deeper into her. He moved within her, pulsing and rocking. She felt his tension grow, felt the muscles of his long legs and his strong back. She felt helpless, but cared for, in his fierce grasp.

Then wondrously, in his passion, she found her own rhythm and rocked in perfect union with him. It was more amazing than she had ever dreamed possible. Then she cried out, taking her own pleasure as he took his.   ◄§

32

THE STAGECOACH jolted along at a snail's pace over the dusty, sagebrush-freckled miles from Buffalo. The passengers, Major Frank Wolcott among them, sat cramped hip-to-hip in the narrow seats. The midday sun beat the dreary landscape into flatness.

Why couldn't the Creator have thought of some other vegetation besides sagebrush when He made the West? Wolcott asked himself. What's so wonderful about the West that all these rustlers and homesteaders are clamoring to come out here? They should all have stayed wherever it is they came from.

The shadows of late day were deepening as the horses strained up the first rise out of Powder River. From the top, one could get a last view of the Big Horns before heading south.

The driver, something of a showman, paused to let the passengers have a look at Black Tooth and Cloud's Peak with the streaks of snow on their sides.

But Wolcott did not hear the stagedriver's speech about the view, for he was contemplating his first drink of the day. Stealthily, so as not to attract the attention of the ladies aboard, he pulled the silver flask from his pocket and took a long swallow, eyes closed to better appreciate it.

He opened his eyes to see a well-dressed woman staring at him disapprovingly. He smiled, and tipped his brown bowler. The lady, offended, tightened her mouth and held the book she was reading before her face.

Damnable stagecoach, Wolcott thought, it's the only means of transportation, and I have not only to put up with discomfort but also with that woman's self-righteousness. Well, at least it's for a good cause.

He comforted himself with the thought that Sturgis would have it worse. He would have to ride all the way to Colorado, across the Big Horns, to buy the necessary horses. At least he himself would change in Cheyenne to a train and enjoy gentlemanly comforts for the rest of the trip. Once in Texas he would make the necessary connections and hire the twenty-two gunfighters—the minimum number he and Adrian and Sturgis had decided they would need.

One week later, a lean, almost gaunt young Texan stood at his regular bar in Paris, Texas. He was in town like so many others, duded up in his finest regalia, spending his pay on women and whiskey. The dark-haired woman he was with was a favorite of his. They were having a drink and coming to terms on her charge for the night.

He barely noticed the well-dressed man enter the bar, although his brown bowler and tailored suit set him apart. This cowboy had other things on his mind.

The woman started ahead of him toward the rooms upstairs. He finished his drink and was trying to catch the bartender's attention to pay for his whiskey and the woman's "tea." He waved his right hand, conscious, as always, that the thumb was missing—it had been severed neatly at the palm line.

As the bartender headed his way, he overheard

something from one of the tables in back of him that caught his attention.

"Powder River County is where you'll be needed," a voice with a distinct British accent was saying. "I've been sent to hire twenty-odd men, the best guns in Texas, and someone told me to look you up. You see, we have a special problem with rustlers. We've got warrants for all of them. You'll be paid five dollars a day plus fifty dollars a head."

Tucker, the young Texan at the bar, turned slowly, trying to get a look at the man who was speaking without himself being noticed.

My God, he thought, it's Major Frank Wolcott, "the Dude." Sounds like the Association is going after a real killing!

"We've got warrants for seventy men," Wolcott was saying. "I'll be needing your answer right away as I'll be leaving first thing in the morning. You'll be back in Texas in two weeks with a year's pay in your pocket."

Tucker did not wait to hear the rest of the conversation. He dropped some coins on the bar and told the bartender to give one to the dark-haired woman who was waiting for him on the stairs. He raced from the saloon, not quite certain what to do first.

He had to get word to Clyde Stewart, for he would certainly be one of the seventy men in Powder River the warrants were out for. But he dared not attempt to send a telegram, for the telegrapher in Cheyenne who would receive it, like everyone else there with a good job, had the Association to thank for his job.

He would have to go to Powder River, Tucker decided, even though being seen near Cheyenne might cost him his life. It was a chance he would have to take. He had to give warning, especially to Stewart and Miss Pruitt. He owed his own life to Miss Pruitt. He'd be dead now if she hadn't cut off his gangrenous thumb. And it was Stewart who had given him a stake so he could leave Powder River and get away from James Adrian.

Early the next morning Major Frank Wolcott and his twenty-two hired guns boarded the train and headed for Cheyenne. D. E. Brooks, also known as the Texas Kid, a youthful sharpshooter, was among the gunhands, along with Jim Dudley, alias Gus Green.

Wolcott sat back in his seat, content with his accomplishment. He had had little trouble picking up the gunfighters. With the money he offered, he hadn't needed to use persuasion, especially after he mentioned the warrants. There were no warrants, but they would find that out later.

As Wolcott sat gloating over his success a gaunt young cowboy passed through his car. For a moment he thought he recognized him but he dismissed the idea as he had seen so many faces in his few days in Texas. He leaned back, removed his bowler, and closed his eyes for a brief nap.

Tucker looked out from under his broad-brimmed Stetson at the Red River that separated Texas from Oklahoma. Paris was just below the Texas border, and it would be days before they reached Wyoming. They would travel clear through Oklahoma and Colorado via Denver and then on to Cheyenne. Tucker would have to keep low and pray he wouldn't be discovered. He never could have gotten to Powder River ahead of Wolcott by stage or horse. The train was the only way. It was a great risk, but the only chance he had. It would have to work.

He slouched into his seat, covered his face with his hat, and feigned sleep.

For days the train rolled across the empty plains. Tucker felt that each added day lessened his chances of keeping out of Wolcott's sight.

* * *

"Denver, one hour," the conductor called, waking Tucker from a nap.

Tucker quickly shook off sleep and looked around the car. Many of the men in it had been hired by Wolcott. They didn't know Tucker, but he knew them. They were among the most notorious men in Texas.

He looked out the window. To the west he could see the Rocky Mountains jutting up from the flat landscape. In another day or two he would be in Cheyenne and from there he would get a horse while Wolcott and the others arranged for a special train to take them to Casper. He had overheard talk of their plan and hoped that while they made their arrangements he could get a head start and beat them to Casper. He knew people there he could trust, and from there the word could be spread. He sank back into his seat, praying he would not be discovered.

He thought about the guns. These twenty-odd men could wipe out the entire population of Powder River in a matter of days. They'd have little resistance among the settlers. Tucker knew his warning was their only hope.

Tucker was uncomfortable. He was going to have to make his once-a-day trip to the toilet. He had limited himself to one for he had to walk the length of his car, and the car behind it, to get to the toilet in the caboose. He had purposely taken a seat in the front of the first car so Wolcott and his hired gunfighters wouldn't be passing him in their constant meanderings. He stood up, pulling at the brim of his Stetson.

He walked back through the car, his hands in his pockets, avoiding the eyes of the other passengers. He opened the door to the next car.

In the middle of the car he could see Wolcott's brown bowler. He sat alone. Cautiously, Tucker proceeded.

Barely breathing, he stepped past Wolcott. Wolcott hadn't moved at all. Hopefully he was asleep. Tucker reached for the door at the end of the car. But as he stepped through he heard, "Tucker, is that you?"

Tucker froze and hesitated. He did not recognize the voice. Suddenly there was a handslap on his back.

"I thought that was you," the voice boomed. "How you been?"

Tucker turned his head slowly to see Buck Garrett standing in back of him. He and Buck had grown up together. Their families had neighboring ranches. He hadn't seen Buck since he had originally left Paris for Powder River.

"Fine, Buck," Tucker said quietly. "And you?"

"Just fine," Buck replied. "I'm on my way now out to Powder River on some official business. Last I heard, that was where you were headed."

"Yeah, Buck, that's right. Look, I'd like to talk, but . . . well. . . ."

Tucker's eyes were drawn past Buck. Wolcott was staring him in the face. Tucker tried to avoid his eyes, but it was too late.

"Garrett, grab hold of that man!" Wolcott hollered.

Garrett looked puzzled. Gus Green jumped from his seat and wedged himself between Tucker and Garrett. He had pinioned Tucker's arms behind him before Tucker knew what he was up to.

"I thought I recognized you the other day, Tucker," Wolcott said, getting up and coming toward him. "Seems like whenever there's trouble you find your way into the middle of it."

He turned and called to two other men in the car.

Tucker didn't know what to expect. If they planned on killing him once they got to Powder River, what was to stop them from starting right here? And what was Garrett's part? Was he one of the guns? Tucker couldn't believe he'd been on the train with him all this time and hadn't seen him before. But then he hadn't been looking, and also had been trying to hide himself.

"I don't know what your intentions are, boy," Wolcott was saying, "but I think, whatever they are, you'd better forget them and head back to Paris for good. If I see your face ever again I'm going to consider that reason enough to kill you. James Adrian would certainly be thankful to me."

Wolcott nodded to the other two men he had called. They pushed their way past Garrett to Green and Tucker in the door.

"Go ahead, men," Wolcott said.

Green and the two men hustled Tucker out onto the open platform and threw him from the moving train.

33

THE "SECRET special," carrying Wolcott and his twenty-two hired gunfighters, got under way from Cheyenne in the late afternoon of Tuesday, September 5, 1892. But they were no longer alone. After the fall stock meeting of the Association adjourned the other members of the expedition sauntered down by twos and threes to the railroad yard, where the special train was made up and waiting. There were fifty-two men in all.

Twenty-four of the men were cattle barons, including the owners and managers of the largest outfits in Powder River; five were stock detectives, Mike Shaunsey among them; and there was one non-combatant, Sam T. Clover, a newspaper correspondent from the Chicago Herald. Acting on a tip received in Chicago, Clover turned up in Cheyenne armed with a letter of introduction from Henry A. Blaire, the Chicago tycoon who owned the Hoe ranch in Powder River, and whose manager was a member of the expedition. Although suspected at first of being a spy, Clover was glib enough to wangle himself an invitation to join the party by using the time-honored newsman's pitch:

"I will see that your side of the story reaches the public."

The train left for Casper, one hundred and fifty miles northwest of Cheyenne, where the party would be supplied and would then proceed overland on horseback for Powder River.

The special Pullman arrived at the outskirts of Casper, with all the blinds down, in the dark of four A.M. on September 6. The cattle barons congratulated themselves that their arrival had gone unobserved.

Elinore left Buffalo the first day of September and headed for Casper. Stewart had insisted that McPherren accompany her.

Elinore felt terrible about leaving, as this was the busiest season with the approaching round-up, the harvesting of the hay, and the general readying for winter. But she had no choice. A few days ago she had received a letter stating that a gentleman by the name of James Adrian had put a claim in for the land she had filed on. In order to clear up the misunderstanding she would have to appear in person with the original documents proving ownership. It was dreadfully inconvenient but absolutely necessary, for if she let matters slide, who knew what schemes Adrian would come up with to take the land from her? His claim was spurious, but Elinore knew his influence and power were far-reaching. How she hated him!

Stewart had tried to comfort her by saying that if it had happened any later traveling would have been difficult, if not impossible, for there were only two seasons in Wyoming, July and winter. He also told her that as long as she was traveling all the way to Casper she could order furniture in anticipation of Jerrine's arrival. Hopefully, they would be sending for Jerrine soon. This elated Elinore and would certainly make the trip, at least in part, a happy one.

It took three full days for Elinore and McPherren

to reach Casper. And then it took another full day at the land office. But the matter was corrected. The government would be notifying James Adrian that he had been mistaken about his claim. Elinore was greatly satisfied. The trip was worth all the effort if it saved her land and thwarted Adrian.

Tuesday, September 5, with all the land business behind her, Elinore intended to spend the full day shopping and ordering furniture for Jerrine. After breakfast at the hotel she walked out onto the streets of Casper. The city was bustling. Elinore hadn't seen such commotion since leaving Denver, and she was amazed at how easily she had forgotten about urban living while staying out on Stewart's ranch.

The entire length of Main Street was strung with telegraph wires, there was a railroad yard at the far end, and well-stocked shops all along it. This was nothing like Buffalo, and Elinore was thrilled to have the day to indulge herself.

By noon she had been to all the smaller shops, avoiding the larger ones favored by the Association elite, but she had not found what she wanted. So, before having lunch, she hesitantly headed for the largest general store in Casper, Clay's.

Cautiously she crossed the avenue, skirting the horse-drawn carriages and the throngs of people. She stepped up from the street to the wood-slat sidewalk and stood at the door of Clay's. Although every store she'd visited that morning had been busy, this one outdid all the rest. There barely seemed room to enter.

She opened the heavy oak door and stepped in. She was the only woman in the shop. Clay's was enormous and all the shelves were filled. It seemed that the object of every cowboy or settler's deepest desire must be somewhere on the shelves or in one of the catalogues that covered an entire table. The din was deafening as the men customers piled their purchases upon the counter.

The way the men were acting, you'd think Clay's was giving their merchandise away, Elinore thought. They tore through the racks of pre-made suits and overcoats, and grabbed up boots and Stetsons from the shelves. It was clear from the way they spoke that they were from Texas. Atop each pile of clothing and supplies was a shiny new breechloading, repeating rifle. Elinore had heard that owning a Winchester was every Texan's dream.

Elinore pushed past the men to the table of catalogues and sat down. The table was directly in front of the cashier so, as she leafed through the illustrations of furniture and other goods, she watched as each man completed his purchase. To her surprise, she found she had little interest in the marble-topped dressers, the braided rugs, or even the bolts of calico with which she could make curtains and dresses for Jerrine. All her interest was taken up with what was going on between the men customers and the cashier.

She watched closely, intent upon the man now at the counter. The shopkeeper beamed with each additional article recorded. Then the Texan simply gave his name, the shopkeeper consulted a list, and the man left. No money was exchanged. The identical thing happened with each succeeding Texan. Elinore could not understand what was going on. But she was determined to find out.

As the last of the cowboys left the shop, Elinore walked over to the shopkeeper who was busy tallying his receipts for the morning. He was obviously pleased.

"Excuse me, sir," Elinore began.

"Yes, ma'am," he said, looking up from his receipts. "May I help you?"

"Yes," she replied. "I've come to order some furniture. I've been here quite a while, but was waiting until you had the time to speak with me. You seemed to be terribly busy when I arrived."

"Yes, ma'am," he said. "I apologize for not taking care of you earlier but I was requested by the Cattlemen's Association to give the gentlemen who just left top priority. Outfitting twenty-two men is a tall order. It's more business than I've ever done in one day."

Now it was clear to Elinore why there had been no exchange of money. These men were obviously in the employ of the Association, Elinore thought. But what had they been hired for? Whatever it was it couldn't be good for anyone who opposed the cattle barons.

Elinore turned and quickly left the shop. She had to find out what was going on.

"But, Madam, what about your furniture?" she heard the shopkeeper call after her.

She pushed through the crowds on Main Street, but then hesitated a moment. She didn't know where she was going, but she knew she didn't want to run into McPherren. He would try to stop her.

She began walking slowly down Main Street toward the railroad yard. Who could she possibly talk to who might be able to tell what the Association was up to now? She didn't know anyone in Casper. She kept walking.

The crowds thinned and she saw ahead of her some of the men who had been at Clay's. They were carrying their purchases and heading for the railroad yard. She followed them.

Once at the yard Elinore couldn't believe her eyes. There were scores of horses being unloaded from three stock cars, three brand-new Studebaker wagons were attached to a flatcar, baggage was being unloaded from a fifth car, and in the rear was a Pullman with the shades drawn. She hid herself behind a large tree and watched.

There was a bustle of preparation going on farther back in the yard. Horses were being branded, gear was being stowed, and wagons were being loaded up.

The branded horses were being led off; each man picking one and galloping away. A few men stayed behind, getting the wagons loaded and off.

The men on horseback rode directly north. The only things north were the plains, Powder River and Buffalo.

Elinore darted from the three to the side of the stationmaster's shack, hoping to be able to overhear what was being said. With her back to the building so she could look out over the yard she moved cautiously around to the rear of the station house.

As she slid around the corner, her shoulders rubbing against the wooden shingles, a hand covered her mouth and a strong hard arm held her immobilized. She tried to scream, but it was useless.

She struggled, but her struggles were futile. The arm holding her loosened; not enough to free her, but enough to let her turn around. The hand still covered her mouth.

Elinore saw the man's scuffed and dust-covered boots, then his torn and dirty dungarees. Her eyes stopped when they came up to his waist for she saw the hand that was holding her. The thumb was missing from it.

Her eyes flew up to the man's face. She couldn't believe what she saw. The familiar gaunt face was smiling down at her. It was Tucker!

Slowly he took his hand from her mouth.

"Sorry to scare you, Miss Pruitt," he said, with his thick Texas drawl. "I saw you coming, but I didn't want you to scream or anything."

Elinore had to get her breath back before she could speak.

"You did give me a scare," she said, "but it's all right. What are you doing here, Tucker?"

"There's big trouble brewin'," Tucker said. "Back in Paris I saw Wolcott hiring gunfighters, and I got on the train when they did to come warn you and Mr.

Stewart. But Wolcott recognized me and they threw me off the train outside of Denver. I got a horse, and I've been riding for a week, hardly stopped. Couldn't trust the telegraph operators to get a message up to Powder River, so I came myself. But I can't let Wolcott see me. He warned me he'd kill me if he did. I was hoping I could steal one of their horses. That's the reason I'm still here. Mine gave out and died."

"Tucker, you're doing a brave thing," Elinore said. "But we'd better hide you. Wolcott meant what he said."

"I ain't hiding nowhere. I started this and I mean to do all I can to stop Wolcott and the Association. I overheard them talking on the train. They plan to march into Buffalo and seize the courthouse and take the militia arms stored there and then carry out their plan."

"What plan?" Elinore asked.

"The Association's made a list of every man in Powder River they consider a rustler or a rustler-sympathizer. There's talk of at least seventy men on the list. Sheriff Angus is on it, and his deputies, and the Johnson County commissioners. I'm certain Mr. Stewart is on it, and Robert Foote, Nate Champion, and you too, probably. They think that if they get rid of the leaders the other people will give up. The hired guns think there are warrants for all these people, and that they're serving the law. They're getting five dollars a day and fifty dollars a head. They've loaded enough ammunition in those wagons to kill all the people in the state of Wyoming."

"We've got to find McPherren and try to get word to Stewart," Elinore said. "The Association's really gone crazy this time. Pull your hat down low over your face, and stay on that side of me so they can't see who I am when we walk off. They'll kill us if they recognize us."

* * *

Back at the hotel Elinore got a room for Tucker so he could get cleaned up and then went looking for McPherren. She found him in the saloon next door.

As she walked into the saloon every head turned. A woman of her kind was never seen in such a place. When McPherren saw her he headed her way.

"Mrs. Stewart," he said. "What are you doing here? It isn't respectable."

"McPherren," she said, "we've got bigger problems. Come outside where we can talk."

He followed her outside, looking anxious.

"I saw some pretty strange things going on in Clay's when I was shopping," Elinore said. "I couldn't figure it out, so I went exploring."

"Mrs. Stewart, your husband will kill me. What are you up to now?"

"It's serious, and a good thing I was curious. Anyway, I followed some men to the railroad yard. There were at least fifty men there, and horses, arms and supplies for all of them."

"So, what are you saying?"

"The men were all members of the Association, or men hired by them. I ran into Tucker."

"Tucker? What's he doing here?"

"He saw Wolcott in his home town of Paris, Texas, hiring guns. Wolcott told them he had warrants for rustlers up in Powder River. Tucker came to warn us. They're planning a big killing. Seventy men at least."

McPherren looked stunned. "Are you sure about all this?"

"I'm sure of it, and Tucker will back me up."

"Well, then we know what we're up against. Now I want you to promise me one thing, Mrs. Stewart. You're not to leave my side from here on out. I promised Stewart I would take care of you. We'll get a wire off to Sheriff Angus right away, and then head back to Powder River."

"Tucker said you couldn't trust anyone to send a message."

"I've got a friend at the telegraph office. We go back a long time. I know I can trust him. I'll ask him to send the telegram on the sly. They've got to be warned."

McPherren took Elinore by the arm and led her down the street to the telegraph office.

"Chuck," he called to the man behind the counter. "I need to talk to you. Got a favor to ask."

Chuck rose and bent over the counter. The office was empty except for the three of them.

"I need you to send a message to Sheriff Angus in Buffalo," McPherren said. "It's urgent and has got to be kept a secret. Will you help me out?"

"Sure thing," Chuck said. "What's the message?"

Elinore spoke up. "The message is 'Cattlemen's Association hired guns headed for Powder River. Planning secret raid to exterminate all opposition. Seventy men on deathlist'."

Chuck looked at Elinore in disbelief. He hesitated.

"Send it," McPherren said, "just the way she said it."

Elinore repeated the message and Chuck wrote it down. He went over to the transmitter and began to tap out the message. Elinore was relieved. At least Stewart and the others would have some warning. Chuck continued to tap. McPherren looked on.

Finally, after tapping out the message several times Chuck looked up at them. "The message isn't getting through. The wires must be down."

"Keep trying," Elinore said.

"I can keep trying, ma'am, but it's no use. Nothing's getting through. I hate to say it, but it seems to me the only wires cut are those to Buffalo. I've been getting through everywhere else."

Elinore looked up at McPherren.

"What are we going to do?" she asked, then answered herself. "We're just going to have to get on horses and beat them to Powder River."

"I agree with you, Mrs. Stewart," McPherren said. "There's nothing else to do. But, Chuck, if you'd keep trying I'd be grateful. And please, not a word of this."

"Thank you ever so much, Chuck," Elinore said as she and McPherren turned to leave.

They went directly to the hotel to pick up Tucker. In less than half an hour the three had horses and supplies and were on their way.

34

On Thursday, September 7, the column of wealthy men and their mercenaries breakfasted out of sight of Casper behind some hills north of the Platte River. During breakfast a number of saddled horses which had been loosely picketed to sagebrush broke loose and stampeded. It was several hours before they were rounded up by the Texans.

Meanwhile, the cattle barons sat back and enjoyed their gentlemanly comforts, which included the services of the Cheyenne Club's manservant, Stephan. The gentlemen of the expedition without exception belonged to the little coterie of early comers who had been running the affairs of Wyoming since the beginning and who dominated the Wyoming Stock Growers' Association, the cattle business, and, for the most part, the politics and government of the state.

"You've done a fine job with the horses, Sturgis," Wolcott said, sipping his coffee. "They're so spirited we're hard put to keep them in hand."

"We're going to need them that way," Sturgis replied. "It's bound to be a rugged week. These were the best horses available in Colorado."

"Everything is the best for this expedition," Adrian said. "And it should be. It will cost one hundred thousand dollars before we're finished. But I'd pay the entire sum out of my own pocket to rid Wyoming of those thieves."

"I've contacted my friends Senators Carey and Warren," Sturgis said. "They've assured me that the state authorities are fully behind us. Governor Barber has instructed the Wyoming National Guard that they're not to assemble their commands except on orders from his headquarters to assist the civil authorities in the enforcement of the laws of the state."

"That's brilliant," Frewen said. "This way, in the unlikely event the thieves are forewarned, they won't be able to call for help."

"I've been assured by those in a position to know that the Republicans in the highest offices know of our plans and condone them fully," Sturgis said.

"Do you mean President Harrison knows of our scheme?" Wolcott asked.

"Everyone knows of our hardships out here, trying to tame this wilderness," Sturgis answered. "It's in their interest to have business be as profitable as possible, and it it means eliminating a little agitation, well. . . ."

"We won't let them down," Wolcott said. "I've seen to it that the telegraph lines to Buffalo have been cut. Buffalo might as well be an island now. In fact, it's Senator Carey's manager Ed David who's been put in charge. He was instructed to cut the wire between two poles and hitch one to a saddle horn and drag it two or three miles into the hills. That's certain to do it. He'll keep the lines cut until we notify him."

"Good," Adrian said, signaling Stephan for more coffee. "Now, Wolcott, lets go over the plan."

"We're going to march into Buffalo," Wolcott said, "and seize the courthouse and the arms of the militia stored there. Reinforcements of sympathizers from in and around Buffalo have been promised to help us take the town. Afterward, we'll swing south. We're going to take Red Angus first, then his deputies and the county commissioners. . . ."

"What?" Adrian interrupted angrily. "We'd agreed that Stewart—"

"We have to get rid of Angus and the others so that a set of officials in sympathy with us can be installed," Wolcott said, interrupting him.

"Well, all right," Adrian conceded grudgingly, "I can see the sense in that."

Wolcott took up his outline of the plan. "None of the seventy on the deathlist are to be taken alive. They're to be hanged or shot. Don't worry, Adrian. This plan is foolproof. Stewart's not going to get away from us. Neither is that redhead he married."

"My only fear," Sturgis said, "is that some of the rustlers will get up into the mountains and escape us."

"Not one will escape," Wolcott said. "Their luck's run out. We've had some setbacks, but we're unstoppable now."

Sam Clover, the newspaper reporter, sat by taking notes. This scoop would make his career.

It was well past noon when a young Texan came up to the cattlemen.

"The horses have all been found and brought back," he said. "We're ready to get started."

The impertinence of that man, not even excusing himself, Adrian thought. He's just like all the rest of the cowpunchers.

The barons lethargically got up, mounted their horses, and the march got underway.

The going was bad. The wagons bogged down. The horses slipped and fell repeatedly in the greasy gumbo mud. They were white with lather under their collars. In the afternoon one of the wagons broke through a bridge.

But the bad going was due mostly to the cumbersome equipment. The Texans marveled at it in disbelief. The men fresh from the armchairs of the Cheyenne Club had provided for their every comfort. The wagons were loaded with tents, camp stools, stoves, china, crystal, silver, even linen, not to mention servants. Consequently, the column was not making good time.

The sun seemed to rise earlier than usual this morning as Elinore rolled herself out of her blankets. With Tucker and McPherren, she had ridden late into the night trying to beat the cattle barons and gunfighters to Buffalo. Along the way they had stopped at every friendly ranch and told their tale. A cyclone of rumors was sweeping the state. Casper, Douglas, Newcastle, and Gillette were spouting wild stories that reached the Denver, Omaha and Chicago papers before they reached Cheyenne. Only Buffalo, with its cut telegraph wires, was silent. It was Buffalo that Elinore and her companions had to reach.

After coffee and a cold roasted potato they were back on their horses. Elinore was so sore from the full day's ride the day before that she feared she couldn't beat the discomfort, but she knew she must. Powder River depended on her to.

"McPherren, do you think we've done the right thing telling people?" she asked. "Maybe we should have kept quiet, like we told Chuck to."

"Neither way is foolproof," McPherren said, "but I was thinking that if we get to Buffalo before the cattle barons we're going to need men, lots of men. The people we've told are undoubtedly on our side. They stand to lose if the barons get away with this. And everybody we've told has been sworn not to tell anybody he couldn't trust with his life. They're not going to give us away. They know what'll happen if the cattle barons win out. They'll see their lands and cattle go, maybe even their lives."

"With any luck we'll be in Buffalo tomorrow," Tucker said. "And the people we've told will be joining us. We wouldn't have had time to recruit help. I think we've done the only possible thing to do."

Elinore nodded and looked ahead of her. The plains seemed to stretch out into eternity. God help us, she thought as she saw rain clouds gathering to the south of them.

35

ON THE seventh of September the invaders were plodding along towards their first destination, Sturgis' ranch sixty-five miles north of Casper. The road was still clogged with gumbo and it was beginning to rain. A decision was handed down by Major Wolcott, the self-appointed commander, that the main body of men would push ahead and just a few men would stay behind with the floundering wagons. For perhaps the last time, everyone agreed.

Wolcott led the vanguard to Sturgis' ranch. It was long after dark when they arrived.

"Men," Adrian called as he dismounted. "You can retire to the bunkhouse and rest. We won't be leaving till the wagons arrive, some time tomorrow."

The Texans dismounted. They were wet and cold and not nearly as enthusiastic as they had been at the start of the march. But the idea of getting out of the rain and having a meal softened their discontent.

The cattle barons retired to the main house for a change of clothes and preprandial cocktails. Wolcott was obviously irritated that Adrian had overstepped him and issued the command to the Texans.

Within the comfort of Sturgis' living room the barons sat sipping port and discussing the next day's move. Soon exhaustion overcame them and they all retired.

The next evening most of the men were drinking heavily in the crowded, smoky room, still waiting for the wagons to arrive. Most were in an ugly mood because of the discomforts suffered during the past days. Dinner was announced and consumed. Soon they were back in the armchairs in Sturgis' living room and Stephan was distributing cognacs. By now everyone was drunk, and their nerves were raw. Wolcott and Adrian were arguing, not so quietly, in the corner.

"We have to have a leader," Wolcott said. "Otherwise there'll be mutiny. These cowpunchers are not that intelligent. They need to know who is in command."

"Fine, Wolcott," Adrian replied. "But who appointed you commander?"

Wolcott's face turned red. He was so angry he had trouble speaking.

"You shouldn't have given the command yesterday for them to go to the bunkhouse," he said at last, through clenched teeth. "I've been in charge, and I've heard no complaints. If the group wishes to replace me, I'll gladly resign."

Adrian smiled. He knew that was a meaningless gesture. Wolcott's pride would never allow him to step down.

Their argument was interrupted by the entrance of Mike Shaunsey. He was staying out in the bunkhouse with the Texans.

"Excuse me, gentlemen," he began. The barons put down their drinks and looked up at the huge Irishman. "The wagons have arrived, but there's trouble. The Texans are getting restless and are asking to see the warrants they're supposed to serve."

"That's impossible, Shaunsey," Adrian called out.

"You know as well as I do that there are no warrants. You'll have to stall them. Assure them they'll get paid. That'll make them forget about the warrants."

Wolcott shot Adrian a glance. Adrian was taking over again.

"Yes, Shaunsey," Wolcott said. "Tell them they have to trust us. After all, we're not the criminals. We're all leading citizens acting within the law."

Shaunsey nodded, and said, "Yes, but these men—"

"But *nothing!*" Wolcott shouted. "They'll have to do as they're told! I'll not tolerate insubordination."

"Yes sir," Shaunsey replied. "Oh, there's one other matter, if I might bring it up."

"Shaunsey, your own behavior is bordering on insubordination!" Wolcott growled.

"Let the man speak," Adrian said. "He's served us well in the past."

"Thank you, Mr. Adrian," Shaunsey said. "What I wanted to say is that I had some scouts out, men of mine, and had them meet me here. They've said, and they're reliable, that Nate Champion and Nick Ray are up at the KC ranch, along with fourteen or fifteen others. The KC's on the way to Buffalo, and these are the most notorious of the rustlers."

"Fine work, Shaunsey," Wolcott said, his temper radically changed. "Take three of the Texans and go scout out the KC. We can be there by early morning."

"Wait a moment, Wolcott," Adrian said. "The plan is to march on Buffalo. We can't change strategy now."

The other men were silent.

"Who's in command here?" Wolcott asked defiantly.

Adrian didn't answer for a moment. He regretted allowing Shaunsey to speak. He knew that Shaunsey had a personal vendetta against Champion. They had been avowed enemies for years. Shaunsey had obviously planned this, and Wolcott was falling into the trap.

"This tactic will set back the invasion by a day," Adrian said. "It's one more day the others will have in which to be warned. I think we should stick to our original plan."

The room was silent. Suddenly the idea of bloodshed—so close at hand now—seemed to sober everyone.

Sam Clover sat in the corner, pen in hand, waiting for the decision.

"Gentlemen, we did not spend one hundred thousand dollars between us to see to the killing of a handful of rustlers," Adrian said. "We must go on as planned and take Buffalo."

Shaunsey was quiet, knowing it was not his place to speak.

"Yes, but if we kill off Champion and his friends now, it will save us backtracking later," Sturgis said.

"Yes, it's less wasted effort and time," Wolcott added. "We'll be done with them at daybreak and be on to Buffalo."

"Wait one moment," Adrian said. "If your reasoning is to go to the KC ranch because it's on the way, then we should certainly hit Stewart's ranch too. It's also on the way to town. And besides, Stewart and his wife are high on the list."

The cattle barons sat quietly, thinking.

"I'll agree to go after Champion and Ray first under one condition," Adrian said. "That Clyde and Elinore Stewart are the next mark."

"All right, Adrian," Wolcott said. "If you insist. Shaunsey, get on out with your scouts. We'll meet you at Fowler's Gulch. Before you go, tell the gunmen to get their rest. We'll be leaving here before midnight."

36

Elinore, Tucker and McPherren were halfway up the last summit on the trail to Buffalo. They were exhausted, and soaked to the skin. The horses strained up the steep hill, weary from the night-long push in the rain.

McPherren pulled his Winchester from his saddle. Tucker and Elinore reached for their six-shooters. Each feared that the rain might have fatally delayed them. Who could know what state the barons' plans were in? Had they sent a special mercenary squad ahead to insure the element of surprise in the invasion?

They spurred their horses one last time, fingering their guns, hoping they had made it in time. No one dared speak. Elinore held her breath as her horse approached the top of the hill.

Once atop the ridge, sheltered by sagebrush, they looked down on Buffalo.

"Can't see anything unusual," McPherren said.

"It could be over by now," Elinore said, fear making her voice a whisper.

Tucker was silent.

"Well, seems like there's only one thing to do," McPherren said. "We'll go in on the far side of this hill so we can't be seen until we reach town. Have your guns ready. Their scouts could be anywhere."

Slowly, they descended the hill, their eyes darting in every direction.

Finally they were on the outskirts of town, their guns drawn. But everything seemed normal. Elinore saw the dark-haired woman Stewart had tipped his hat to on the Fourth of July sitting leisurely on her front porch. There were women shopping, and children playing on the street. Robert Foote stood outside his store.

McPherren turned to the others and nodded. Simultaneously they spurred their horses and headed for the courthouse. They dismounted quickly.

McPherren cautiously pushed the door open and entered. Elinore and Tucker followed. But the courthouse was empty.

"What's going on?" a voice called from behind them.

McPherren spun around, leveling his Winchester at the voice.

But Elinore had recognized it. She whirled about with a glad cry. Stewart rushed toward her.

Suddenly her exhaustion overcame her. Her legs would no longer hold her up. She crumbled to the floor. Stewart knelt and picked her up in his arms.

"Elinore, what's the matter?" he asked anxiously. "What happened, McPherren? What are you doing here, Tucker?"

"Stewart, there's big trouble heading for Buffalo," McPherren said. "We know at least fifty armed men are headed here from Casper. We tried to wire you but the lines have been cut."

"We knew the lines were down," Stewart said. "But we thought they had just blown over again."

"The Association's hired gunfighters to kill seventy

men from around Powder River," Tucker said. "Wolcott and some others from the Association are riding with them."

Stewart put aside his surprise at seeing Tucker. "My God! We'd better get to the sheriff!"

"Clyde, they could be here any minute," Elinore said. "The others have got to be warned. They—"

"I'm taking you to the hotel before I do anything else," Stewart interrupted. "You're wet through, and obviously worn out. You've got to get dry and get some rest or you'll take a fever."

"I'll meet you at the sheriff's, Stewart," McPherren said. "But then I've got to go out and see that my family's safe." He paused and turned to Tucker. "You come with me."

The two men left.

"Clyde, what are you doing in town?" Elinore asked.

"I came in to meet you," he said. "I thought I'd take care of a few errands today and see you some time tomorrow."

Elinore slid her arms around his neck and laid her head on his shoulder, thankful for the safety of his arms. "It looks really bad," she whispered.

"We'll send for the militia," Stewart said. "Everything will be fine." But his eyes betrayed his concern.

Stewart entered the hotel with Elinore in his arms. He nodded to the desk clerk and headed up the stairs. The clerk hurried ahead of him with the key and unlocked a door at the end of the hallway, then went discreetly back downstairs.

When they were in the room Stewart put Elinore on her feet. "Get yourself dry, and then get some rest," he said. He took her face in his hands and looked deeply into her eyes. "Take care of yourself. For me. I've learned how much I can miss you." He kissed her, then let her go. "I'll be back as soon as I can."

"Be careful!" Elinore called after him as he left, "Oh Clyde, be careful!"

Elinore awoke with a start. There was a commotion in the streets. She ran to the window. She looked out to see Robert Foote, his long blond beard flying, dashing up and down the street calling the citizens to arms.

"Come out and take sides," he shouted. "Citizens come out and protect all that is yours and that you hold dear. The foe is approaching! Come and protect your common manhood, your land, your women, your children!"

From the window Elinore could see armed men around the perimeter of Buffalo. There was a lookout, Winchester in hand, atop the steeple of the Episcopal church.

She hurriedly pulled on her still-soggy dress and rushed down the stairs of the hotel, past the desk clerk, and out onto the street. Buffalo was going mad! The streets were filling with incoming armed men from the nearer ranches, while other armed men were riding out, galloping to the distant parts of the county to summon help.

Elinore pushed through the crowds, heading for the courthouse. Finally, she reached the front door and looked inside. Stewart stood surrounded by a group of men, each clutching a rifle.

"We've stationed men all around Buffalo and sent out scouts," Stewart was saying. "The man on the church steeple will signal with a red neckerchief if the cattlemen are spotted."

"We know they left Casper with fifty men," Angus said. "But they could have five hundred by now."

"Can't we set up an ambush?" someone asked.

"We've considered it, but it's out of the question," Stewart replied. "We're untrained, and there are too many unknowns. At least, in Buffalo we have a make-shift fortress."

"Have you sent word to Fort McKinney?" Elinore asked, coming into the room.

Stewart looked surprised to see her. "Yes," he said in answer to her question. "One of our fastest riders has been sent to the Fort." He came up to her. "Eli," he said in a low voice, "I think you ought to have gotten a little more rest before—"

"Clyde, those men may be over the next hill," Elinore said. "There's everything to do yet. Have you given any thought to how you're all going to be fed? I'll go over to the church and get the women organized."

"All right," Stewart said. "I think you'll be safe here in Buffalo. All the Association members who were here have left, getting out before the trouble starts. You women get whatever you need at Robert Foote's. He's thrown open his store to all Johnson County defenders. Help yourselves to bacon, flour, any other food supplies. And tell any men who come there that he's offering guns, ammunition, blankets and warm clothing to all who need them."

"You Scotsmen are incredible," Elinore said.

"Do you have a gun?" Stewart asked.

Elinore twisted her hip around to show him the six-shooter hanging there. It was the gun James Adrian had given her.

Stewart recognized it, but he only nodded. "Remember, I love you," he said.

Elinore smiled. She gave him a hug and ran out.

She headed up past the brothels of Laurel Avenue to the Episcopal church. She entered to find the church already half-filled with women, most of whom were hysterical. Others sat murmuring prayers.

"You women are going to have to pull yourselves together," Elinore called from the back of the church. "I know you're scared. I am too. But it's our homes, our land, and our families too. We've got to help our men."

The women all looked back at Elinore. Slowly, one by one they unfolded their hands or put away their handkerchiefs, and stood up.

"Your men will be proud of you," Elinore said. "Any of you who have a gun keep it handy. Let's get to work now. Some of you go over and bring supplies from Foote's. The rest come with me and we'll get started in the kitchen."

Once inside the kitchen, Elinore no longer had to give orders. The small children were put in a corner and given spoons to play with while the older children were given simple chores. In a matter of minutes pots were being scrubbed, vegetables were being pulled from bins, scraped and peeled. The women's fears seemed to subside as their work absorbed them. Each woman was familiar with the church's kitchen from the multitude of bazaars and church dinners they had prepared there.

Elinore sat down discontentedly to the women's work of peeling potatoes. In a moment she looked up to see a bunch of new recruits, dressed in silks and finery. They were the women of Laurel Avenue. The dark-haired woman Elinore remembered from the Fourth of July led them.

"We've come to help," the woman said.

"Thank you for coming," Elinore said, ignoring the disapproval on the faces of some of the other women.

"Our houseboy is bringing things from our supply-house," the dark-haired woman said. "We've plenty of coffee and whiskey."

She sat down next to Elinore and began peeling potatoes.

"It's very kind of you to come, and generous to offer your supplies," Elinore said after a silence. She couldn't forget Stewart tipping his hat to the woman. A wave of nausea ran through her.

"Powder River is our home too," the woman replied, "though there are some that wouldn't think so."

Elinore nodded.

"Mrs. Stewart," the woman began, "I saw you on the Fourth. I know you were upset by Mr. Stewart's gesture and I would like to—"

"It's not necessary to explain," Elinore began, I—"

"Please, Mrs. Stewart. Let me finish. Your husband is a gentleman and would never snub me like the others. You see, my husband worked for Mr. Stewart, but he died two winters ago. Your husband tried to help me get along, but eventually I had to stand on my own feet. I had no home to go back to, so I took up business here." The woman paused. "So you see, it's nothing like you thought."

Elinore looked at the woman. She was so ashamed of her jealousy.

"I'm sorry about your husband," she said, "and about my misunderstanding. You see, Clyde never spoke of you."

"He's not the type of man who talks about the good he's done. By the way, my name is Mary Elizabeth."

The women shook hands warmly.

"Call me Elinore," Elinore said.

A commotion at the kitchen door disrupted their conversation. When Elinore looked up she told herself she should have known. It was Mrs. O'Shaughnessy, her merry blue eyes darting about the room till she spotted Elinore.

"Elinore!" she said, running over and wrapping her arms around her. "How are you, my little cub? Heard you've been snooping around those barons again. Still aiming to get yourself killed?"

Before Elinore could answer Mrs. O'Shaughnessy went on. "Well, as usual, you did good."

Elinore introduced Mrs. O'Shaughnessy and Mary Elizabeth.

"Would you mind if I went over to the courthouse to see what the men are up to?" Elinore asked.

"I knew you'd be bored with this women's work soon enough," Mrs. O'Shaughnessy said. "Do as you like. Mary Elizabeth and I can handle this. But be careful. If I know that scoundrel Adrian, he wants you dead over any rustler in Powder River."

Elinore nodded, ignoring Mrs. O'Shaughnessy's warning. She wiped her hands on her skirt, looked around the bustling church kitchen, and in a moment was off to the courthouse.

She found Clyde right away and ran over and hugged him.

"How's everything going?" she asked.

"Not so good," Stewart replied. "I'm worried about Nate Champion. He's certainly on the deathlist, and we haven't heard from him. And still no word from Fort McKinney. We'll only be able to hold out for a short while if we don't get help from the Fort. And once they get us surrounded we'll be cut off from any new recruits and supplies."

They looked at each other, disheartened, knowing they could only ready themselves as best they could and wait.   ⮑

37

IT WAS just after midnight, the morning of the ninth,
in the teeth of frozen rain and wind, that Wolcott
and the others started again on their way. For three
hours horses and men breasted the storm with scarcely a word exchanged between the riders. The frozen
rain beat with savage violence against the exposed
faces of the men, blinding them so that it was impossible to see a foot beyond their horses' heads, while
beards and mustaches became masses of ice. Chilled
to the marrow and stiff in every joint, the determined
men pushed ahead and before daybreak were within
four miles of the KC ranch.

The invaders stopped in a deep ravine, Fowler's
Gulch, where they built sagebrush fires to thaw out.
Sam Clover was so stiff he had to be lifted from his
horse.

It was an hour's wait before Shaunsey and his scouts
appeared.

"Champion and three others are there," Shaunsey
said, not hiding his eagerness. "They're playing the
fiddle and having themselves a time."

"Good news, Shaunsey," Wolcott said. "There'll be no trouble surprising them."

At daylight the party was dismounting on the river bluff half a mile south of the still-sleeping KC. Below the bluff there was a cutbank stream with cottonwoods, box elders, and willows marking its course. In the foreground was a huddle of log buildings.

Major Wolcott took charge immediately.

"Men, surround the house," he ordered, strutting back and forth in his riding breeches, crop in hand. "No one must escape. I want some of you behind the stable, some of you in the brush down by the river, and who's left I want to take positions along the loop of the Middle Fork of Powder River."

The men began to scatter, leaving their horses tied behind.

"Wolcott," Adrian said, "may I ask something?"

"Of course, Adrian. What is it?"

"No one seems to have noticed that there are a freighter's wagon and a buckboard in front of the house. It can only mean one thing. Those rustlers have company, and we don't know who it is. We can't just riddle the house with bullets. We're going to have to wait and see who comes out."

Wolcott was obviously peeved by this reference to his oversight, but he quickly regained his aplomb.

"Yes, Adrian, you're right," he said, resuming his strutting. "We're executioners, not wanton murderers. We have vowed to kill only those on the list or those who foolishly come to their aid. There is nothing to do but wait and see."

Sturgis nodded his agreement. Adrian turned his back and walked away from the group.

These men are idiots, he thought, his teeth clenched. How did I ever get involved in this travesty? And what happened to Shaunsey's fifteen rustlers? There are only four we're sure of, and certain of the identity of only two of those—Nate Champion and Nick Ray. Shaunsey's using Wolcott to get his revenge on Champion and Wolcott's too dumb to know it. A hundred thousand dollar invasion jeopardized in order to help a commoner avenge himself!

Adrian positioned himself behind the stable next to the Texas sharpshooters. They shared one purpose— to shoot down any man who stepped outside the house, to finish the business here and push on to Buffalo.

For nearly two hours the invaders lay prone in the cold mud with their Winchesters ready, watching the cabin for signs of life.

Presently an old man appeared. The besiegers tensed themselves and took aim, awaiting the order to fire. The old man walked down toward the river, tin bucket in hand, to get water for breakfast. He continued past the stable unmolested, but the moment he was out of sight of the house he found himself staring at two Winchesters.

"Who are you?" Adrian asked.

"I don't want no trouble," the old man stammered. "My name is Ben Jones. I'm known in these parts as a peaceful man. Make my living trapping. Just stopped the night to get out of the rain, me and my partner Bill Walker."

Adrian stared at the man for a moment. The Texans looked to Adrian for an order. The old man was shaking by now, knowing that his life depended on the nod of this man's head.

"I think he's all right," Adrian said. "Besides, if we shoot him now it will warn the others. Later on we can decide whether or not to let him go. Old man, I want you to sit over there and not move a muscle or say a word."

Relieved, the old man did as he was told.

In about a half hour Bill Walker appeared, and after he passed the stable he too was taken prisoner.

Luckily for the two men their stories were the same.

"The men you're after are still asleep," Walker said. "My partner and me are trappers just stopped for the night."

Adrian ordered him to go sit with the old man.

The gunfighters and Adrian repositioned themselves, waiting for the next man to show himself. The muddy water was seeping through their clothes. The guns were uncomfortable and they were getting restless.

Adrian cursed the cold mud beneath him. This was not for gentlemen, he thought. The Association should have paid the gunfighters to do the job and waited in comfort to hear the results.

Suddenly Adrian looked up to see Nick Ray coming out of the house. Ray was looking around suspiciously. When he was ten steps from the door Adrian heard Wolcott's shout.

"Fire!"

The Texas Kid's Winchester cracked and the big body of Nick Ray doubled over, his hand gripping his gut. The Texas Kid had just earned his first fifty dollars.

A dozen Winchesters cracked simultaneously. Nick Ray staggered and fell. With a great effort he started crawling on his hands and knees toward the door of the cabin. As he reached the door another shot hit him in the back. He let out a loud groan and fell forward on the doorstep. Nate Champion, who had been appearing in the door at intervals to fire at the stable, opened the door and dragged the wounded man inside.

For an hour or two the besiegers poured lead into the open windows of the house. Sam Clover borrowed a gun from one of the Texans and banged away with the others. Round after round blasted the small cabin. The barons, finally, having decided that they were only wasting ammunition, withdrew to their camp for consultation.

Stephan served coffee.

Meanwhile, Nate Champion was writing laboriously in a pocket notebook.

"Me and Nick was getting breakfast when the attack took place. Two men was with us—Ben Jones and his partner. The old man went after water and didn't come back. His friend went to see what was the matter and he did not come back. Nick started out and I told him to look out that I thought there was somebody at the stable would not let them come back.

Nick is shot but not dead yet. He's hurt bad. I have to stop writing now and go wait on him.

It's been two hours since the first shot was fired. Nick is still alive.

They are still shooting and are all around the house. Boys, there is bullets coming like hail.

Them fellows is in such shape I can't get at them. They are shooting from the stable and the river and the back of the house.

Nick is dead. He died about nine o'clock. I see smoke down behind the stable.

It is about noon now. There is somebody at the stable yet. They are throwing a rope at the door and dragging it back. I guess it is to draw me out. I wish that duck would show himself so I could get a shot at him.

Boys, I don't know what they have done with them two fellows that stayed here last night.

Boys, I feel pretty lonesome right now. I wish there was somebody here with me so we could watch all sides at once. They ain't gonna let me go this time."

"Wolcott, let's get on with this," Adrian demanded, pacing the camp. "This strategy will ruin us if we don't push on quickly. Fire that house and get Champion out in the open! Use anything! That buckboard of the trappers will do."

"Fine with me," Wolcott said, though obviously not pleased with Adrian's arrogance. "Men, gather up any hay you can find in the barn, and chop up the pitch-pine posts around the corral. Load the buckboard high enough to protect the men who'll push it against the house." He looked around. "I need volunteers for that."

Six of the Texans immediately offered. They were anxious to get on to bigger game. Only one man in that house meant only fifty dollars to be had out of it.

In no time the buckboard was loaded high and ignited. The six volunteers backed it against one of the windows of the house, while the others poured a hail of bullets into the cabin to prevent Champion from firing at them.

Once the combustible load was lodged against the house the volunteers set fire to it and sprinted back to cover. The wind from the river drove the flames through the open window.

The roof of the house was the first to catch on fire. The fire spread rapidly downward until the north wall was a sheet of flames. Huge puffs of smoke poured out of the open windows and, in a short time, through the plastered cracks of the log house.

Still Nate Champion remained doggedly concealed. The cordon of sharpshooters stood ready to fire the instant he appeared. The flames grew fiercer and hotter until every part of the house was ablaze.

"I suppose the thief has shot himself," Wolcott shouted to his men. "No one could stay in that inferno and still be alive."

The men relaxed their aims. But in a moment came a shout.

"There he goes!"

Nate Champion ran through the volume of black smoke. He was carrying a Winchester, and a revolver was in his belt. He started off across the open space surrounding the cabin. He jumped into a ravine just south of the house thinking he would be safe. But he met with two of the best shots in the outfit who stood waiting with leveled Winchesters.

Champion saw them, but it was too late. A bullet struck his rifle arm. The rifle fell from his nerveless grasp. Before he could draw his revolver a second shot struck him in the chest, and a third and fourth ripped through his heart.

Nate Champion was dead. He lay prone on his back, a look of mingled defiance and determination on his face. He had met his fate without even a groan.

The entire band of regulators gathered round to see their victim. Nate Champion's red sash was tied around him. His half-closed, steely blue-gray eyes stared up at his avowed enemy, Mike Shaunsey. Shaunsey looked down and kicked the bullet-ridden body, grinning malevolently.

Sam Clover made a sign and pinned it to the blood-soaked vest: "Cattle thieves, beware." Pawing through Champion's pockets he discovered the diary and stuffed it in his own pocket.

The regulators rapidly withdrew from the scene of the double killing, leaving their prisoners behind. The trappers were warned to stay out of sight.

The cattle barons camped once again a half mile from the burning cabin where Nick Ray's body was being incinerated, confident in their overwhelming strength, feeling no sense of urgency.

The Texans were urged by the barons to push on to Buffalo. Adrian agreed, warning that their success depended on swift action. But Wolcott and the rest of the Cheyenne Club were unable to entertain the idea of failure.

So the barons sat on camp stools they'd had unpacked and set up, sipping brandy to warm themselves and waited for Stephan to serve the afternoon repast. Adrian seethed.

38

THE PEOPLE in Buffalo were tense and raw-nerved on Sunday, September 10, waiting for a sign of the cattle barons.

But it didn't come. Even the scouts they had sent out couldn't find a trace of them.

All that day recruits flocked into town, unshaven, on wiry horses, wearing six-shooters and carrying rifles.

Elinore, Stewart and Red Angus stood on the sidewalk in front of the courthouse, waiting like all the others. Suddenly from the west they saw an old man on a spent horse riding frantically up Main Street. He rode directly to them and threw himself off the horse.

"What's up, Ben?" Angus asked worriedly.

"I've just come from Champion's," the old man burst out, gasping and trying to get his breath. "They killed Nick Ray and Nate! They burned up the house! Burned Nick Ray up in it!"

"How do you know?" Stewart asked.

"Me and my partner spent the night there," Ben Hill said. "They had us prisoner, but they let us go. Told us to keep out of sight. But soon as they left I took one of Nate's horses and come riding to tell the sheriff."

Stewart turned to Angus. "Can this man be trusted?" he asked quietly.

"Sure can," Angus replied. "Ben's been out here forever. He's a cowpuncher. Just trapping to get through the winter. He's a good man."

"Do you know where they're headed?" Elinore asked Ben.

"I heard them sayin' something about Wolcott's TA ranch," Ben answered, "but there was a lot of arguing going on."

"My God, the TA is a fortress with a connecting barn," Elinore said.

"I'll send scouts out," Angus said, and turned toward the courthouse where a large crowd of men was gathered. Stewart followed him.

"We can't thank you enough for the risk you took," Elinore said to Ben.

"Took it on my own account as much as on anybody else's," the old man said. "I'm a cattleman myself. I'd take more risk than that to stop those bastards."

"Go on over to the church and get yourself some food," Elinore said.

"Thanks, I'm needing something to eat," he said, tipping his crumpled hat and leaving.

Elinore turned and ran into the courthouse. The people in the room were inflamed. *Murderers!* The term was on every tongue. There was no longer any doubt in these men's minds that the cattle barons intended to drive them from their homes, seize their cattle and kill all who opposed them.

"I want volunteers," Red Angus called out. "First, someone has to go out to the KC and verify that Nick and Nate are dead. Then I'll need a posse to go check the barons' location. The TA is out by Independence Rock. Looks like they've changed their plans, or they'd have been here by now. We've got to find out what they're up to."

The mention of Independence Rock sent the men further into murderous rage. That was where the barons' arrogance first spilled over into murder with the hanging of Cattle Kate. Every man present wanted to volunteer after a year of waiting for justice. The citizens and rustlers, as they were now being called, were united, ready to risk all.

Stewart was deputized and would lead the men to the TA. Sheriff Angus would stay behind in Buffalo organizing and directing recruits. If the barons were at the TA, Angus would join Stewart there at daybreak.

Stewart took fifty men and on Sunday evening, September 10, started for the TA ranch. He left only one order behind: Elinore was not to leave Buffalo. ❧

39

A CHILLY morning dawned on the TA ranch Monday the eleventh of September. Wolcott and the others began to rouse themselves. Stephan and Wolcott's cook prepared coffee and breakfast.

As the barons were about to sit down to their morning meal the Texas Kid burst into the room from the connecting barn.

"Have any of you gentlemen had a look outside?" he shouted.

"What is the meaning of this impertinence?" Wolcott demanded. "You had orders to stay in the barn."

"We're surrounded, you fool," the Texas Kid said. "Take a look."

Adrian jumped up and ran to the window. He couldn't believe his eyes. Everywhere he looked were knots of heavily armed men—there must be at least five hundred, and all their guns were trained on the ranch house.

"No need to push on, eh, Wolcott?" he shouted. "Come have a look at what your arrogance has brought. We're surrounded!"

All the men ran to the windows to see for themselves.

"What now, Major?" Adrian asked sarcastically.

Wolcott hesitated. Finally, he said, "We can send twenty of the Texans on foot to attack. I doubt that rabble would fight back."

Adrian sneered. "You're an ass, Wolcott," he said. "Those men out there might be common, but they're not stupid enough for your tactics. They'd pick off the Texans like so many crows."

The men were all stunned into silence. Stephan replenished their coffee cups and then set brandy and glasses on the table.

"Perhaps we could take twenty of our men and make a break for it," Wolcott suggested.

"Fool!" Adrian shouted, "don't you understand? We're surrounded! They're not going to let us just go riding off to the Cheyenne Club for cocktails and cigars!"

"Damned mutineer!" Wolcott snarled, turning on Adrian.

"And where are all the reinforcements we were promised we could count on?" Adrian jeered at Sturgis.

"All this arguing is just costing us time," the Texas Kid said.

Adrian and Wolcott scowled at him. But they knew he was right.

"I've just had a load of lumber delivered," Wolcott said, regaining his composure. "It's in the barn. We'll blast up all the doors and windows to a man's height. That'll protect us and give us barricades to shoot from. We'll do the same to the barn." He looked at the Texan. "Well, get going! Get your men started on it! Their necks are in this too!"

The Texas Kid turned to leave. "The house first!" Wolcott shouted after him. "Barricade the house first!"

When the Kid had left he turned to the barons. "Any other problems, gentlemen?" His eyes were fixed on Adrian.

Adrian was silent, for whatever Wolcott lacked as a leader he was making up for as an engineer. Fortification would be crucial.

How did I ever get involved with these fools? Adrian thought. They'll be the ruin of me.

The previous night, once Stewart had verified that the cattle barons were at the TA, he sent word to Red Angus in Buffalo. Then he put his men to work digging rifle pits and fortifying their position. Scouts were posted in every direction to insure they wouldn't be caught by a surprise attack.

Red Angus sent back word that instead of coming directly there he was going himself to Fort McKinney to find out what the delay was and to appeal to his old friend Colonel Van Horn to send militia with all speed.

Throughout the night reinforcements arrived, coming out of the sparsely populated region of rugged mountains and vast expanses of sagebrush. By morning there were upwards of three hundred men gathered for the attack on the TA ranch.

At daylight Stewart and Jack Flagg paced among the recruits waiting for the first rifle shots from the TA. The cattle barons had seen their outposts. They knew they were there.

But no shots came. The waiting was maddening.

"Why don't we storm them?" Flagg asked. "The scout you sent up there last night said there couldn't be much more than fifty men inside. The count of their horses backs him up. We outnumber them by far. And who knows but what they have reinforcements coming, and how many there'll be? This may be our only chance to take them."

"If help comes for them we'll have plenty of warn-

ing. I've got scouts posted in every direction," Stewart
said. "As for storming the house, it would have made
sense if we could have done it last night and taken
them by surprise. But we didn't have enough men
then. It would be suicide to do it now. They're warned
and ready for us. We can't see them, but we're staring
into the muzzles of at least twenty sharpshooters."

"Yeah, you're right," Flagg admitted, "and most of
the barons are good shots. But what are we supposed
to do?"

"I'm hoping that when Red Angus comes he'll be
coming with a company of militia. The barons aren't
going to take on the militia. They'll have to surrender."

"What if militia doesn't come? Seems to me if the
commander had been going to send it, it would have
been here by now. We need a contingency plan."

Stewart paced back and forth a few minutes. Then
he said, "All right, Flagg. I guess you're right. Have
some men unload a couple of wagons and lash them
together. Have them stack logs on them—two thick-
nesses—and wire them together. I want them up to a
height of six feet. If all else fails, we have a vehicle
we can roll close enough to the house to dynamite the
building. But only if all else fails."

Flagg nodded and left to get a work force and
supervise the construction of the movable fort.

Elinore sat in the kitchen of the church preparing
supplies to be sent out to the men at the TA ranch.
She was glad to be of help but she hated having to be
so far away from the action, doing women's work.

As she wrapped the roasted meats to be sent she
thought back to all of Adrian's heinous actions. He
had killed Cattle Kate and John Tisdale. He had
tried to kill her. She would be dead now if it hadn't
been for Stewart. And then his attempt to disgrace
her and Stewart by accusing them of unlawful co-

habitation. What a pleasure it had been to foil his scheme, and now, because of it, she had a real marriage to a wonderful man.

Her mind returned to the afternoon she and Adrian had spent at the TA. That was worse in some ways than the attempt on her life because she was to blame. How could she have been so stupid? How could she have believed his intentions were honorable? She went over every detail of that awful afternoon—the picnic, the rain, what had happened in Wolcott's cellar—hoping to purge herself of the self-hatred she lived with.

Suddenly she remembered something Adrian had said about the cellar. It was now used for wine, but it had originally been built to camouflage an escape route in case of Indian attack. There was a tunnel that led from the cellar to the far hill that looked over Independence Rock. Only Adrian and Wolcott knew of it.

I wonder if they might try to escape through it? Elinore thought. Wolcott wouldn't, she decided. Pompous and arrogant as he was, he wasn't a coward. He wouldn't desert the others. But Adrian was cowardly enough to attempt it!

She had to warn Stewart. Adrian could be escaping even now!

Elinore made an excuse and ran from the church kitchen. In minutes she was on her horse and headed for the TA ranch, determined to outrace anybody who tried to stop her. Adrian and the barons weren't going to get away this time!

The crack of rifle fire was incessant. The Texans inside the TA ranch house wouldn't be held down and had started sniping. Every shot they fired was returned tenfold. All were wasted shots on both sides.

"Wolcott, we're doomed if we don't get supplies and

reinforcements," Adrian said. "The food's not going to hold out, and neither is the ammunition at this rate. We've got to send someone for help."

"It would be suicide," Wolcott said. "None of the Texans will go. We'll have to wait it out."

Both men sat and thought.

A one hundred thousand dollar mission, with the backing of the most powerful men in the country, thwarted by homesteaders! The idea was too humiliating to even entertain. Something must be done.

"We can't just wait it out, Wolcott," Adrian said after a moment. "Have you forgotten how we got Champion out of his fortress with the flaming wagon? These men could easily do the same. We'll be picked off one by one."

"We've got to get a message to Governor Barber to send the cavalry," Wolcott said.

There was a pause.

"Wait," Wolcott said. "I've got it. We can send one of the Texans out through the secret tunnel after dark. It's beyond their fortifications. I had forgotten all about it."

"Great thinking, Wolcott," Adrian said. "I had forgotten about the tunnel, too. I hope it is still passable."

Wolcott went for a volunteer immediately. He returned to tell Adrian of his choice, but couldn't find him.

"Where's Adrian?" he asked the barons stationed in the front room. But no one could hear him over the din of rifle shots.

Elinore approached the ridge behind the TA with her gun drawn. She could hear the crack of rifle fire and see the muzzle flashes all about the perimeter of the buildings.

From what Adrian had said, she knew she was near the exit of the tunnel. By the time she found Stewart and brought him here, it might be too late.

She pulled her horse to a stop behind the crest of the hill and dismounted and tied her reins to a bush. Then she slowly walked in circles, looking for any indication of the exit. She found it suddenly and unexpectedly. Under the mass of brush beneath her feet she felt a hardness that wasn't earth—it was wood. She knelt down and scrabbled under the brush. This was it! A trap door!

Elinore moved back and sat on the little incline near the trap door, behind it, so that she wouldn't be seen until it was too late for whoever came out to duck back inside. She aimed her gun and waited.

Her back was aching from the strain of sitting so still, and the muscles in her forearms were trembling from the tension of holding her aim before she finally heard a rustling sound and saw the brush over the trap door move. She took a deep breath and extended her arms, gripping the six-shooter with both hands.

The door concealed under the brush was pushed up, hiding from Elinore whoever was coming out. Then she saw a black hat appear above it, and the shoulders of a man in a black suit. The muzzle end of a Winchester pointed upwards. Elinore was too tense and scared to breathe. Then the man was out of the tunnel and dropping the door closed.

It was Adrian.

With his foot, he pushed the brush back over the door. No one else would be coming out of the tunnel.

"Drop it, Adrian," Elinore said clearly. "Drop the Winchester."

Adrian's back jerked in surprise. He tossed the rifle to the ground in front of him and turned around. His eyes flared when he saw Elinore.

She got to her feet, gun still held at arm's length in both hands. She prayed her legs would hold her.

Adrian's eyes darted around.

"What are you looking for, Adrian? Help from the friends you've deserted?"

"Elinore, I—"

"Don't you dare call me Elinore!"

"Shall I call you the fool you are?" he sneered. "Put the gun down, Elinore. You know you're not going to use it."

"I'll use it if I have to, but I don't plan on murdering anyone. You'll hang for what you've done, you arrogant bastard!"

"You're a fool! President Harrison himself backed this mission! If you believe I'll hang you're as naive as you were the day I first had you."

At the outrage on Elinore's face he laughed aloud, pulling a pistol from under his jacket.

Before he could aim, Elinore leveled her six-shooter and fired. Adrian doubled over, gripping his gut, and fell to the ground.

Elinore stood over him and watched as blood oozed from between his fingers and colored the dirt.

She bent over and picked up his pistol and Winchester.

"A slow, agonizing death is too good for you, Adrian," Elinore said, "but it will have to do." She turned her back on him and coolly walked away. ◂§

Epilogue

Powder River, November 1892

STEWART AND Elinore sat in the buckboard bundled against the piercing wind and snow. Jerrine sat between them as they rode toward the Sioux settlement. Jerrine was adjusting wonderfully to her new home and was excited about seeing real Indians, particularly the children, and Stewart was taking to fatherhood very well. In fact, he paid Jerrine so much attention that Elinore had felt a tinge of jealousy from time to time. But deep down, she couldn't have been more contented.

As Elinore looked out over the bare plains to the snow-topped Big Horns her thoughts drifted back to the events of the past few weeks. The barons had surrendered just as the citizens were about to dynamite the ranch. But after a humiliating march through Buffalo and a brief imprisonment the Governor freed them before they could be tried. Adrian had been right about their power and influence.

Elinore couldn't help thinking that if Adrian had

not been such a coward, and attempted to desert, he would be alive that day.

But life wouldn't have been the same for him, for although the barons hadn't been prosecuted, they had lost their suffocating hold and most of them had returned to their lives back East or in England.

Sam Clover had made the scoop of his career with the publishing of Nate Champion's diary in the Chicago *Herald.*

But that day Elinore would finally put all the ugliness behind her. They were riding out to the Sioux to return the ring the old man had sold to Cattle Kate. Bette had finally answered Elinore's last letter. She had sent back the ring, wanting no reminders of a man such as Adrian.

When they reached the settlement Stewart pulled the buckboard to a stop and jumped down and raised his hands to Jerrine. Jerrine laughed as she jumped into his arms. This had become one of their favorite games. Elinore followed.

A squaw appeared from one of the tents. Elinore said she wanted to see the old man. The squaw directed Stewart and Jerrine to a tent where they could keep warm. She led Elinore to another.

Elinore lifted the flap and entered. The old man sat on the floor. He gestured for Elinore to sit down.

Elinore sat down and took out the ring from the pouch and held it out to him in her hand. The old Sioux was obviously puzzled.

"The ring has been recovered," Elinore said, "and since you never received your yearlings in payment, I feel the ring is rightfully yours."

She admired the ring one last time and gave it to him. He held it a moment, paused, and then gave it back.

"No, it is rightfully yours," the old man said quietly. "Cattle Kate was my friend. I know she would want you to have the ring." ◆⑤